Best True
GHOST
STORIES

Books by Hans Holzer

Non-Fiction

The Aquarian Age
Astrology: What It Can Do for
    You
Beyond Medicine
Beyond this Life
Charismatics
The Directory of the Occult
Elvis Presley Speaks (From the
    Beyond)
ESP and You
Ghost Hunter
Ghosts I've Met
The Ghosts that Walk in
    Washington
Gothic Ghosts
The Habsburg Curse
The Handbook of Parapsychology
Hans Holzer's Haunted Houses
Haunted Hollywood
Hidden Meanings in Dreams
Houses of Horror
How to Win at Life
The Human Dynamo
Inside Witchcraft
Life After Death: the Challenge
    and the Evidence
Murder in Amityville
Patterns of Destiny
Phantoms of Dixie
The Power of Hypnosis
The Powers of the New Age

The Primer of Reincarnation
The Prophets Speak
Psychic Healing
The Psychic Side of Dreams
Psycho-Ecstasy
Some of My Best Friends Are
    Ghosts
Speed Thinking
Star Ghosts
The Truth About ESP
The Truth About Witchcraft
The UFOnauts: New Facts on
    Extraterrestrial Landings
The Vegetarian Way of Life
Window to the Past
The Witchcraft Report
Yankee Ghosts

Fiction

The Alchemist
The Alchemy Deception
The Amityville Curse
Circle of Love
The Clairvoyant
The Entry
Heather, Confessions of a Witch
The Red Chindvit Conspiracy
Star of Destiny
The Unicorn
The Zodiac Affairs

Best True GHOST STORIES

Hans Holzer

Prentice-Hall, Inc. Englewood Cliffs, New Jersey

Editoras Prentice-Hall do Brasil, Ldta., *Rio de Haneiro*
Prentice-Hall International, Inc., *London*
Prentice-Hall of Australia, Pty. Ltd., *Sydney*
Prentice-Hall of Canada, Inc., *Toronto*
Prentice-Hall of India Private Ltd., *New Delhi*
Prentice-Hall of Japan, Inc., *Tokyo*
Prentice-Hall of Southeast Asia Pte. Ltd., *Singapore*
Whitehall Books, Ltd., *Wellington, New Zealand*

Library of Congress Cataloging in Publication Data

Holzer, Hans
   Best true ghost stories.

   1. Ghosts—United States. I. Title.
BF1472.U6H6373 1983   133.1   82-23143
ISBN 0-13-071936-6
ISBN 0-13-071928-5 {PBK.}

Printed in the United States of America

Introduction

Ghosts, haunted houses, and the so-called inexplicable have come of age: no longer do witnesses to such extraordinary happenings risk being declared mentally unstable or fraudulent.

Parapsychology, a young science dealing with mankind's oldest faculty, extrasensory perception, takes such reports very seriously. Many turn out to be authentic and indicative of man's continued existence beyond death.

In my investigations, I have always made sure that my witnesses were reliable and that the facts were as reported; when working with sensitives (mediums), I make sure they know nothing at all about the case they are helping me to investigate.

To be sure, there is no such thing as the supernatural. All the phenomena reported in these pages deals with extensions of human experience into areas that previously were not fully understood: the mind, the psyche and man's ability to break through the conventional time-space barrier.

More and more universities are paying attention to psychic research today, and students want to pursue careers in parapsychology. The 1982-83 television season alone has half a dozen pilots dealing with the subject matter in various stages of development. I myself have just taped a half-hour pilot discussion show called "Beyond the Five Senses," during which my guests, an investigative reporter from a large weekly and a police detective, discussed their valid experiences with psychic events.

If acceptance of the existence of ghosts, hauntings and other psychic phenomena that indicate continuance of life beyond physical death, seem to defy the concepts of modern science, then we must widen our scientific inquiry to accommodate the evidence we find, rather than label it unscientific or, as some have done, nonexistent. What for centuries was the exclusive province of religion has now become a legitimate area of proper and unbiased scientific inquiry. Incapable of being artificially recreated in the laboratory, the phenomena of the psyche are

5

nevertheless real and telling. Proper and frequent observation of these phenomena as they occur in life, along with the correlation of that material, helps us gain scientific understanding of man's very nature.

Prof. Hans Holzer, Ph.D.

Contents

Introduction   5

1. How It All Began   9
2. The Haunted Trailer   19
3. The Reality of Ghosts   25
4. The Strange Death of Valerie K.   49
5. The Last Ride   59
6. A California Ghost Story   64
7. A Haunted House Is Not a Home   76
8. Yankee Phantoms and Dixie Ghosts   98
9. The Stay-Behinds   116
10. The Ghostly Usher of Minneapolis   141
11. The Ghostly Adventures of a North Carolina Family   146
12. Reba's Ghosts   153
13. Henny from Brooklyn   158

chapter 1

How It All Began

"ENOUGH OF THIS NONSENSE," the kindergarten teacher, Miss Seidler, said sternly, and a hush fell upon the assembled children. There were seven or eight boys and girls, roughly three or four years old, grouped around a boy of three who sat on a wooden chair in the middle of an imperfect circle. Imperfect was right. The teacher did not approve of our activities. I was the little boy in the middle, and I had been telling the kids some of the wildest ghost stories ever heard anywhere since Edgar Allan Poe was in knee pants.

Tales of the supernatural seemed to come to me easily, as if I had been born to tell them; where I got my raw materials is still a mystery to me. But apparently the plots hit home; parents started to complain that their offspring wouldn't sleep nights, demanding more and better ghost stories, and what the heck were they teaching their youngsters at Miss Seidler's?

It was clear that Miss Seidler did not intend to make ghost-story telling a regular—or even an irregular—part of the curriculum.

"Hans," she now demanded, "let me see that."

"That" was the book of wisdom I had been holding in my hands, pretending to read from it. It was a little futuristic, for I could neither read nor write at that point, but I had seen grownups doing it, so I copied the action. My book was no ordinary book, however. It was my father's trolley car pass, expired, in a nice black leather cover. Miss Seidler was not impressed.

After a moment of silence, she returned the *legitimation* or pass to me, and told me to stop telling ghost stories.

But you can't keep a good man down. By the time I was six, I was regaling my mothers's family in Moravia with tales told me, allegedly,

9

by the wood sprites in the trees along the little river that flows through the city of Bruenn, where I spent every summer. My beginnings in the psychic field were humble, to say the least, and about as far from fact as you can go.

Fortunately, my uncle Henry was a dreamer and understanding. At his side, I had my first whiff of the real thing: psychic experiences really existed, I was informed, and my interest was now doubly aroused. Uncle Henry of course did not treat me like a parapsychologist: I was a boy of maybe nine or ten who liked adventure, and that was precisely what he was going to give me. In his room, furnished exclusively with eighteenth-century furniture and antiques, we held seances by candlelight. He had some early books dealing with the occult, and used to read from them the way a minister interprets the Bible. Since most of it was in distorted Latin, the sound but not the meaning penetrated my consciousness, and it was all very exciting.

Uncle Henry did not say there were ghosts and spirits; neither did he say there weren't. It was all I needed in getting my secret work cut out for me; a responsible adult approved, so I was doing the right thing!

As the years passed, my interests veered toward science and the unconquered territories of electronics and radio. A new rationalism grew in my mind and I became very cocky in my attitude toward anything I could not touch, see, hear, or feel at this point: how *could* such things as spirits exist?

There had to be a "natural" explanation, regardless of the evidence presented! I was completely unwilling to regard an unseen world around us as anything but pure fantasy, as remnants of childhood memories and totally incompatible with my brave new world of electronics.

I was about ten at the time, and such silly attitudes were perhaps normal for my age. But I know some mature, intelligent adults who have exactly the same sort of reasoning. There is that television producer, for instance, who patiently listened to all the evidence for the existence of psychic phenomena, looked carefully at the photographs taken under test conditions, and even managed to have an experience with strange pictures himself—to no avail.

"There's got to be some other explanation," he would intone regularly. He, like many others in our materialistic world today, is incapable of accepting the truth unless that truth conforms to his preconceived notions as to what that truth must look like. It is a little like the bed of Procrustes. Procrustes, you may recall, was a highwayman in ancient Greece whose particular brand of fun consisted of placing unwary travelers into his "special" bed: if they were too long, he'd cut them down, if they were too short, he'd stretch them to fit.

I did not attend the ordinary, tuition-free high school in my ancestral city of Vienna, Austria, but managed to get into a *Gymnasium*, a combination of high school and junior college, with emphasis on the humanities. My electronics spirit had somehow departed along the way, and was now replaced by a burning desire to become an archaeologist. Children often change their plans dozens of times during their school days, depending on what influences them in the world around them. But in my case, at least, the label stuck, and I did indeed become an archaeologist—at least at first.

This was in the 1930s, when Europe seethed with political unrest and the madman of Berlin had already cast a heavy shadow upon smaller countries around Germany such as the Austria I grew up in. It seemed foolish, on the fact of it, to study history and the humanities in *Gymnasium* in order to continue at the university in the hopes of eventually becoming an archaeologist, at a time when more practical pursuits might have been wiser. I also evinced a strong interest in writing, and it was clear to me that I would be a *Schriftsteller,* an author, of some kind—exactly what I have become, of course. But in the 1930s, when I was in my early teens, this was really quite outlandish to my parents and friends.

In the second half of my *Gymnasium* period, when I was sixteen years old, I was profoundly impressed by one of my teachers, Franz Spunda. This, of course, brought me into immediate disrepute with most of my classmates, since Dr. Spunda was one of the least-liked teachers and one of the most feared.

The reasons for this were in the man's character: he was a taciturn, dour man who seldom joked or said an unnecessary word, and whose scholastic behavior was stern and uncompromising. Other teachers you could soften up, but not him. What impressed me about Franz Spunda, however, was not the fact that he was disliked by my classmates, of course, for I am not a nonconformist for its own sake. Spunda was a well-known writer of historical novels who, like so many authors, even successful ones, was forced to augment his income by teaching.

Perhaps he resented this, for it interfered with his more important work, but his storehouse of knowledge was greater than called for in his teaching position. His classes dealt with literature, as was to be expected, but I soon discovered that Dr. Spunda had a deep interest in the occult, just as I used to have in the old Uncle Henry days.

I read some of Spunda's books, which led to other books on occult subjects, notably the very technical books on parapsychology by Professor Oesterreicher and by G. W. Gessmann, both published in the 1920s, which I acquired in 1935 when I was fifteen. Suddenly I realized that there was truth in these accounts, and that it was worthy of my further efforts to involve myself in the study of the occult. Whenever I had an opportunity, I let Dr. Spunda know that I shared his interests in these fields. On one occasion, I picked as the topic for a paper the rather cumbersome title of "Dr. von Schrenck-Notzing's Theory of

the Telekinetic, Teleplastic. Ideoplasticity," and confounded my classmates by just the title, to say nothing of the contents!

But not Dr. Spunda. After I was through reading my paper, he
remarked that it was a hodgepodge of several theories and proceeded
to criticize my statements with the experienced approach of an inside
man. After this, it became clear to my classmates that I was something
special, and many avoided me afterwards in anything but the most
superficial relationships. It suited me fine, for I preferred a few close
friends to general and shallow popularity.

Many years later, when I returned to Vienna as an American
foreign correspondent, I met my erstwhile teacher again in the stillness
of his cottage in the suburbs of Vienna. We talked freely of the past
and he admitted his errors of a political nature: Spunda had welcomed
the Hitler movement at first with the unrealistic emotional optimism
of a Wagnerian revivalist of Pan-Germanic days, only to find the bitter
truth difficult to accept. Essentially a religious man, he realized in the
later war years that the German cause had been betrayed by the Third
Reich, but he had a difficult time cleansing himself of his association
with it for many years after. And yet, he had never done anything
overt, and never denied his mistakes. Eventually his books were published
again and some are still in print, especially his very profound work on
the rose cross, *Jacob Boehme,* which Bauer republished recently. Spunda
has since gone on in a manner worthy of his Olympian philosophy: he
died of a heart attack during a trip exploring once again the beauty of
ancient Greece.

At the University of Vienna, my days were occupied with the
formal studies of archaeology and history, and psychic matters had to
wait. In 1938, we decided that the threatening war clouds would soon
erupt into rainstorms of blood and destruction, and I went to live in
New York where my father had spent many years at the turn of the
century as an immigrant. All this time, my interest in the world of the
sixth sense lay dormant, though far from dead. In 1946, I met for the
first time Eileen Garrett, whose work has influenced my thinking profoundly, even though we do not always agree on the conclusions to be
drawn from it.

I was making a reasonably good living as a writer and associate
editor of a magazine called *Numismatic Review,* a position utilizing
my knowledge of archaeology and ancient numismatics, but none of
my ESP talents.

The latter grew quietly in the dark, like mushrooms in a tunnel,
until suddenly there was need to display them.

I have always maintained that people form links in chains of destiny,
each of us furnishing a vital step forward in a journey someone else
may be taking, without our knowledge of where it may lead him or
her. This is our duty then, to serve so that someone else might prosper

or succeed, and in turn be served on another occasion by someone else in the same manner. Thus it was that the British actor, writer, and comedian Michael Bentine touched off a new wave of psychic interest within me when we met backstage at the Hippodrome Theatre in London in 1950, where he was then starring.

Our friendship blossomed particularly when we discovered our common interest in psychic research. When Michael came to New York the following year, we met again.

It so happened that I had also become friendly with the late Danton Walker, the Broadway columnist of the New York *Daily News* who was, as I discovered, psychic, and very much interested in my favorite subject.

Somehow the Michael Bentine link led to the next link, Walker, when Walker asked me to arrange an interview with Bentine. Now there were three of us, meeting over a drink in Manhattan. During that afternoon, Walker started to tell us of his haunted house in the country and Michael immediately offered to go there with him. But his commitments called him back to England before this could be arranged, and it was I alone who went. Also present was the famous medium Eileen Garrett, who acted as a "telephone between worlds," using the James Crenshaw description of this gift. Dr. Robert Laidlaw came as an observer and arbiter of the investigation that followed.

I have, of course, reported this remarkable case in my earlier book, *Ghost Hunter,* and it has always stood out in my mind as one of the most interesting cases of a haunting I have ever witnessed—and I have had several thousand cases since. I don't know whether it was the stark tragedy of a Colonial runner being clubbed to death by the British soldiery and its vivid reenactment in trance by the medium, or the quality of the witnesses who had experienced the uncanny phenomena I came to know over and over again in the years that followed, but the Rockland County Ghost helped convince me that man does indeed have an immortal component. What this component was began to occupy my time more and more after my involvement with this case.

Still, I knew only that sometimes things go wrong in life and someone dies tragically, and something stays behind and becomes a "ghost" of the event. Was it the exception from the norm, and did we usually leave no residue upon expiring? That question occupied my mind a great deal. It seemed entirely consistent with my knowledge of electronics to postulate that man's emotional tensions might constitute an electromagnetic field similar to a radiation field in the atmosphere. Could it be that these ghosts were really impressions like photographs in the "ether" or atmosphere of old houses, and had no relationship to living human beings? That too seemed vaguely possible under my set of rules. After all, if an atomic explosion can make a part of the atmosphere radioactive for many years, why couldn't a miniature outburst such as sudden death have some effect?

At this point in my studies, I was still trying to find some "natural" way of explaining the phenomena I had witnessed, to correlate them with the known facts of science and nature, even though they might be new aspects or little-known facts within the customary framework of human knowledge and understanding. But the Rockland case threw me for a loop: for all intents and purposes, this was not a shallow impression of a past event, but a seemingly living human being from the past, temporarily using the body of the medium to act out his problems.

I could not reconcile what I observed with the concept of a "dead" impression left behind in the atmosphere, devoid of all further life or power to react to those making a fresh contact with it. I began to get uncomfortable as I realized what I was trying to do: that is, to select my evidence not on the basis of truth, but instead to make the facts fit the theory. Fortunately I am a very honest fellow. I can't live with half-truths and I don't fool myself about anything when I know, deep within me, that it is wrong.

Consequently, it began to dawn on me that there were psychic cases involving lifeless "impressions" in the atmosphere, and that there were also cases of authentic hauntings, where a human being was continually reliving his emotional tragedy of the past.

For me, the search was on for the proof of personal survival, that is to say, scientific evidence that man does survive physical death and continues his existence as a full individual in another dimension.

I realized that ghosts were not exactly ideal cases with which to prove or disprove the nature of that "other side" of the universe. It had become clear to me that all ghosts were either psychotic or at least psychologically disoriented minds, not balanced individuals who had passed on. Obviously, if the survival of a personality was a fact, it would be far more common than hauntings, and the evidence for it should be capable of verification on a much larger scale. More people die "normally" than under tragic conditions, and even among the latter class, those turning up as "ghosts" are again a small portion of the total thus "qualified."

Where was I to turn to find evidence for this so-called spirit world about which the spiritualists had been talking so nicely for so long, without ever convincing me of its reality?

As for so many others raised in the upper middle class, all emotional religions were alien to my way of life. I grew up considering spiritualist mediums as either outright fakes or misguided self-styled prophets at best, and the practice of seances in questionable taste. Should I now reverse myself and seek out some medium and try my hand at a seance, just so I could discover for myself what went on? This was not easy, since I hated the dark and wouldn't sit in total darkness for anything.

Torn between letting the matter rest and feeling an aroused curiosity, I attended a number of spiritualist lectures, the kind that attracts a rather motley crowd ranging from frustrated old maids of both sexes, to earnest seekers of truth, to students of the occult, to just plainly curious people more in need of a fortuneteller than a medium.

On one such occasion, I was approached by a man in the crowd just as the meeting broke up. He explained to me that he had some talents as a medium that he wished to improve upon, and was therefore trying to arrange a little group to "sit" with him. He hastened to explain that he was also a clerk in Brooklyn and that no money was involved in this project. I saw nothing wrong with it and gladly agreed to join him and some others in at least one such meeting. As it happened, they needed a quiet place in which to meet, so I suggested my offices on Fifty-Ninth Street, in New York City, after business hours.

That was agreeable, and six ladies I had never seen before came up to my office the following evening. They looked like typical New York housewives in their forties and fifties, which is what they were. I pulled down the shades, and the gentleman I had met the night before seated himself in one of the chairs and closed his eyes. For a few moments, we were all very quiet and the traffic rumbling by downstairs was all we could hear. Then his breathing became a bit labored and his head fell upon his shoulders.

Rapidly he kept calling out names and bits of information about people who evidently were recognized by one or another person in the room. Of course I immediately suspected that this was because he knew these ladies and was trying to please them by "bringing in" their favorite deceased relative. After the seance, I questioned them separately and satisfied myself that they had only met him the night before, as I had, at the lecture hall. Evidently, my observation that night had not been as good as it should have been, since I did not recall seeing these ladies there, but it had been a rather large crowd.

After the fourth or fifth person had spoken through the medium, his head turned in my direction and, in a strangely distorted voice resembling his normal speaking voice, he addressed me.

"Someone here who knows you . . . named Eric . . . says he died short time ago . . . bad accident . . . wants you to tell loved ones he's all right. . . ."

That was all.

But it was enough for me. Half a year before this seance, a friend of mine had died tragically in an accident while still quite young. His wife had been completely inconsolable since that time, taking the death of her husband of only a few months very hard. His name was Eric.

Of all the people I knew who had passed away in my family, not one of them had evidently decided to speak through this medium. But there was certainly something urgent about the message from Eric. His wife needed this bit of news.

I called her and told her, and though she did not really believe in the possibility of personal spiritual survival after death, she was not entirely sure that it didn't exist. An indication that it was possible was all that was needed to help her gradually get over the tragedy, and so she did.

In 1953, I got to know a group that met regularly at the New York headquarters of the Association for Research and Enlightenment, better known as the Edgar Cayce Foundation. This was a study group, and mediums worked with them to learn more about their own abilities. One such budding medium was Ethel Johnson Meyers, who has since become one of our more famous psychics and one of the people I frequently work with in my investigations.

At that time, however, she was just a singing teacher with mediumship who wanted to find out more about herself.

At that time, Ethel's controls—spirit personalities operating her psychic channels to regulate the flow of information and to keep out intruders—were her late husband Albert and a Tibetan named Toto Himalaya. I must confess that Toto sounded absolutely phony to me, somewhat like a vaudeville Indian making grunting noises and behaving very much like a synthetic Tibetan, or one manufactured by the unconscious of the medium herself. This, of course, is an age-old question: are these "controls" real people or are they parts of the personality of the medium that act out consciously during a trance and which the medium cannot act out when awake?

I have never been able to prove satisfactorily the reality of these controls, and some trance mediums like Sybil Leek don't have them. But I haven't any evidence to say that they are anything except what they claim to be, and am of late persuaded to accept them as indeed real human beings who have crossed the threshold into the nonphysical world. Even so great a medium and human being as Eileen Garrett has not been able to make up her own mind on this difficult question.

When I first met Toto via the entranced Ethel Meyers we had our difficulties, for I don't take kindly to generalities and bits of philosophy that seem to waste both a medium's and an investigator's time.

But if Toto was indeed an ancient Tibetan priest, he had a right to preach. I just wasn't particularly ready to listen to the sermon at that point. Instead, I decided to test Ethel's psychometry talents. Psychometry is the gift of touching an object and describing instantly its history or owners. Naturally, the medium must not know anything about the object or see its shape or outline, in order to avoid any conscious clues as to its identity.

Consequently, I took the object I had in mind, wrapped it several times in paper, then in pieces of cloth, until it became a shapeless parcel of about an arm's length and weighing perhaps three pounds. With this thing under my arm, I came down to the Association where Ethel Meyers was already in the midst of psychometrizing objects. At the first free moment, I thrust the parcel into her outstretched hands and watched for her reactions.

For a moment Mrs. Meyers sat as if stunned. Then, with a shriek, she rose from her chair, at the same time throwing the parcel onto the floor as if I had handed her a stick of dynamite with a lit fuse.

Even though it was early spring, she was sweating and I could tell she was upset.

"I see a sacrifice," she mumbled, and shuddered.

"This is some kind of ceremony . . . a dagger . . . don't like it." She looked at me sternly, almost reproachfully.

"It's all right, Ethel," I said, "I shan't ask you to touch it again."

With that, I picked up the package and started to unravel it. The others present had formed a circle around us as layer upon layer of cloth and paper disappeared. Eventually, I held in my hand a gleaming *dorje* or Tibetan sacrificial scepter, at the end of which was a dagger. I had meant to make Toto Himalaya feel at home, and all I had succeeded in doing was getting Mrs. Meyers upset!

The following year, after attending dozens upon dozens of meetings at the Association, I made a special visit because my friends had told me of a new medium who had recently joined the experimental group and seemed interesting. I was late in arriving and took a seat in the rear of the already darkened room. At the far end, a woman sat with her eyes closed, while a small red light burned next to her, casting an eerie glow over the assembled people.

This went on for about fifteen minutes—utter silence while the medium slept. Then she awoke and gave messages to some of those present. It was her brand of mediumship, this going out "alone," and then returning and talking. Most mediums go into trance and talk during, not after, the trance state. The lights came on now, and I arose to leave. I had walked down the corridor part of the way when the medium I had just observed came after me and stopped me.

"Are you Hans Holzer?"

I nodded, sure someone had told her my name. But nobody had, as I later discovered.

"Then I have a message for you. From an uncle."

Now I have lots of uncles, some dead, some living, and I was not impressed. I looked at her blankly.

The dark-haired woman shook her head impatiently.

"His initials are O. S." she said rapidly, "and he's got a wife named Alice. She's a blonde."

All at once I felt shivers down my spine.

Many years before, an uncle of mine named Otto Stransky had died tragically. I was not particularly close to him, and had not thought of him for years. There had been no reason to do so; his family lived thousands of miles away, in South America, and there was almost no contact.

Whatever it was, the medium certainly had not read my unconscious mind.

His wife's name was indeed Alice. When he had been alive, she had been a blonde, but by now, however, Alice's hair had long since turned white. Yet, to the timeless memory of her loving husband, the hair would forever be blonde!

That was the first time I had come in contact with a clearcut message from a departed relative or friend that could not be explained by fraud, coincidence, mind reading or some otherwise explainable cause. It had to be the survival of human personality. I thanked the lady, not realizing at the time that she would also play a large role in my future work. She is probably one of the finest clairvoyant mediums in America today. Her name is Betty Ritter.

Now I knew that in some instances at least, proof of survival could be shown. Then why not in all? Why not indeed. My mind was made up to turn my attention to this end: to give the average person the facts of afterlife, in terms he can both understand and accept; to be a scientist but not a negative doubter. Truth does not need interpretation, just exposure.

That's how I became a Psychic Investigator.

chapter 2

The Haunted Trailer

SOMETIMES, ONE WOULD THINK, the work of a Psychic Investigator must be downright drab. Little old ladies have nightmares, imaginative teenagers let off steam over frustrations in directions as yet unexplored, neurotics of uncertain sex fantasize about their special roles and talents. All this is grist for the investigator's mill, poor chap, and he has to listen and nod politely, for that's how he gets information. (As when Peter Lorre whispered across the screen, "Where is the information?" this question is the beacon toward which the psychic sleuth must be drawn.)

And in fact it is perfectly possible for such people to have genuine ESP experiences. Anybody can play this game. All he needs is to be alive and kicking. ESP comes to just about everyone, and there's nothing anyone can do about it one way or the other.

It is therefore necessary to have a completely open mind as to the kind of individual who might have a valid psychic experience. I can attest to this need to my regret. Several years ago, people approached me who had witnessed the amazing Ted Serios demonstrate his thought photography and who wanted me to work with the fellow. But my quasi-middle-class sense of propriety shied away from the midwestern bellhop when I realized that he drank and was not altogether of drawing-room class. How wrong I was! A little later, Professor Jule Eisenbud of the University of Colorado showed better sense and less prejudice as to a person's private habits, and his work with Serios is not only a scientific breakthrough of the first order, but was turned into a successful book for Eisenbud as well.

Of course, I don't expect all my subjects to be proprietors of New England mansions about to collapse, or Southern plantation owners drinking mint juleps on their lawns, but I have yet to hear from a truck driver who has seen a ghost, or a State Department man with premonitions. Hindsight maybe, but not precognition.

So it was with more than casual interest that I received a communication (via the U.S. mail) from a comely young lady named Rita Atlanta.

Her initial letter merely requested that I help her get rid of her ghost. Such requests are not unusual, but this one was—and I am not referring to the lady's occupation—exotic dancing in sundry nightclubs around the more or less civilized world.

What made her case unusual was the fact that "her" ghost appeared in a thirty-year-old trailer near Boston.

"When I told my husband that we had a ghost," she wrote, "he laughed and said, 'Why should a respectable ghost move into a trailer? We have hardly room in it ourselves with three kids.' "

It seemed the whole business had started during the summer when the specter made its first sudden appearance. Although her husband could not see what she saw, Miss Atlanta's pet skunk evidently didn't like it and moved into another room. Three months later, her husband passed away and Miss Atlanta was kept busy hopping the Atlantic (hence her stage name) in quest of nightclub work.

Ever since her first encounter with the figure of a man in her Massachusetts trailer, the dancer had kept the lights burning all night long. As someone once put it, "I don't believe in ghosts, but I'm scared of them."

Despite the lights, Miss Atlanta always felt a presence at the same time that her initial experience had taken place—between three and three-thirty in the morning. It would awaken her with such a regularity that at last she decided to seek help.

At the time she contacted me, she was appearing nightly at the Imperial in Frankfurt, taking a bath onstage in an oversize champagne glass filled with under-quality champagne. The discriminating clientele that frequents the Imperial loved the French touch, and Rita Atlanta was and is a wow.

I discovered that her late husband was Colonel Frank Bane, an Air Force ace who had originally encouraged the Vienna-born girl to change from ballet to belly dancing, and eventually to what is termed "exotic" dancing, but which is better described as stripping.

I decided to talk to the "Champagne Bubble Girl" on my next overseas trip. She was working at that time in Stuttgart, but she came over to meet us at our Frankfurt Hotel, and my wife was immediately taken with her pleasant charm and lack of "show business" phonyness. Then it was discovered that Rita was a Libra, like Catherine, and we repaired for lunch to the terrace of a nearby restaurant to discuss the ups and downs of a hectic life in a champagne glass, not forgetting the three kids in a house trailer.

I asked Rita to go through an oriental dance for my camera (minus champagne glass, but not minus anything else) and then we sat down to discuss the ghostly business in earnest. In September of the previous year, she and her family had moved into a brand-new trailer in Peabody, Massachusetts. After her encounter with the ghost, Rita made some inquiries about the nice grassy spot where she had chosen to park the trailer. Nothing had ever stood on the spot before. No ghost stories. Nothing. Just one little thing.

One of the neighbors in the trailer camp, which is at the outskirts of greater Boston, came to see her one evening. By this time Rita's heart was already filled with fear, fear of the unknown that had suddenly come into her life here. She freely confided in her neighbor, a girl by the name of Birdie Gleason.

To her amazement, the neighbor nodded with understanding. She, too, had felt "something," an unseen presence in her house trailer next to Rita's.

"Sometimes I feel someone is touching me," she added.

"What exactly did *you* see?" I interjected, while outside the street noises of Frankfurt belied the terrifying subject we were discussing.

"I saw a big man, almost seven foot tall, about three hundred fifty pounds, and he wore a long coat and a big hat."

But the ghost didn't just stand there glaring at her. Sometimes he made himself comfortable on her kitchen counter, with his ghostly legs dangling down from it. He was as solid as a man of flesh and blood, except that she could not see his face clearly since it was in the darkness of early morning.

Later, when I visited the house trailer with my highly sensitive camera, I took some pictures in the areas indicated by Miss Atlanta: the bedroom, the door to it, and the kitchen counter. In all three areas, strange phenomena manifested on my film. Some mirrorlike transparencies developed in normally opaque areas, which could not and cannot be explained.

When it happened the first time, she raced for the light and turned the switch, her heart beating wildly. The yellowish light of the electric lamp bathed the bedroom in a nightmarish twilight. But the spook had vanished. There was no possible way a real intruder could have come and gone so fast. No way out, no way in. Because this was during the time Boston was being terrorized by the infamous Boston Strangler, Rita had taken special care to double-lock the doors and secure all the windows. Nobody could have entered the trailer without making a great deal of noise. I have examined the locks and the windows—not even Houdini could have done it.

The ghost, having once established himself in Rita's bedroom, returned for additional visits—always in the early morning hours. Sometimes he appeared three times a week, sometimes even more often.

"He was staring in my direction all the time," Rita said with a slight Viennese accent, and one could see that the terror had never really left her eyes. Even three thousand miles away, the spectral stranger had a hold on the woman.

Was he perhaps looking for something? No, he didn't seem to be. In the kitchen, he either stood by the table or sat down on the counter. Ghosts don't need food—so why the kitchen?

"Did he ever take his hat off?" I wondered.

"No, never," she said and smiled. Imagine a ghost doffing his hat to the lady of the trailer!

What was particularly horrifying was the noiselessness of the apparition. She never heard any footfalls or rustling of his clothes as he silently passed by. There was no clearing of the throat as if he wanted to speak. Nothing. Just silent stares. When the visitations grew more frequent, Rita decided to leave the lights on all night. After that, she did not *see* him any more. But he was still there, at the usual hour, standing behind the bed, staring at her. She knew he was. She could almost feel the sting of his gaze.

One night she decided she had been paying huge light bills long enough. She hopped out of bed, turned the light switch to the off position and, as the room was plunged back into semidarkness, she lay down in bed again. Within a few minutes her eyes had gotten accustomed to the dark. Her senses were on the alert, for she was not at all sure what she might see. Finally, she forced herself to turn her head in the direction of the door. Was her mind playing tricks on her? There, in the doorway, stood the ghost. As big and brooding as ever.

With a scream, she dove under the covers. When she came up, eternities later, the shadow was gone from the door.

The next evening, the lights were burning again in the trailer, and every night thereafter, until it was time for her to fly to Germany for her season's nightclub work. Then she closed up the trailer, sent her children to stay with friends, and left with the faint hope that on her return in the winter, the trailer might be free of its ghost. But she wasn't at all certain.

It was getting dark outside now, and I knew Miss Atlanta soon had to fly back to Stuttgart for her evening's work. It was obvious to me that this exotic dancer was a medium, as only the psychic can "see" apparitions.

I queried her about the past, and reluctantly she talked of her earlier years in Austria.

When she was a schoolgirl of eight, she suddenly felt herself compelled to draw a picture of a funeral. Her father was puzzled by the choice of so somber a subject by a little girl. But as she pointed out who the figures in her drawing were, ranging from her father to the more distant relatives, her father listened with lips tightly drawn. When the enumeration was over, he inquired in a voice of incredulity mixed with fear, "But who is being buried?"

"Mother," the little girl replied, without a moment's hesitation, and no more was said about it.

Three weeks later to the day, her mother was dead.

The war years were hard on the family. Her father, a postal employee, had a gift for playing the numbers, allegedly on advice from his deceased spouse. But Germany's invasion ended all that and eventually Rita found herself in the United States and married to an Air Force Colonel.

She had forgotten her psychic experiences of the past, when the ghost in the trailer brought them all back only too vividly. She was frankly scared, knowing her abilities to receive messages from the beyond. But who was this man?

I decided to visit Peabody with a medium to see what we could learn, but it wasn't until the winter of the same year that I met Rita and she showed me around her trailer. It was a cold and moist afternoon.

Her oldest son greeted us at the door. He had seen nothing and neither believed nor disbelieved his mother. But he was willing to do some legwork for me to find out who the shadowy visitor might be.

It was thus that we learned that a few years ago a man had been run over by a car very close by. Had the dead man, confused about his status, sought refuge in the trailer—the nearest "house" in his path?

Was he trying to make contact with what he could sense was a medium, who would be able to receive his anxious pleas?

It was at this time that I took the unusual photographs of the areas Rita pointed out as being haunted. Several of these pictures show unusual mirrorlike areas, in which "something" must have been present in the atmosphere. But the ghost did not appear for me or, for that matter, Rita.

Perhaps our discovery of his "problem" and our long and passionate discussion of this had reached his spectral consciousness and he knew that he was out of his element in a trailer belonging to people not connected with his world.

Was this his way of finally, belatedly, doffing his hat to the lady of the house trailer, with an apology for his intrusions?

I haven't had any further word from Rita Atlanta, but the newspapers carry oversize ads now and then telling some city of the sensational performance of the girl in the champagne glass.

It is safe to assume that she can take her bath in the glass completely alone, something she had not been sure of in the privacy of her Massachusetts trailer. For Rita, the eyes of a couple hundred visiting firemen in a Frankfurt nightclub are far less bothersome than one solitary pair of eyes staring from another world.

chapter 3

The Reality of Ghosts

WHAT EXACTLY IS A GHOST? Something people dream up in their cups or on a sickbed? Something you read about in juvenile fiction? Far from it. Ghosts—apparitions of "dead' people or sounds associated with invisible human beings—are the surviving emotional memories of people. They are people who have not been able to make the transition from their physical state into the world of the spirit—or as Dr. Joseph Rhine of Duke University has called it, the world of the *mind*. Their state is one of emotional shock induced by sudden death or great suffering, and because of it the individuals involved cannot understand what is happening to them. They are unable to see beyond their own immediate environment or problem, and so they are forced to continually relive those final moments of agony until someone breaks through and explains things to them. In this respect they are like psychotics being helped by the psychoanalyst, except that the patient is not on the couch, but rather in the atmosphere of destiny. Man's electromagnetic nature makes this perfectly plausible; that is, since our individual personality is really nothing more than a personal energy field encased in a denser outer layer called the physical body, the personality can store emotional stimuli and memories indefinitely without much dimming, very much like a tape recording that can be played over and over without losing clarity or volume.

Those who die normally under conditions of adjustment need not go through this agony, and they seem to pass on rapidly into that next state of consciousness that may be a "heaven" or a "hell," according to what the individual's mental state at death might have been. Neither state is an objective place, but is a subjective state of being. The sum total of similar states of being may, however, create a quasi-objective state approaching a condition or "place" along more orthodox religious lines. My contact with the confused individuals unable to depart from the earth's sphere, those who are commonly called "ghosts" or earth-bound spirits, is through a trance medium who will lend her physical body temporarily to the entities in difficulty so that they can speak through the medium and detail their problems, frustrations, or unfinished business. Here again, the parallel with psychoanalysis becomes apparent: in telling their tales of woe, the restless ones relieve themselves of their pressures and anxieties and thus may free themselves of their bonds. If fear is the absence of information, as I have always held, then knowledge is indeed the presence of understanding. Or view it the other way round, if you prefer. Because of my books, people often call on me to help them understand problems of this nature. Whenever someone has seen a ghost or heard noises of a human kind that do not seem to go with a body, and feel it might be something I ought to look into, I usually do.

To be sure, I don't always find a ghost. But I frequently do find one, and moreover, I find that many of those who have had the uncanny experiences are themselves mediumistic, and are therefore capable of being communications vehicles for the discarnates. It is more common than most people realize, and, really quite natural and harmless.

At times, it is sad and shocking, as all human suffering is, for man is his worst enemy, whether in the flesh or outside of it. But there is nothing mystical about the powers of ESP or the ability to experience ghostly phenomena.

Scoffers like to dismiss all ghostly encounters by cutting the witnesses down to size—their size. The witnesses are probably mentally unbalanced, they say, or sick people who hallucinate a lot, or they were tired that day, or it must have been the reflection from (pick your light source), or finally, in desperation, they may say yes, something probably happened to them, but in the telling they blew it all up so you can't be sure any more what really happened.

I love the way many people who cannot accept the possibility of ghosts being real toss out their views on what happened to strangers. "Probably this or that," and from "probably," for them, it is only a short step to "certainly." The human mind is as clever at inventing away as it is at hallucinating. The advantage in being a scientifically trained reporter, as I am, is the ability to dismiss people's interpretations and find the facts themselves. I talked of the *Ghosts I've Met* in a book a few years ago that bore that title. Even more fascinating are the people I've met who encounter ghosts. Are they sick, unbalanced, crackpots, or other unrealistic individuals whose testimony is worthless?

Far from it.

Those who fall into that category never get to me in the first place. They don't stand up under my methods of scrutiny. Crackpots, beware!

I call a spade a spade, as I proved when I exposed the fake spiritualist camp practices in print some years ago.

The people who come across ghostly manifestations are people like you.

Take the couple from Springfield, Illinois, for instance. Their names are Gertrude and Russell Meyers and they were married in 1935. He worked as a stereotyper on the local newspaper, and she was a high-school teacher. Both of them were in their late twenties and couldn't care less about such things as ghosts.

At the time of their marriage, they had rented a five-room cottage which had stood empty for some time. It had no particular distinction but a modest price, and was located in Bloomington where the Meyerses then lived.

Gertrude Meyers came from a farm background and had studied at Illinois Wesleyan as well as the University of Chicago. For a while she worked as a newspaperwoman in Detroit, later taught school, and as a sideline has written a number of children's books. Her husband Russell, also of farm background, attended Illinois State Normal University at Normal, Illinois, and later took his apprenticeship at the Bloomington Pantograph.

The house they had rented in Bloomington was exactly like the house next to it, and the current owners had converted what was formerly *one* large house into two separate units, laying a driveway between them.

In the summer, after they had moved into their house, they went about the business of settling down to a routine. Since her husband worked the night shift on the newspaper, Mrs. Meyers was often left alone in the house. At first, it did not bother her at all. Sounds from the street penetrated into the house and gave her a feeling of people nearby. But when the chills of autumn set in and the windows had to be closed to keep it out, she became aware, gradually, that she was not really alone on those lonely nights.

One particular night early in their occupancy of the house, she had gone to bed leaving her bedroom door ajar. It was ten-thirty and she was just about ready to go to sleep when she heard rapid, firm footsteps starting at the front door, inside the house, and coming through the living room, the dining room, and finally approaching her bedroom door down the hall leading to it.

She leapt out of bed and locked the bedroom door. Then she went back into bed and sat there, wondering with sheer terror what the intruder would do. But nobody came.

More to calm herself than because she really believed it, Mrs.

Meyers convinced herself that she must have been mistaken about those footsteps.

It was probably someone in the street. With this reassuring thought on her mind, she managed to fall asleep.

The next morning, she did not tell her new husband about the nocturnal event. After all, she did not want him to think he had married a strange woman!

But the footsteps returned, night after night, always at the same time and always stopping abruptly at her bedroom door which, needless to say, she kept locked.

Rather than facing her husband with the allegation that they had rented a haunted house, she bravely decided to face the intruder and find out what this was all about. One night she deliberately waited for the now familiar brisk footfalls. The clock struck ten, then ten-thirty. In the quiet of the night, she could hear her heart pound in her chest.

Then the footsteps came, closer and closer, until they got to her bedroom door. At this moment, Mrs. Meyers jumped out of bed, snapped on the light, and tore the door wide open.

There was nobody there, and no retreating footsteps could be heard.

She tried it again and again, but the invisible intruder never showed himself once the door was opened.

The winter was bitterly cold, and it was Russell's habit of building up a fire in the furnace in the basement when he came home from work at three-thirty A.M. Mrs. Meyers always heard him come in, but did not get up. One night he left the basement, came into the bedroom and said, "Why are you walking around this freezing house in the middle of the night?"

Of course she had not been out of bed all night, and told him as much. Then they discovered that he, too, had heard footsteps, but had thought it was his wife walking restlessly about the house. Meyers had heard the steps whenever he was fixing the furnace in the basement, and by the time he got upstairs they had ceased.

When Mrs. Meyers had to get up early to go to her classes, her husband would stay in the house sleeping late. On many days he would hear someone walking about the house and investigate, only to find himself quite alone.

He would wake up in the middle of the night thinking his wife had gotten up, but immediately reassured himself that she was sleeping peacefully next to him. Yet there was *someone* out there in the empty house!

Since everything was locked securely, and countless attempts to trap the ghost had failed, the Meyerses shrugged and learned to live with their peculiar boarder. Gradually the steps became part of the atmosphere of the old house, and the terror began to fade into the darkness of night.

In May of the following year, they decided to work in the garden and, as they did so, they met their next-door neighbors for the first time. Since they lived in identical houses, they had something in common, and conversation between them and the neighbors—a young man of twenty-five and his grandmother—sprang up.

Eventually the discussion got around to the footsteps. They, too, kept hearing them, it seemed. After they had compared notes on their experiences, the Meyerses asked more questions. They were told that before the house was divided, it belonged to a single owner who had committed suicide in the house. No wonder he liked to walk in *both* halves of what was once his home!

You'd never think of Kokomo, Indiana as particularly haunted ground, but one of the most touching cases I know of occurred there some time ago. A young woman by the name of Mary Elizabeth Hamilton was in the habit of spending many of her summer vacations there in her grandmother's house. The house dates back to 1834 and is a handsome place, meticulously kept up by the grandmother.

Miss Hamilton had never had the slightest interest in the supernatural, and the events that transpired that summer, when she spent four weeks at the house, came as a complete surprise to her. One evening she was walking down the front staircase when she was met by a lovely young lady coming up the stairs. Miss Hamilton, being a female, noticed that she wore a particularly beautiful evening gown. There was nothing the least bit ghostly about the woman, and she passed Miss Hamilton closely, in fact so closely that she could have touched her had she wanted to.

But she did notice that the gown was of a filmy pink material, and her hair and eyes dark brown, and the latter full of tears. When the two women met, the girl in the evening gown smiled at Miss Hamilton and passed by.

Since she knew that there was no other visitor in the house, and that no one was expected at this time, Miss Hamilton was puzzled as to who the lady might be. She turned her head to follow her up the stairs, when she saw the lady in pink reach the top of the stairs and vanish—into thin air.

As soon as she could, she reported the matter to her grandmother, who shook her head and would not believe her account. She would not even discuss it, so Miss Hamilton let the matter drop out of deference to her grandmother. But the dress design had been so unusual, she decided to check it out in a library. She found, to her amazement, that the lady in pink had worn a dress of the late 1840s period.

In September of the next year, her grandmother decided to redecorate the house. In this endeavor she used many old pieces of furniture, some of which had come from the attic of the house. When Miss Hamilton arrived and saw the changes, she was suddenly stopped by a portrait hung in the hall.

It was a portrait of her lady of the stairs. She was not wearing the pink gown in this picture but, other than that, it was the same person.

Miss Hamilton's curiosity about the whole matter was again aroused and, since she could not get any cooperation from her grandmother, she turned to her great aunt for help. This was particularly fortunate since the aunt was a specialist in family genealogy.

Finally the lady of the stairs was identified. She turned out to be a distant cousin of Miss Hamilton's, and had once lived in this very house.

She had fallen in love with a ne'er-do-well, and after he died in a brawl, she threw herself down the stairs to her death.

Why had the family ghost picked on her to appear before, Miss Hamilton wondered.

Then she realized that she bore a strong facial resemblance to the ghost. Moreover, their names were almost identical—Mary Elizabeth was Miss Hamilton's, and Elizabeth Mary the pink lady's. Both women even had the same nickname, Libby.

Perhaps the ghost had looked for a little recognition from her family and, having gotten none from the grandmother, had seized upon the opportunity to manifest for a more amenable relative?

Miss Hamilton is happy that she was able to see the sad smile on the unfortunate girl's face, for to her it is proof that communication, though silent, had taken place between them across the years.

Mrs. Jane Eidson is a housewife in suburban Minneapolis. She is middle-aged and her five children range in age from nine to twenty. Her husband Bill travels four days each week. They live in a cottage-type brick house that is twenty-eight years old, and they've lived there for the past eight years.

The first time the Eidsons noticed that there was something odd about their otherwise ordinary-looking home was after they had been in the house for a short time. Mrs. Eidson was in the basement sewing, when all of a sudden she felt that she was not alone and wanted to run upstairs. She suppressed this strong urge but felt very uncomfortable. Another evening, her husband was down there practicing a speech when he had the same feeling of another presence. His self-control was not as strong as hers, and he came upstairs. In discussing their strange feelings with their next-door neighbor, they discovered that the previous tenant also had complained about the basement. Their daughter, Rita, had never wanted to go to the basement by herself and, when pressed for a reason, finally admitted that there was a man down there. She described him as dark-haired and wearing a plaid shirt.

Sometimes he would stand by her bed at night and she would become frightened, but the moment she thought of calling her mother, the image disappeared. Another spot where she felt his presence was the little playhouse at the other end of their yard.

The following spring, Mrs. Eidson noticed a bouncing light at the top of the stairs as she was about to go to bed in an upstairs room, which she occupied while convalescing from surgery.

The light followed her to her room as if it had a mind of its own!

When she entered her room the light left, but the room felt icy. She was disturbed by this, but nevertheless went to bed and soon had forgotten all about it as sleep came to her. Suddenly, in the middle of the night, she woke and sat up in bed.

Something had awakened her. At the head of her bed she saw a man who was "beige-colored," as she put it. As she stared at the apparition it went away, again leaving the room very chilly.

About that same time, the Eidsons noticed that their electric appliances were playing tricks on them. There was the time at five A.M. when their washing machine went on by itself as did the television set in the basement, which could only be turned on by plugging it into the wall socket. When they had gone to bed, the set was off and there was no one around to plug it in.

Who was so fond of electrical gadgets as to turn them on in the small hours of the morning?

Finally Mrs. Eidson found out. In May of 1949, a young man who was just out of the service had occupied the house. His hobby was electrical wiring, it seems, for he had put in a strand of heavy wires from the basement underground through the yard to the other end of the property. When he attempted to hook them up with the utility pole belonging to the electric company, he was killed instantly. It happened near the place where Mrs. Eidson's girl had seen the apparition. Since the wires are still in her garden, Mrs. Eidson is not at all surprised that the dead man likes to hang around.

And what better way for an electronics buff to manifest as a ghost than by appearing as a bright, bouncy light? As of this writing, the dead electrician is still playing tricks in the Eidson home, and Mrs. Eidson is looking for a new home—one a little less unusual than their present one.

Eileen Courtis is forty-seven years old, a native of London, and a well-balanced individual who now resides on the West coast but who lived previously in New York City. Although she has never gone to college, she has a good grasp of things, an analytical mind, and is not given to hysterics. When she arrived in New York at age thirty-four, she decided to look for a quiet hotel and then search for a job.

The job turned out to be an average office position, and the hotel she decided upon was the Martha Washington, which was a hotel for women only on Twenty-Ninth Street. Eileen was essentially shy and a loner who only made friends slowly.

She was given a room on the twelfth floor and, immediately on crossing the threshold, she was struck by a foul odor coming from the room. Her first impulse was to ask for another room, but she was in no mood to create a fuss so she stayed.

"I can stand it a night or two," she thought, but did not unpack. It turned out that she stayed in that room for six long months, and yet she never really unpacked.

Now all her life, Eileen had been having various experiences of what we now call extrasensory perception, and her first impression of her new "home" was that someone had died in it. She examined the walls inch by inch. There was a spot where a crucifix must have hung for a long time, judging by the color of the surrounding wall. Evidently it had been removed when someone moved out . . . permanently.

That night, after she had gone to bed, her sleep was interrupted by what sounded like the turning of a newspaper page. It sounded exactly as if someone were sitting in the chair at the foot of her bed reading a newspaper. Quickly she switched on the light and she was, of course, quite alone. Were her nerves playing tricks on her? It was a strange city, a strange room. She decided to go back to sleep. Immediately the rustling started up again, and then someone began walking across the floor, starting from the chair and heading toward the door of the room.

Eileen turned on every light in the room and it stopped. Exhausted, she dozed off again. The next morning she looked over the room carefully. Perhaps mice had caused the strange rustling. The strange odor remained, so she requested that the room be fumigated. The manager smiled wryly, and nobody came to fumigate her room. The rustling noise continued, night after night and Eileen slept with the lights on for the next three weeks.

Somehow her ESP told her this presence was a strong-willed, vicious old woman who resented others occupying what she still considered "her" room. Eileen decided to fight her. Night after night, she braved it out in the dark, only to find herself totally exhausted in the morning. Her appearance at the office gave rise to talk. But she was not going to give in to a ghost. Side by side, the living and the dead women now occupied the same room without sharing it.

Then one night, something prevented her from going off to sleep. She lay in bed quietly, waiting.

Suddenly she became aware of two skinny but very strong arms extended over her head, holding a large downy pillow as though to suffocate her!

It took every ounce of her strength to force the pillow off her face.

Next morning, she tried to pass it off to herself as a hallucination. But was it? She was quite sure that she had not been asleep.

But still she did not move out and, one evening when she arrived home from the office with a friend, she felt a sudden pain in her back, as if she had been stabbed. During the night, she awoke to find herself in a state of utter paralysis. She could not move her limbs or head. Finally, after a long time, she managed to work her way to the telephone receiver and call for a doctor. Nobody came. But her control seemed to start coming back and she called her friend, who rushed over only to find Eileen in a state of shock.

During the next few days she had a thorough examination by the company physician, which included the taking of X-rays to determine if there was anything physically wrong with her that could have caused this condition. She was given a clean bill of health and her strength had by then returned, so she decided to quit while she was ahead.

She went to Florida for an extended rest, but eventually came back to New York and the hotel. This time she was given another room, where she lived very happily and without incident for over a year.

One day a neighbor who knew her from the time she had occupied the room on the twelfth floor saw her in the lobby and insisted on having a visit with her. Reluctantly, for she is not fond of socializing, Eileen agreed. The conversation covered various topics until suddenly the neighbor came out with "the time you were living in that haunted room across the hall."

Since Eileen had never told anyone of her fearsome experiences there, she was puzzled. The neighbor confessed that she had meant to warn her while she was occupying that room, but somehow never had mustered enough courage. "Warn me of what?" Eileen insisted.

"The woman who had the room just before you moved in," the neighbor explained haltingly, "well, she was found dead in the chair, and the woman who had it before her also was found dead in the bathtub."

Eileen swallowed quickly and left. Suddenly she knew that the pillowcase had not been a hallucination.

The Buxhoeveden family is one of the oldest noble families of Europe, related to a number of royal houses and—since the eighteenth century when one of the counts married the daughter of Catherine the Great of Russia—also to the Russian Imperial family. The family seat was Lode Castle on the island of Eesel, off the coast of Estonia. The castle, which is still standing, is a very ancient building with a round tower somewhat apart from the main building. Its Soviet occupants have since turned it into a museum.

The Buxhoevedens acquired it when Frederick William Buxhoeveden married Natalie of Russia; it was a gift from mother-in-law Catherine.

Thus it was handed down from first-born son to first-born son, until it came to be in the hands of an earlier Count Anatol Buxhoeveden. The time was the beginning of this century, and all was right with the world.

Estonia was a Russian province, so it was not out of the ordinary that Russian regiments should hold war games in the area, and on one occasion when the maneuvers were in full swing, the regimental commander requested that his officers be put up at the castle. The soldiers were located in the nearby town, but five of the staff officers came to stay at Lode Castle. Grandfather Buxhoeveden was the perfect host, but was unhappy that he could not accommodate all five in the main house. The fifth man would have to be satisfied with quarters in the tower. Since the tower had by then acquired a reputation of being haunted, he asked for a volunteer to stay in that particular room.

There was a great deal of teasing about the haunted room before the youngest of the officers volunteered and left for his quarters.

The room seemed cozy enough and the young officer congratulated himself for having chosen so quiet and pleasant a place to spend the night after a hard day's maneuvers.

And being tired, he decided to get into bed right away. But he was too tired to fall asleep quickly, so he took a book from one of the shelves lining the walls, lit the candle on his night table, and began to read for a while.

As he did so, he suddenly became aware of a greenish light toward the opposite end of the circular room. As he looked at the light with astonishment, it changed before his eyes into the shape of a woman. She seemed solid enough and, to his horror, came over to his bed, took him by the hand and demanded that he follow her. Somehow he could not resist her commands, even though not a single word was spoken. He followed her down the stairs into the library in the castle itself. There she made signs indicating that he was to remove the carpet. Without questioning her, he flipped back the rug. She then pointed at a trap door that was underneath the carpet. He opened the door and followed the figure down a flight of stairs until they came to a big iron door that barred their progress. Now the figure pointed to the right corner of the floor and he dug into it. There he found a key, perhaps ten inches long, and with it he opened the iron gate. He now found himself in a long corridor that led him to a circular room. From there another corridor led on and again he followed eagerly, wondering what this was all about.

This latter corridor suddenly opened into another circular room which seemed familiar—he was back in his own room. The apparition was gone.

What did it all mean? He sat up trying to figure it out, and when he finally dozed off it was already dawn. Consequently he overslept and came down to breakfast last. His state of excitement immediately drew the attention of the Count and his fellow officers. "You won't believe this," he began and told them what had happened to him.

He was right. Nobody believed him.

But his insistence that he was telling the truth was so convincing that the Count finally agreed, more to humor him than because he believed him, to follow the young officer to the library to look for the alleged trap door.

"But," he added, "I must tell you that on top of that carpet are some heavy bookshelves filled with books which have not been moved or touched in over a hundred years. It is quite impossible for any one man to flip back that carpet."

They went to the library, and just as the Count had said, the carpet could not be moved. But Grandfather Buxhoeveden decided to follow through anyway and called in some of his men. Together, ten men were able to move the shelves and turn the carpet back. Underneath the carpet was a dust layer an inch thick, but it did not stop the intrepid young officer from looking for the ring of the trap door. After a long search for it, he finally located it. A hush fell over the group when he pulled the trap door open. There was the secret passage and the iron gate. And there, next to it, was a rusty iron key. The key fit the lock. The gate, which had not moved for centuries perhaps, slowly and painfully swung open and the little group continued their exploration of the musty passages. With the officer leading, the men went through the corridors and came out in the tower room, just as the officer had done during the night.

But what did it mean? Everyone knew there were secret passages— lots of old castles had them as a hedge in time of war.

The matter gradually faded from memory, and life at Lode went on. The iron key, however, was preserved and remained in the Buxhoeveden family until some years ago, when it was stolen from Count Alexander's Paris apartment.

Ten years went by, until, after a small fire in the castle, Count Buxhoeveden decided to combine the necessary repairs with the useful installation of central heating, something old castles always need. The contractor doing the job brought in twenty men who worked hard to restore and improve the appointments at Lode. Then one day, the entire crew vanished to a man—like ghosts. Count Buxhoeveden reported this to the police, who were already being besieged by the wives and families of the men who had disappeared without leaving a trace.

Newspapers of the period had a field day with the case of the vanishing workmen, but the publicity did not help to bring them back, and the puzzle remained.

Then came the revolution and the Buxhoevedens lost their ancestral home. Count Alexander and the present Count Anatol, my brother-in-law, went to live in Switzerland. The year was 1923. One day the two men were walking down a street in Lausanne when a stranger approached them, calling Count Alexander by name.

"I am the brother of the Major Domo of your castle," the man explained. "I was a plumber on that job of restoring it after the fire."

So much time had passed and so many political events had changed the map of Europe that the man was ready at last to lift the veil of secrecy from the case of the vanishing workmen.

This is the story he told: when the men were digging trenches for the central heating system, they accidentally came across an iron kettle of the kind used in the Middle Ages to pour boiling oil or water down on the enemies besieging a castle. Yet this pot was not full of water, but rather of gold. They had stumbled onto the long-missing Buxhoeveden treasure, a hoard reputed to have existed for centuries but which was never found. Now, at this stroke of good fortune, the workmen became larcenous. To a man, they opted for distributing the find among themselves, even though it meant leaving everything behind—their families, their homes, their work—and striking out fresh somewhere else. But the treasure was large enough to make this a pleasure rather than a problem, and they never missed their wives, it would seem, finding ample replacements in the gentler climes of western Europe, where most of them went to live under assumed names.

At last the apparition that had appeared to the young officer made sense: it had been an ancestor who wanted to let her descendants know where the family gold had been secreted. What a frustration for a ghost to see her efforts come to naught, and worse yet, to see the fortune squandered by thieves while the legal heirs had to go into exile. Who knows how things might have turned out for the Buxhoevedens if *they* had gotten to the treasure in time.

At any rate there is a silver lining to this account: since there is nothing further to find at Lode Castle, the ghost does not have to put in appearances under that ghastly new regime. But Russian aristocrats and English lords of the manor have no corner on uncanny phenomena. Nor are all of the haunted settings I have encountered romantic or forbidding. Certainly there are more genuine ghostly manifestations in the American Midwest and South than anywhere else in the world. This may be due to the fact that a great deal of violence occurred there during the nineteenth and early twentieth centuries. Also, the American public's attitude toward such phenomena is different from that of Europeans. In Europe, people are inclined to reserve their accounts of bona fide ghosts for those people they can trust. Being ridiculed is not a favorite pastime of most Europeans.

Americans, by contrast, are more independent. They couldn't care less what others think of them in the long run, so long as their own people believe them. I have approached individuals in many cases with an assurance of scientific inquiry and respect for their stories. I am not a skeptic. I am a searcher for the truth, regardless of what this truth looks or sounds like.

Some time ago, a well-known TV personality took issue with me concerning my conviction that ESP and ghosts are real. Since he was not well informed on the subject, he should not have ventured forth into an area I know so well. He proudly proclaimed himself a skeptic.

Irritated, I finally asked him if he knew what being a skeptic meant. He shook his head.

"The term skeptic," I lectured him patiently, "is derived from the Greek word *skepsis*, which was the name of a small town in Asia Minor in antiquity. It was known for its lack of knowledge and people from skepsis were called skeptics."

The TV personality didn't like it at all, but the next time we met on camera, he was a lot more human and his humility finally showed.

I once received a curious letter from a Mrs. Stewart living in Chicago, Illinois, in which she explained that she was living with a ghost and didn't mind, except that she had lost two children at birth and this ghost was following not only her but also her little girl. This she didn't like, so could I please come and look into the situation?

I could and did. On July 4, I celebrated Independence Day by trying to free a hung-up lady ghost on Chicago's South Side. The house itself was an old one, built around the late 1800s, and not exactly a monument of architectural beauty. But its functional sturdiness suited its present purpose—to house a number of young couples and their children, people who found the house both convenient and economical.

In its heyday, it had been a wealthy home, complete with servants and backstairs for them to go up and down on. The three stories are even now connected by an elaborate buzzer system which, however, hasn't worked for years.

I did not wish to discuss the phenomena at the house with Mrs. Stewart until after Sybil Leek, who was with me, had had a chance to explore the situation. My good friend Carl Subak, a stamp dealer, had come along to see how I worked. He and I had known each other thirty years ago when we were both students, and because of that he had overcome his own—ah—skepticism—and come along. Immediately on arrival, Sybil ascended the stairs to the second floor as if she knew where to go! Of course she didn't; I had not discussed the matter with her at all. But despite this promising beginning, she drew a complete blank when we arrived in the apartment upstairs. "I feel absolutely nothing," she confided and looked at me doubtfully. Had I made a mistake? She seemed to ask. On a hot July day, had we come all the way to the South Side of Chicago on a wild ghost chase?

We gathered in a bedroom where there was a comfortable chair and windows on both sides that gave onto an old-fashioned garden; there was a porch on one side and a parkway on the other. The furniture, in keeping with the modest economic circumstances of the owners, was old and worn, but it was functional and they did not seem to mind.

In a moment, Sybil Leek had slipped into trance. But instead of a ghost's personality, the next voice we heard was Sybil's own, although it sounded strange. Sybil was "out" of her own body, but able to observe the place and report back to us while still in trance.

The first thing she saw were maps, in a large round building somehow connected with the house we were in.

"Is there anyone around?" I asked.

"Yes," Sybil intoned, "James Dugan."

"What does he do here?"

"Come back to live."

"When was that?"

"1912."

"Is there anyone with him?"

"There is another man. McCloud."

"Anyone else?"

"Lots of people."

"Do they live in this house?"

"Three, four people . . . McCloud . . . maps . . . "

"All men?"

"No . . . girl . . . Judith . . . maidservant . . . "

"Is there an unhappy presence here?"

"Judith . . . she had no one here, no family . . . that man went away . . . Dugan went away . . . "

"How is she connected with this Dugan?"

"Loved him."

"Were they married?"

"No. Lovers."

"Did they have any children?"

There was a momentary silence, then Sybil continued in a drab, monotonous voice.

"The baby's dead."

"Does she know the baby's dead?"

"She cries . . . baby cries . . . neglected . . . by Judith . . . guilty . . . "

"Does Judith know this?"

"Yes."

"How old was the baby when it died?"

"A few weeks old."

Strange, I thought, that Mrs. Stewart had fears for her own child from this source. She, too, had lost children at a tender age.

"What happened to the baby?"

"She put it down the steps."

"What happened to the body then?"

"I don't know."

"Is Judith still here?"

"She's here."

"Where?"

"This room . . . and up and down the steps. She's sorry for her baby."

"Can you talk to her?"

"No. She cannot leave here until she finds—You see if she could get Dugan—"

"Where is Dugan?"

"With the maps."

"What is Dugan's work?"

"Has to do with roads."

"Is he dead?"

"Yes. She wants him here, but he is not here."

"How did she die?"

"She ran away to the water . . . died by the water . . . but is here where she lived . . . baby died on the steps . . . downstairs . . . "

""What is she doing here, I mean how does she let people know she is around?"

"She pulls things . . . *she cries . . .* "

"And her Christian name?"

"Judith Vincent, I think. Twenty-one. Darkish, not white. From an island."

"And the man? Is he white?"

"Yes."

"Can you see her?"

"Yes."

"Speak to her?"

"She doesn't want to, but perhaps . . . "

"What year does she think this is?"

"1913."

"Tell her this is the year 1965."

Sybil informed the spirit in a low voice that this was 1965 and she need not stay here any longer. Dugan is dead, too.

"She has to find him," Sybil explained and I directed her to explain that she need only call out for her lover in order to be reunited with him "Over There."

"She's gone . . . " Sybil finally said, and breathed deeply.

A moment later she woke up and looked with astonishment at the strange room, having completely forgotten how we got here, or where we were.

There was no time for explanations now, as I still wanted to check out some of this material. The first one to sit down with me was the owner of the flat, Mrs. Alexandra Stewart. A graduate of the University of Iowa, twenty-five years old, Alexandra Stewart works as a personnel director. She had witnessed the trance session and seemed visibly shaken. There was a good reason for this. Mrs. Stewart, you see, had met the ghost Sybil had described.

The Stewarts had moved into the second floor apartment in the winter of 1964. The room we were now sitting in had been hers. Shortly after they moved in, Mrs. Stewart happened to be glancing up toward the French doors, when she saw a woman looking at her. The figure was about five feet three or four, and wore a blue-gray dress with a shawl, and a hood over her head, for which reason Mrs. Stewart could not make out the woman's features. The head seemed strangely bowed to her, almost as if the woman were doing penance.

I questioned Mrs. Stewart on the woman's color in view of Sybil's description of Judith. But Mrs. Stewart could not be sure; the woman could have been white or black. At the time, Mrs. Stewart had assumed it to be a reflection from the mirror, but when she glanced at the mirror, she did not see the figure in it. When she turned her attention back to the figure, it had disappeared. It was toward evening and Mrs. Stewart was a little tired, yet the figure was very real to her. Her doubts were completely dispelled when the ghost returned about a month later. In the meantime she had had the dresser that formerly stood in the line of sight moved farther down, so that any reflection as explanation would simply not hold water. Again the figure appeared at the French doors. She looked very unhappy to Mrs. Stewart, who felt herself strangely drawn to the woman, almost as if she should help her in some way as yet unknown.

But the visual visitations were not all that disturbed the Stewarts. Soon they were hearing strange noises, too. Above all there was the crying of a baby, which seemed to come from the second-floor rear bedroom. It could also be heard in the kitchen though less loud, and it seemed to come from the walls. Several people had heard it and there was no natural cause to account for it. Then there were the footsteps. It sounded like someone walking down the backstairs, the servants' stairs, step by step, hesitatingly, and not returning, but just fading away!

They dubbed their ghostly guest "Elizabeth," for want of a better name. Mrs. Stewart did not consider herself psychic, nor did she have any interest in such matters. But occasionally things had happened to her that defied natural explanations such as the time just after she had lost a baby. She awoke from a heavy sleep with the intangible feeling of a presence in her room. She looked up and there, in the rocking chair across the room, she saw a woman, now dead, who had taken care of her when she herself was a child. Rocking gently in the chair, as if to reassure her, the Nanny held Mrs. Stewart's baby in her arms. In a moment the vision was gone, but it had left Alexandra Stewart with a sense of peace. She knew her little one was well looked after.

The phenomena continued, however, and soon they were no longer restricted to the upstairs. On the first floor in the living room, Mrs. Stewart heard the noise of someone breathing close to her. This had happened only recently, again in the presence of her husband and a friend. She asked them to hold their breath for a moment, and still she heard the strange breathing continue as before. Neither of the men could hear it or so they said. But the following day the guest came back with another man. He wanted to be sure of his observation before admitting that he too had heard the invisible person breathing close to him.

The corner of the living room where the breathing had been heard was also the focal point for strange knockings that faulty pipes could not explain. On one occasion they heard the breaking of glass, and yet there was no evidence that any glass had been broken. There was a feeling that someone other than the visible people was present at times in their living room, and it made them a little nervous even though they did not fear their "Elizabeth."

Alexandra's young husband grew up in the building trade, and now works as a photographer. He too has heard the footsteps on many occasions, and he knows the difference between them and a house settling or timbers creaking—these were definitely human noises.

Mrs. Martha Vaughn is a bookkeeper who had been living in the building for two years. Hers is the apartment in the rear portion of the second floor, and it includes the back porch. Around Christmas of 1964, she heard a baby crying on the porch. It was a particularly cold night, so she went to investigate immediately. It was a weird, unearthly sound—to her it seemed right near the porch, but there was nobody around. The yard was deserted. The sound to her was the crying of a small child, not a baby, but perhaps a child of from one to three years of age. The various families shared the downstairs living room "like a kibbutz," as Mrs. Stewart put it, so it was not out of the ordinary for several people to be in the downstairs area. On one such occasion Mrs. Vaughn also heard the breaking of the *invisible* glass.

Richard Vaughn is a laboratory technician. He too has heard the baby cry and the invisible glass break; he has heard pounding on the wall as have the others. A skeptic at first, he tried to blame these noises on the steam pipes that heat the house. But when he listened to the pipes when they were acting up, he realized at once that the noises he had heard before were completely different.

"What about a man named Dugan? Or someone having to do with maps?" I asked.

"Well," Vaughn said, and thought back, "I used to get mail here for people who once lived here, and of course I sent it all back to the post office. But I don't recall the name Dugan. What I do recall was some mail from a Washington Bureau. You see, this house belongs to the University of Chicago and a lot of professors used to live here."

"Professors?" I said with renewed interest.

Was Dugan one of them?

Several other people who lived in the house experienced strange phenomena. Barbara Madonna used to live there too. But in May of that year she moved out. She works three days a week as a secretary and moved into the house in November of the previous year. She and her husband much admired the back porch when they first moved in, and had visions of sitting out there drinking a beer on warm evenings. But soon their hopes were dashed by the uncanny feeling that they were not alone, that another presence was in their apartment, especially around the porch. Soon, instead of using the porch, they studiously avoided it, even if it meant walking downstairs to shake out a mop. Theirs was the third-floor apartment, directly above the Stewart apartment.

A girl by the name of Lolita Krol also had heard the baby crying. She lived in the building for a time and bitterly complained about the strange noises on the porch.

Douglas McConnor is a magazine editor, and he and his wife moved into the building in November of the year Barbara Madonna moved out, first to the second floor and later to the third. From the very first, when McConnor was still alone—his wife joined him in the flat after their marriage a little later—he felt extremely uncomfortable in the place. Doors and windows would fly open by themselves when there wasn't any strong wind.

When he moved upstairs to the next floor, things were much quieter, except for one thing: always on Sunday nights, noisy activities would greatly increase toward midnight. Footsteps, the sounds of people rushing about, and of doors opening and closing would disturb Mr. McConnor's rest. The stairs were particularly noisy. But when he checked, he found that everybody was accounted for, and that no living person had caused the commotion.

It got to be so bad he started to hate Sunday nights.

I recounted Sybil's trance to Mr. McConnor and the fact that a woman named Judith had been the central figure of it.

"Strange," he observed, "but the story also fits my ex-wife who deserted her children. She is of course very much alive now. Her name is Judith."

Had Sybil intermingled the impression a dead maidservant with the imprint left behind by an unfit mother? Or were there two Judiths? An any rate the Stewarts did not complain further about uncanny noises, and the girl in the blue-gray dress never came back.

On the way to the airport, Carl Subak seemed unusually silent as he drove us out to the field. What he had witnessed seemed to have left an impression on him and his philosophy of life.

"What I find so particularly upsetting," he finally said, "is Sybil's talking about a woman and a dead baby—all of it borne out afterwards by the people in the house. But Sybil did not know this. She couldn't have."

No, she couldn't.

In September, three years later, a group consisting of a local television reporter, a would-be psychic student, and an assortment of clairvoyants descended on the building in search of psychic excitement. All they got out of it were more mechanical difficulties with their cameras. But the ghosts were long gone.

Ghosts are not just for the thrill seekers, nor are they the hallucinations of disturbed people. Nothing is as democratic as seeing or hearing a ghost, for it happens all the time to just about every conceivable type of person. Neither age nor race nor religion seem to stay these spectral people in their predetermined haunts.

Naturally I treat each case reported to me on an individual basis. Some I reject on the face of the report, and others only after I have been through a long and careful investigation. But other reports have the ring of truth about them and are worthy of belief, even though some of them are no longer capable of verification because witnesses have died or sites have been destroyed.

A good example is the case reported to me recently by a Mrs. Edward Needs, Jr., of Canton, Ohio. In a small town by the name of Homeworth, there is a stretch of land near the highway that is today nothing more than a neglected farm with a boarded-up old barn still standing. The spot is actually on a dirt road, and the nearest house is half a mile away, with wooded territory in between. This is important, you see, for the spot is isolated and a man might die before help could arrive . . . On rainy days, the dirt road is impassable. Mrs. Needs has passed the spot a number of times, and does not particularly care to go there. Somehow it always gives her an uneasy feeling. Once, the Needs's car got stuck in the mud on a rainy day, and they had to drive through open fields to get out.

It was on that adventure-filled ride that Mr. Needs confided for the first time what had happened to him at that spot on prior occasions. It was the year when Edward Needs and a friend were on a joy ride after dark. At that time Needs had not yet married his present wife, and the two men had been drinking a little, but were far from drunk. It was then that they discovered the dirt road for the first time.

On the spur of the moment, they followed it. A moment later they came to the old barn. But just as they were approaching it, a man jumped out of nowhere in front of them. What was even more sobering was the condition this man was in: engulfed in flames from head to toe!

Quickly Needs put his bright headlights on the scene, to see better. The man then ran into the woods across the road, and just disappeared.

Two men never became cold sober more quickly. They turned around and went back to the main highway fast. But the first chance they had, they returned with two carloads full of other fellows. They were equipped with strong lights, guns, and absolutely no whiskey. When the first of the cars was within twenty feet of the spot where Needs had seen the apparition, they all saw the same thing: there before them, was the horrible spectacle of a human being blazing from top to bottom, and evidently suffering terribly as he tried to run away from his doom. Needs emptied his gun at the figure: it never moved or acknowledged that it had been hit by the bullets. A few seconds later, the figure ran into the woods—exactly as it had when Needs had first encountered it.

Now the ghost posse went into the barn, which they found abandoned although not in very bad condition. The only strange thing was spots showing evidence of fire: evidently someone or something had burned inside the barn without, however, setting fire to the barn as a whole. Or had the fiery man run outside to save his barn from the fire?

Betty Ann Tylaska lives in a seaport in Connecticut. Her family is a prominent one going back to Colonial days, and they still occupy a house built by her great-great-great-grandfather for his daughter and her husband back in 1807.

Mrs. Tylaska and her husband, a Navy officer, were in the process of restoring the venerable old house to its former glory. Neither of them had the slightest interest in the supernatural, and to them such things as ghosts simply did not exist except in children's tales.

The first time Mrs. Tylaska noticed anything unusual was one night when she was washing dishes in the kitchen.

Suddenly she had the strong feeling that she was being watched. She turned around and caught a glimpse of a man standing in the doorway between the kitchen and the living room of the downstairs part of the house. She saw him only for a moment, but long enough to notice his dark blue suit and silver buttons. Her first impression was that it must be her husband, who of course wore a Navy blue uniform. But on checking she found him upstairs, wearing entirely different clothes.

She shrugged the matter off as probably a hallucination due to her tiredness, but the man in blue kept returning. On several occasions, the same uncanny feeling of being watched came over her, and when she turned around, there was the man in the dark blue suit.

It came as a relief to her when her mother confessed that she too had seen the ghostly visitor—always at the same spot, between living room and kitchen. Finally she informed her husband, and to her surprise, he did not laugh at her. But he suggested that if it were a ghost, perhaps one of her ancestors was checking up on them.

Perhaps he wanted to make sure they restored the house properly and did not make any unwanted changes. They were doing a great deal of painting in the process of restoring the house, and whatever paint residue was left they would spill aginst an old stone wall in the back of the house.

Gradually the old stones were covered with paint of various hues.

One day Mr. Tylaska found himself in front of these stones. For want of anything better to do at the moment, he started to study them. To his amazement, he discovered that one of the stones was different from the others: it was long and flat. He called his wife and they investigated the strange stone; upon freeing it from the wall, they saw to their horror that it was a gravestone—her great-great-great-grandfather's tombstone, to be exact.

Inquiry at the local church cleared up the mystery of how the tombstone had gotten out of the cemetery. It seems that all the family members had been buried in a small cemetery nearby. But it filled up, and one day a larger cemetery was started. The bodies were removed to it and a larger monument had been erected over great-great-great-grandfather's tomb. Since the original stone was of no use any longer, it was left behind. Somehow the stone got used when the old wall was being built. But evidently great-great-great-grandfather did not like the idea. Was that the reason for his visits? After all, who likes having paint splashed on one's precious tombstone? I ask you.

The Tylaska family held a meeting to decide what to do about it. They could not very well put two tombstones on grandad's grave. What would the other ancestors think? Everybody would want to have two tombstones then; and while it might be good news to the stonecutter, it would not be a thing to do in practical New England.

So they stood the old tombstone upright in their own backyard. It was nice having grandad with them that way, and if he felt like a visit, why, that was all right with them too.

From the moment when they gave the tombstone a place of honor, the gentleman in the dark blue suit and the silver buttons never came back. But Mrs. Tylaska does not particularly mind. Two Navy men in the house might have been too much of a distraction anyway.

Give a ghost his due, and he'll be happy. Happy ghosts don't stay around: in fact, they turn into normal spirits, free to come and go (mostly go) at will. But until people come to recognize that the denizens of the Other World are real people like you and me, and not some benighted devils or condemned souls in a purgatory created for the benefit of a political church, people will be frightened of ghosts quite needlessly. Sometimes even highly intelligent people shudder when they have a brush with the uncanny.

Take young Mr. Bentine, for instance, the son of my dear friend Michael Bentine, the British TV star. He, like his father, is very much interested in the psychic. But young Bentine never bargained for first hand experiences.

It happened at school, Harrow, one of the finest British "public schools" (in America they are called private schools), one spring. Young Bentine lived in a dormitory known as The Knoll. One night around two A.M., he awoke from sound sleep. The silence of the night was broken by the sound of footsteps coming from the headmaster's room. The footsteps went from the room to a nearby bathroom, and then suddenly came to a halt. Bentine thought nothing of it, but why had it awakened him? Perhaps he had been studying too hard and it was merely a case of nerves. At any rate, he decided not to pay any attention to the strange footsteps. After all, if the headmaster wished to walk at that ungodly hour, that was his business and privilege.

But the following night the same thing happened. Again, at two A.M. he found himself awake, and there came the ominous footsteps. Again they stopped abruptly when they reached the bathroom. Coincidence? Cautiously young Bentine made some inquiries. Was the headmaster given to nocturnal walks, perhaps? He was not.

The third night, Bentine decided that if it happened again, he would be brave and look into it. He fortified himself with some tea and then went to bed. It was not easy falling asleep, but eventually his fatigue had the upper hand and our young man was asleep in his room.

Promptly at two, however, he was awake again. And quicker than you could say, "Ghost across the hall," there were the familiar footsteps!

Quickly our intrepid friend got up and stuck his head out of his door, facing the headmaster's room and the bathroom directly across the corridor.

The steps were now very loud and clear. Although he did not see anyone, he heard someone move along the passage.

He was petrified. As soon as the footsteps had come to the usual abrupt halt in front of the bathroom door, he crept back into his own room and bed. But sleep was out for the night. The hours were like months, until finally morning came and a very tired Bentine went down to breakfast, glad the ordeal of the night had come to an end.

He had to know what this was all about, no matter what the consequences. To go through another night like that was out of the question.

He made some cautious inquiries about that room. There had been a headmaster fourteen years ago who had died in that room. It had been suicide, and he had hanged himself in the shower. Bentine turned white as a ghost himself when he heard the story. He immediately tried to arrange to have his room changed. But that could not be done as quickly as he had hoped, so it was only after another two and a half weeks that he was able to banish the steps of the ghostly headmaster from his mind.

His father had lent him a copy of my book, *Ghost Hunter*, and he had looked forward to reading it when exams eased up a bit. But now, even though he was in another room without the slightest trace of a ghost, he could not bring himself to touch my book. Instead, he concentrated on reading humor.

Unfortunately nobody did anything about the ghostly headmaster, so it must be that he keeps coming back down that passage to his old room, only to find his body still hanging in the shower.

You might ask, "What shall I do if I think I have a ghost in the house? Shall I run? Shall I stay? Do I talk to it or ignore it? Is there a rule book for people having ghosts?" Some of the questions I get are like that. Others merely wish to report a case because they feel it is something I might be interested in. Still others want help: free them from the ghost and vice versa. Some are worried: how much will I charge them for the house-cleaning job? When I explain that there is no charge and that I will gladly do it, they are relieved. This is because ghostly manifestations often occur to people with very little money.

But so many people have ghosts—almost as many as have termites, not that there is any connection—that I cannot personally go after each and every case brought to my attention by mail, telephone, telegram, or television.

In the most urgent cases, I try to come and help the people involved. Usually I do this in connection with a TV show or lecture at the local university, for *someone* has to pay my expenses. The airlines don't accept ghost money, nor do the innkeepers. And thus far I have been on my own, financially speaking, with no Institute or Research Foundation to take up the slack. For destruction and bombs there is always money, but for research involving the psychic, hardly ever.

Granted, I can visit a number of people with haunted-house problems every year, but what do the others do when I can't see them myself? Can I send them to a local ghost hunter, the way a doctor sends patients to a colleague if he can't or does not wish to treat them?

Even if I could, I wouldn't do it. When they ask for my help, they want my approach to their peculiar problems and not someone else's. In this field every researcher sees things a little differently from the next one. I am probably the only parapsychologist who is unhesitatingly pro-ghost. Some will admit they exist, but spend a lot of time trying to find "alternate" explanations if they cannot discredit the witnesses.

I have long, and for good scientific reasons, become convinced that ghosts exist. Ghosts are ghosts. Not hallucinations, necessarily, and not mistakes of casual observers. With that sort of practical base to start from, I go after the cases by concentrating on the situation and problems, rather than, as some researchers will do, trying hard to change the basic stories reported to me. I don't work on my witnesses; I've come to help them. To try and shake them with the sophisticated apparatus of a trained parapsycholoist is not only unfair, but also foolish. The original reports are straight reports of average people telling what has happened in their own environment. If you try to shake their testimony, you may get a different story—but it won't be the truth, necessarily. The more you confuse the witnesses, the less they will recall that which is firsthand information.

My job begins when the witnesses have told their story for the first time.

In the majority of cases I have handled, I have found a basis of fact for the ghostly "complaint." Once in a while, a person may have thought something was supernormal when it was not, and on rare occasions I have come across mentally unbalanced people living in a fantasy world of their own. There just aren't that many kooks who want my help: evidently my scientific method, even though I am convinced of the veracity of ghostly phenomena, is not the kind of searchlight they wish to have turned on their strange stories.

What to do until the Ghost Hunter arrives? Relax, if you can. Be a good observer, whether or not you are scared stiff. And remember, please—ghosts are also people.

There, but for the grace of God, goes someone like you.

chapter 4
The Strange Death of Valerie K.

SOMETIMES being a psychic investigator puts a heavy moral burden on one, especially where there may be a possibility of preventing someone's death. Of course, you're never sure that you can. Take the case of Valerie K., for instance. I am not using her full name because the case is far from closed. The police won't talk about it, but her friends are only too sure there is something mysterious about her death, and they *will* talk about it. They speak mainly to me, for that's about all they can do about it—now.

To start at the beginning, one April I got a phone call from Sheila M.—an English girl whom I had met through a mutual friend—inviting my wife and me to a cocktail party at her house on New York's East Side. Now if it's one thing my wife and I hate it's cocktail parties, even on the East Side, but Sheila is a nice person and we thought she was likely to have only nice friends, so I said we'd come. The party was on April 20, and when we arrived everybody was already there, drinking and chatting, while the butler passed between the guests, ever so quietly seeing after their needs.

Since I don't drink, I let my wife talk to Sheila and sauntered over to the hors d'oeuvres, hopefully searching for some cheese bits, for I am a vegetarian and don't touch meat or fish. Next to the buffet table I found not only an empty chair, unusual at a cocktail party, but also a lovely young woman in a shiny silver Oriental-style dress. In fact, the young lady was herself an Oriental, a very impressive-looking girl perhaps in her middle twenties, with brown hair, dark eyes, and a very quiet, soigné air about her. It turned out that the girl's name was Valerie K., and I had been briefly introduced to her once before on the telephone when Sheila had told her of my interest in psychic research, and she had wanted to tell me some of her experiences.

We got to talking about our mutual interest in ESP. She sounded far away, as if something was troubling her, but I had the impression she was determined to be gay and not allow it to interfere with her enjoyment of the party. I knew she was Sheila's good friend and would not want to spoil anything for her. But I probed deeper, somehow sensing she needed help. I was right, and she asked me if she could talk to me sometime privately.

There were several eager young men at the party whose eyes were on the lovely Oriental, so I thought it best not to preempt her time, since I knew she was not married. I gave her my telephone number and asked her to call me whenever she wanted to.

About an hour later we left the party, and when we got home I suppressed a desire to telephone this girl and see if she was all right. I dismissed my feeling as undue sentimentality, for the girl had seemed radiant, and surely the reason for her wanting to see me would have to be psychic rather than personal in the usual sense.

All through the weekend I could not get her out of my mind, but I was busy with other work and decided to call her first thing the following week.

Monday night, as I read the *Daily News,* my eye fell on a brief article tucked away inside the newspaper, an article telling of the death of two women a few hours before. The paper's date was Tuesday morning. The deaths had occurred early Monday morning. One of the two women was Valerie K.

With a shudder I put down the paper and closed my eyes.

Could I have prevented her death? I will let you be the judge. But first let me show you what happened in the final hours of this girl's life on earth. Every word is the truth . . . .

Valerie K. came from a well-to-do Chinese family residing in Hawaii. She was as American as anyone else in her speech, and yet there was that undefinable quality in the way she put her words together that hinted at Eastern thought. After an unhappy and brief marriage to a Hong Kong businessman, she came to New York City to try living on her own. Never particularly close to her parents, she was now entirely self-supporting and needed a job. She found a job vaguely described as a public relations assistant, but in fact was the secretary to the man who did publicity for the company. Somehow she was not quite right for the job or the job for her, and it came to a parting of the ways.

The new girl hired to take her place was Sheila. Despite the fact that the English girl replaced her, they struck up a friendship that developed into a true attachment to each other, so much so that Valerie would confide in Sheila to a greater extent than she would in anyone else.

When Valerie left the office, there was no job waiting for her; fortunately, however, she had met the manager of a firm owned by the same company, and the manager, whose initial was G., took her on for somewhat selfish reasons. He had a sharp eye for beauty and Valerie was something special. Thus she found herself earning considerably more than she would have been paid in a similar job elsewhere. Soon the manager let her know that he liked her and she got to like him, too. Between August and October of the year before her death, they became close friends.

But in October of that year she called her friend Sheila to complain bitterly of the humiliation she had been put through. G. had found another girl to take her place. Innocently, the new girl, Lynn, became the pawn in the deadly game between the manager and the Chinese beauty.

G. found fault with her very appearance and everything she did, criticizing her and causing her to lose face—to an Oriental an important matter not easily forgotten.

Still, she cared for the man and hoped that he would resume his former attentions. He didn't, and after a miserable Christmas which she partially shared with Sheila, the axe fell. He fired her and gave her two weeks' pay, wishing her the best.

When Sheila heard about this she suggested that Valerie register at the Unemployment Office. Instead, the proud girl took sleeping pills. But she either did not take enough or changed her mind in time, for she was able to telephone Sheila and tell her what she had done. A doctor was called and she was saved. She had a session with a psychiatrist after that and seemed much more cheerful.

But the humiliation and rejection kept boiling within her. Nothing can be as daring as a person whose affections have been rejected, and one day Valerie wrote a personal letter to the owner of the companies she had once worked for, denouncing the manager and his work.

As if nourished by her hatred, her psychic abilities increased and she found she was able to infuence people through telepathy, to read others' thoughts and to put herself into a state of excitement through a form of meditation.

All this of course was for the purpose of getting even, not only with the manager but with the world that had so often hurt her.

Nobody knew for sure if she ever got a reply to her letter. But she was a regular at an Oriental restaurant near her apartment and became friendly with the owners. There she talked about her plans and how she would show the world what sort of girl she was.

Meanwhile the manager found himself short of help and asked her back. Despite her deep hatred for the man, she went back, all the time scheming and hoping her fortunes would take a turn for the better. But she did confide in Sheila that she had taken a big gamble, and if it worked she'd be all right in more ways than one. The owner of the restaurant saw her on Friday, April 21—a day after the party at which I had met her for the first time—and she seemed unusually happy.

She would marry a prominent European, she told him; she had been asked and would say yes. She was almost obsessed at this point with the desire to tell the whole world she would marry him; her parents in Hawaii received a letter requesting them to have formal Chinese wedding attire made up for her in Paris because she would marry soon. Had the idea of getting even with G. robbed her of her senses? It is difficult to assess this, as the principals involved quite naturally would not talk, and even I prefer that they remain anonymous here.

That weekend—April 22 and 23—the pitch of her "wedding fever" rose higher and higher. A neighbor who had dropped in on her at her apartment found her clad only in a bikini and drinking heavily. She observed her running back and forth from her telephone, trying to reach the man overseas she said she would marry. But she couldn't get through to him. In the meantime, she started giving possessions away, saying she would not need them any longer now that she would marry so rich a man.

She also drew up a list of all those whom she would help once she had become the wife of the millionaire. The neighbor left rather perturbed by all this, and Valerie stayed alone in her apartment—or did she?

It was four A.M. when the police received a call from her telephone. It was a complaint about excessive noise. When an officer—initialed McG.—arrived on the scene at four-twenty A.M., Valerie herself opened the door in the nude.

"Go away," she said, and asked to be left alone. The officer quickly surveyed the scene. She became rude and explained she was expecting a phone call and did not wish to be disturbed. The officer reported that she had been alone and was drinking, and there the matter stood.

The minutes ticked away. It was early Monday morning, April 24.

At precisely five A.M., the building superintendent looked out his window and saw something heavy fall on his terrace.

Rushing to the scene, he discovered Valerie's broken body. She had been killed instantly. The girl had taken two roses with her—but one somehow remained behind on the window sill of the open window from which she had plunged to her death. The other sadly fluttered to earth even as she did.

The police officers found themselves back at the apartment sooner than they had expected, only this time there was a cause for action. After a routine inspection of the girl's tenth floor apartment, her death was put down to accidental death or suicide by falling or jumping from her window. Since she had been drinking heavily, they were not sure which was the actual cause of death.

Monday night Sheila called me frantically, wondering what she should do. There was no one to claim the girl's body. Neither her sister Ethel nor her parents in Hawaii could be reached. I told her to calm down and keep trying, meanwhile berating myself for not having called Valerie in time to prevent her death.

Eventually the parents were found and a proper funeral arranged. But the puzzle remained. Had she committed suicide or not?

Did that call from Europe finally come and was it so humiliating that Valerie could no longer face the world? Was there not going to be a wedding after all—then at least there must be a funeral?

Valerie had been particularly fond of two things in life—flowers and jewelry. To her, losing a favorite piece of jewelry was bad luck.

Lynn, the girl who now worked at Valerie's office, is a rather matter-of-fact person not given to emotional scenes or superstitions.

Valerie owned a pair of jade earrings that G. had had made for her in the days when they were close. About a month before her death, Valerie gave those earrings to Lynn as a gift. There was a special stipulation, however. She must not wear them around the office, since people had seen Valerie wear them and presumably knew their history.

Lynn agreed not to wear them around the office, but when she wore them outside a most unusual phenomenon took place. Suddenly the earrings would not stay put. One and then the other would drop off her ears as if pulled by some unseen force. That was on April 13, and Valerie was still alive though she had seemed very distraught.

Word of Lynn's concern with the falling earrings got back to the former owner, and finally Valerie called to assure her the falling was a "good omen." Then a week later, on Saturday April 22, she suddenly called Lynn shortly before midnight and asked her to wear "her" earrings at the office. Lynn promised she would wear them to work Monday.

That was the day Valerie died. The following day, Lynn was still wearing the earrings, which now seemed to cling properly to her ears. She found herself in the ladies' room, when she felt her right earring forced off and thrown into the toilet. It felt as if it had been snatched from her ear by an unseen hand.

Returning to her desk, she noticed that an unusual chill pervaded the area where Valerie's desk had stood. It disappeared at 4:30, which was the time Valerie usually left for home.

All this proved too much for Lynn and she went on a week's vacation.

Sheila was still very upset when a male friend dropped in to help her in this sorry matter. The gentleman, a lawyer by profession, had taken off his jacket when he suddenly felt a cufflink leave his shirt. It was a particularly intricate piece of jewelry, and no matter how they searched it was never found.

Was the dead girl trying to show her hand? Too fantastic, and yet . . . .

There was no rational explanation for the sudden disappearance, in plain light and in the presence of two people, of so definite an object as a cufflink.

On Friday of that week, after the girl had been buried, her sister, Ethel, who had finally arrived in town, went to the apartment to find out what she could about her sister's effects.

As soon as she entered the apartment, she realized that a terrific fight had taken place in it. Nothing had been touched from the moment of death until her arrival, as the apartment had been sealed. Three knives were lying on the floor and the place was a shambles. On the table she noticed two glasses, one partially filled with Scotch and one almost empty. When she called the police to report the strange appearance of the place, she was given the cold shoulder.

Who was the person Valerie had entertained during her last hours on earth?

The superintendent reported to the sister that Valerie had received two letters since her death, but when they looked in the mailbox, it was empty.

A friend, the owner of the restaurant Valerie had frequented, notified the telephone company to cut off service and forward the final bill to her. She was told the bill could not be found.

And so it went. Was someone covering up his traces? Sheila heard these things and went to work. To her, something was terribly wrong about her friend's death and she was going to find out what. Questioning both the restaurant owner and the girl's sister again, she came upon another strange fact. The ash trays Ethel had found in the apartment had two different types of cigarettes in them—L&M and Winston. Valerie always smoked L&M, but who smoked Winston?

The police seem not particularly interested in pursuing the matter. They think it was Valerie herself who called them the first time, and that she just decided to end it all in a drunken stupor. That at least is the impression they gave Sheila.

The following day, Saturday, the window was still open. The rose Valerie had left behind was still on the sill, despite the windy weather of April.

That night when Sheila was putting on her jacket, she felt somebody helping her into it. She was alone, or so she thought.

It occurred to her then that Valerie's spirit was not at rest and that I might be able to help. The very least I could do was talk to her *now,* since fate had prevented me from getting to her in time.

I arranged with Betty Ritter to be ready for me the following weekend, without telling her where we would be going, of course. The date was May 6, the time three P.M., and Sheila was to meet us at the apartment that once belonged to Valerie, but now was cleaned out and ready for the next occupant. The superintendent agreed to let us in, perhaps sensing why we had come or not caring. At any rate he opened the tenth floor apartment and left us alone inside.

As we reached the eleevator of the East Sixty-Third Street building, Betty Ritter suddenly remarked that she felt death around her. I nodded and we went upstairs.

As soon as we had stepped through the door into Valerie's place, Betty became a psychic bloodhound. Making straight for the window—now closed—she touched it and withdrew in horror, then turned around and looked at me.

"There is a man here jumping around like mad," she said, but there is also someone else here—I am impressed with the initial E." She then took off her coat and started to walk toward the bathroom. There she stopped and looked back at me.

"I hear a woman screaming . . . I saw blood . . . now I see the initial M . . . she was harmed . . . it is like suicide . . . as if she couldn't take it any more."

Betty had difficulty holding back her emotions and was breathing heavily.

"She left *two* behind," she said. "I see the initials L. and S."

Betty Ritter, not a trance medium but essentially a clairvoyant, is very strong on initials, names, letters, and other forms of identification and she would naturally work that way even in this case.

"I heard her say, 'Mama, Mama'—she is very agitated."

"I also get a man's spirit here . . . initial J."

"How did this girl die?" I interjected at this point.

"She couldn't take it any more. She shows the initial R. This is a living person. She gulped something, I think."

I thought that Betty was picking up past impressions now and wanted to get her away from that area into the current layer of imprints.

"How exactly did she die?" I queried the medium. Betty had no idea where she was or why I had brought her here.

"I think she tried . . . pills . . . blood . . . one way or the other . . . in the past. She was a little afraid but she did plan this. She is very disturbed now and she does not know how to get out of this apartment. I get the initial G. with her."

I asked Betty to convey our sympathies to her and ask her if there was something she wished us to do.

While Betty talked to the spirit woman in a low voice, I reflected on her evidence so far. The initials given—E. was the first initial of Valerie's sister's name, Ethel, M. was Mary, her mother, and G. the manager of the company with whom she had had a relationship—it all seemed to make sense. Betty Ritter had also correctly "gotten" the attempted suicide by pills and pointed out the window as a "hot" area.

What was to follow now?

"She is crying," Betty reported. "She wants her loved ones to know that she didn't mean it. She shows me the head of an Indian and it is a symbol of a car—a brand name I think—it's red—the initial H. comes with this and then she shows me writing, something she has left unfinished. She asks her mother to forgive her because she could not help herself."

I decided to ask Valerie some important questions through the medium. Was she alone at the time of her death?

"Not alone. Initial A. A man, I feel him walking out of the door. Agitating her, agitating her."

"Was he with her when she died or did he leave before?"

"She says, 'I slammed the door on him.' And then she says, 'And then I did it.' "

"Why?"

"I had gone completely out of my mind . . . could not think straight . . . he drove me to it . . ."

"This man is a living person?"

"Yes."

"Is he aware of what happened to her?" ·

"Yes."

"Did she know him well?"

"Yes, definitely."

"What was his connection with her?"

Betty was herself pretty agitated now; in psychic parlance, she was really hot.

"I see a bag of money," she reported, "and the letters M. or W."

I handed her some personal belongings of Valerie's, brought to the scene in a shopping bag by Sheila and now placed on the stove for Betty to touch. She first took up a pendant—costume jewelry—and immediately felt the owner's vibrations.

"How I loved this," she mumbled. "I see D. R., Doctor . . . this was given to her and there is much love here in connection with this . . . this goes way back . . ."

Somehow the personalities of Betty Ritter and Valerie K. melted into one now and Betty, not quite herself, seemed not to listen any more to my queries, but instead kept talking as if she were Valerie, yet with Betty's own voice and intonation.

"There's so much I wanted to say and I couldn't at the time . . . ."

Now returning to herself again, she spoke of a man in spirit, who was very agitated and who had possessed the woman, not a ghost but someone who had died . . . an older man who had a link with her in the past. **J.W.** Dark-skinned, but not Negro—India or that part of the world."

It struck me suddenly that she might be talking of Valerie's late husband, the man she had married long ago in Hong King; he was much older than she at the time.

"I have a feeling of falling," Betty suddenly said, "I don't know why. May have something to do with her."

I decided to let her walk around the entire apartment and to try to pick up "hot" areas. She immediately went for the lefthand window.

"Something terrible happened here . . . this is the room . . . right here . . . stronger here . . ."

"Is there another woman involved in this story?" I asked.

"I see the initial M." Betty replied, "and she is with a man who is living, and there is also some jealousy regarding a woman's boyfriend . . . she could not take it."

I decided to start the exorcism immediately.

"It's such a short time ago that she went," Betty remarked. "She wants to greet Mary . . . or Marie . . . and an L. To tell L. she is relieved now. Just carry on as usual."

L. was the initial of Lynn, the girl at the office who had encountered the strange happenings with the earrings.

I decided to test this connection.

"Did she communicate with L. in any way?" I asked.

"Yes," Betty nodded, "I see her by L.'s bed . . . perhaps she frightened her . . . but now she knows . . . didn't mean to frighten her . . . she is leaving now, never wants to get back again . . . ."

We were quiet for a moment.

"She's throwing us kisses now," Betty added.

"She would do that," Sheila confirmed, "that was the way she would do it."

And that was that.

Betty lit a cigarette and relaxed, still visibly shaken by the communications for which she had been the carrier.

We put Valerie's pitiful belongings back into the paper bag and left the apartment, which now looked shiny and new, having been given a hasty coat of paint to make it ready for the next occupant.

No further snatching of jewelry from anyone's ears occurred after that, and even Sheila, my friend, no longer tried to reopen the case despite her belief that there was more to it than met the eyes of the police.

We decided to allow Valerie a peaceful transition and not to stir up old wounds that would occur with a reopening of the case.

But somehow I can't quite bring myself to forget a scene, a scene I only "saw" through the eyes of a laconic police detective making a routine report: the tall, lovely Oriental woman, intoxicated and nude, slamming the door on the police . . . and two liquor glasses on her table.

Who was that other glass for . . . and who smoked the second cigarette, the brand Valerie never smoked?

Who, then, was the man who left her to die?

chapter 5

The Last Ride

CORONADO BEACH is a pleasant seaside resort in southern California not far from San Diego. You get there by ferry from the mainland and the ride itself is worth the trip. It takes about fifteen minutes, then you continue by car or on foot into a town of small homes, none grand, none ugly—pleasantly bathed by the warm California sunshine, vigorously battered on the oceanside by the Pacific, and becalmed on the inside of the lagoon by a narrow body of water.

The big thing in Coronado Beach is the U.S. Navy; either you're in it and are stationed here, or you work for them in one way or another: directly, as a civilian, or indirectly by making a living through the people who are in the Navy and who make their homes here.

Mrs. Francis Jones is the wife of an advertising manager for a Sidney, Ohio, newspaper, who had returned to Coronado after many years in the Midwest. She is a young woman with a college background and above-average intelligence, and has mixed Anglo-Saxon and Austrian background. Her father died a Navy hero while testing a dive bomber, making her mother an early widow.

Gloria Jones married fairly young, and when her husband took a job as advertising manager in Sidney, Ohio, she went right along with him. After some years, the job became less attractive, and the Joneses moved right back to Coronado where Jones took up work for the Navy.

They have a thirteen-year-old daughter, Vicki, and live a happy, well-adjusted life; Mr. Jones collects coins and Mrs. Jones likes to decorate their brick house surrounded by a garden filled with colorful flowers.

One January, Mrs. Jones sought me out to help her understand a series of most unusual events that had taken place in her otherwise placid life. Except for an occasional true dream, she had not had any contact with the psychic and evinced no interest whatever in it until the events that so disturbed her tranquility had come to pass. Even the time she saw her late father in a white misty cloud might have been a dream. She was only ten years old at the time, and preferred later to think it was a dream. But the experiences she came to see me about were not in that category. Moreover, her husband and a friend were present when some of the extraordinary happenings took place.

Kathleen Duffy was the daughter of a man working for the Convair company. He was a widower and Kathleen was the apple of his eye. Unfortunately the apple was a bit rotten in spots; Kathleen was a most difficult child. Her father had sent her away to a Catholic school for girls in Oceanside, but she ran away twice; after the second time she had to be sent to a home for "difficult" children.

Gloria Jones met Kathleen when both were in their teens. Her mother was a widow and Mr. Duffy was a widower, so the parents had certain things in common. The two girls struck up a close friendship and they both hoped they might become sisters through the marriage of their parents, but it did not happen.

When Kathleen was sent away to the Anthony Home, a reform school at San Diego, Gloria was genuinely sorry. That was when Kathleen was about sixteen years of age. Although they never met again, Kathleen phoned Gloria a few times. She wasn't happy in her new environment, of course, but there was little that either girl could do about it.

In mounting despair, Kathleen tried to get away again but did not succeed. Then one day, she and her roommate, June Robeson, decided to do something drastic to call attention to their dissatisfied state. They set fire to their room in the hope that they might escape in the confusion of the fire.

As the smoke of the burning beds started to billow heavier and heavier, they became frightened. Their room was kept locked at all times, and now they started to bang at the door, demanding to be let out.

The matron came and surveyed the scene. The girls had been trouble for her all along. She decided to teach them what she thought would be an unforgettable "lesson." It was. When Kathleen collapsed from smoke inhalation, the matron finally opened the door. The Robeson girl was saved, but Kathleen Duffy died the next day in the hospital.

When the matter became public, the local newspapers demanded an investigation of the Anthony Home. The matron and the manager of the Home didn't wait for it. They fled to Mexico and have never been heard from since.

Gradually, Gloria began to forget the tragedy. Two years went by and the image of the girlfriend receded into her memory.

One day she and another friend, a girl named Jackie Sudduth, were standing near the waterfront at Coronado, a sunny, wind-swept road from which you can look out onto the Pacific or back toward the orderly rows of houses that make up Coronado Beach.

The cars were whizzing by as the two girls stood idly gazing across the road. One of the cars coming into view was driven by a young man with a young girl next to him who seemed familiar to Gloria. She only saw her from the shoulders up, but as the car passed close by she knew it was Kathleen. Flabbergasted, she watched the car disappear.

"Did you know that girl?" her friend Jackie inquired.

"No, why?"

"She said your name," her friend reported.

Gloria nodded in silence. She had seen it too. Without uttering a sound, the girl in the passing car had spelled the syllables "Glo-ri-a" with her lips.

For weeks afterward, Gloria could not get the incident out of her mind. There wasn't any rational explanation, and yet how could it be? Kathleen had been dead for two years.

The years went by, then a strange incident brought the whole matter back into her consciousness. It was New Year's Eve, twelve years later. She was now a married woman with a daughter. As she entered her kitchen, she froze in her tracks: a bowl was spinning counterclockwise while moving through the kitchen of its own volition.

She called out to her husband and daughter to come quickly. Her daughter's girlfriend, Sheryl Konz, age thirteen, was first to arrive in the kitchen. She also saw the bowl spinning. By the time Mr. Jones arrived, it had stopped its most unusual behavior.

Over dinner, topic A was the self-propelled bowl. More to tease her family than out of conviction, Mrs. Jones found herself saying, "If there is anyone here, let the candle go out." Promptly the candle went out.

There was silence after that, for no current of air was present that could have accounted for the sudden extinguishing of the candle.

The following summer, Mrs. Jones was making chocolate pudding in her kitchen. When she poured it into one of three bowls, the bowl began to turn—by itself. This time her husband saw it too. He explained it as vibrations from a train or a washing machine next door. But why did the other two bowls not move also?

Finally wondering if her late friend Kathleen, who had always been a prankster, might not be the cause of this, she waited for the next blow.

On New Year's Day that following year, she took a Coke bottle out of her refrigerator, and set it down on the counter. Then she turned her back on it and went back to the refrigerator for some ice. This took only a few moments. When she got back to the counter, the Coke bottle had disappeared.

Chiding herself for being absent-minded, she assumed she had taken the bottle with her to refrigerator and had left it inside. She checked and there was no Coke.

"Am I going out of my mind?" she wondered, and picked up the Coke carton. It contained five bottles. The sixth bottle was never found.

Since these latter incidents took place during the three years when they lived in Sidney, Ohio, it was evident that the frisky spirit of Kathleen Duffy could visit them anywhere they went—if that is who it was.

In late May of that year, back again in Coronado, both Mr. and Mrs. Jones saw the bread jump out of the breadbox before their very eyes. They had locked the breadbox after placing a loaf of bread inside. A moment later, they returned to the breadbox and found it open. While they were still wondering how this could be, the bread jumped out.

A practical man, Mr. Jones immediately wondered if they were having an earthquake. They weren't. Moreover, it appeared that their neighbors' breadboxes behaved normally.

They shook their heads once more. But this time Mrs. Jones dropped me a letter.

On June 3, I went to San Diego to see the Joneses. Sybil Leek and I braved the bus ride from Santa Ana on a hot day, but the Joneses picked us up at the bus terminal and drove us to the Anthony Home where Kathleen had died so tragically.

Naturally Sybil was mystified about all this, unless her ESP told her why we had come. Consciously, she knew nothing.

When we stopped at the Home, we found it boarded up and not a soul in sight. The day was sunny and warm, and the peaceful atmosphere belied the past that was probably filled with unhappy memories. After the unpleasant events that had occurred earlier, the place had been turned into a school for retarded children and run as such for a number of years. At present, however, it stood abandoned.

Sybil walked around the grounds quietly and soaked up the mood of the place.

"I heard something, maybe a name," she suddenly said. "It sounds like Low Mass."

Beyond that, she felt nothing on the spot of Kathleen's unhappy memories. Was it Kathleen who asked for a Low Mass to be said for her? Raised a strict Catholic, such a thought would not be alien to her.

"The place we just left," Sybil said as we drove off, "has a feeling of sickness to it—like a place for sick people, but not a hospital."

Finally we arrived at the corner of Ocean Avenue and Lomar Drive in Coronado, where Gloria Jones had seen the car with Kathleen in it. All through the trip, on the ferry, and down again into Coronado Island, we avoided the subject at hand.

But now we had arrived and it was time to find out if Sybil felt anything still hanging on in this spot.

"I feel a sense of death," she said slowly, uncertainly. "Despite the sunshine, this is a place of death." It wasn't that there was a presence here, she explained, but rather that someone had come here to wait for another person. The noise around us—it was Sunday—did not help her concentration.

"It's a foreign face I see," Sybil continued. "Someone—a man, with very little hair—who is alien to this place. I see an iris next to his face."

Was the man using the symbol to convey the word Irish perhaps? Was he an ancestor of Kathleen's from over there?

I turned to Mrs. Jones.

"I think what you witnessed here was the superimposition on a pair of motorists of the spirit image of your late friend. These things are called transfigurations. I am sure if the car had stopped, you would have found a stranger in it. Kathleen used her so that you could see her familiar face, I think."

Perhaps Kathleen Duffy wanted to take one more ride, a joy ride in freedom, and, proud of her accomplishment, had wanted her best friend to see her taking it.

There have been no further disturbances or prankish happenings at the Jones house since.

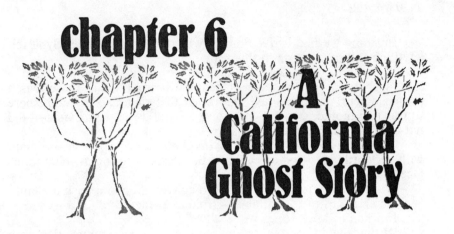

chapter 6
A California Ghost Story

LITTLE DID I KNOW when I had successfully investigated the haunted apartment of Mrs. Verna Kunze in San Bernardino, that Mrs. Kunze would lead me to another case equally as interesting as her own, which I reported on in my book, *Ghosts of the Golden West*.

Mrs. Kunze is a very well-organized person, and a former employee in the passport division of the State Department. She is used to sifting facts from fancy. Her interest in psycho-cybernetics had led her to a group of like-minded individuals meeting regularly in Orange County. There she met a gentleman formerly with the FBI by the name of Walter Tipton.

One day, Mr. Tipton asked her help in contacting me concerning a most unusual case that had been brought to his attention. Having checked out some of the more obvious details, he had found the people involved truthful and worthy of my time.

So it was that I first heard of Mrs. Carole Trausch of Santa Ana.

What happened to the Trausch family and their neighbors is not just a ghost story. Far more than that, they found themselves in the middle of an old tragedy that had not yet been played out fully when the moved into their spanking new home.

Carole Trausch was born in Los Angeles of Scottish parentage and went to school in Los Angeles. Her father is a retired policeman and her mother was born in Scotland. Carole married quite young and moved with her husband, a businessman, to live first in Huntington Beach and later in Westminster, near Santa Ana.

Now in her early twenties, she is a glamorous-looking blonde who belies the fact that she has three children aged eight, six, and two, all girls.

Early the previous year, they moved into one of two hundred two-story bungalows in a new development in Westminster. They were just an ordinary family, without any particular interest in the occult. About their only link with the world of the psychic were some peculiar dreams Carole had had.

The first time was when she was still a little girl. She dreamed there were some pennies hidden in the rose bed in the garden. On awakening, she laughed at herself, but out of curiosity she did go to the rose bed and looked. Sure enough, there were some pennies in the soil below the roses. Many times since then she has dreamed of future events that later came true.

One night she dreamed that her husband's father was being rolled on a stretcher, down a hospital corridor by a nurse, on his way to an operation. The next morning there was a phone call informing them that such an emergency had indeed taken place about the time she dreamed it. On several occasions she sensed impending accidents or other unpleasant things, but she is not always sure what kind. One day she felt sure she or her husband would be in a car accident. Instead it was one of her little girls, who was hit by a passing car.

When they moved into their present house, Mrs. Trausch took an immediate disliking to it. This upset her practical-minded husband. They had hardly been installed when she begged him to move again. He refused.

The house is a white-painted two-story bungalow, which was built about five years before their arrival. Downstairs is a large, oblong living room, a kitchen, and a dining area. On the right, the staircase leads to the upper story. The landing is covered with linoleum, and there are two square bedrooms on each side of the landing, with wall-to-wall carpeting and windows looking onto the yard in the rear bedroom and onto the street in the front room.

There is a large closet along the south wall of the rear bedroom. Nothing about the house is unusual, and there was neither legend nor story nor rumor attached to the house when they rented it from the local bank that owned it.

And yet there was something queer about the house. Mrs. Trausch's nerves were on edge right from the very first when they moved in. But she accepted her husband's decision to stay put and swept her own fears under the carpet of everyday reason as the first weeks in their new home rolled by.

At first the children would come to her with strange tales. The six-year-old girl would complain of being touched by someone she could not see whenever she dropped off for her afternoon nap in the bedroom upstairs. Sometimes this presence would shake the bed, and then there was a shrill noise, somewhat like a beep, coming from the clothes closet. The oldest girl, eight years old, confirmed the story and reported similar experiences in the room.

Carole dismissed these reports as typical imaginary tales of the kind children will tell.

But one day she was resting on the same bed upstairs and found herself being tapped on the leg by some unseen person.

This was not her imagination; she was fully awake, and it made her wonder if perhaps her intuition about this house had not been right all along.

She kept experiencing the sensation of touch in the upstairs bedrooms only, and it got to be a habit with her to make the beds as quickly as possible and then rush downstairs where she felt nothing unusual. Then she also began to hear the shrill, beeplike sounds from the closet. She took out all the children's clothes and found nothing that could have caused the noise. Finally she told her husband about it, and he promptly checked the pipes and other structural details of the house, only to shake his head. Nothing could have made such noises.

For several months she had kept her secret, but now that her husband also knew, she had Diane, the oldest, tell her father about it as well.

It was about this time that she became increasingly aware of a continuing presence upstairs. Several times she would hear footsteps walking upstairs, and on investigation found the children fast asleep. Soon the shuffling steps became regular features of the house. It would always start near the closet in the rear bedroom, then go toward the stair landing.

Carole began to wonder if her nerves weren't getting the better of her. She was much relieved one day when her sister Kathleen Bachelor, who had come to visit her, remarked about the strange footsteps upstairs. Both women knew the children were out. Only the baby was upstairs, and on rushing up the stairs, they found her safely asleep in her crib. It had sounded to them like a small person wearing slippers.

Soon she discovered, however, that there were two kinds of footsteps: the furtive pitter-patter of a child, and the heavy, deliberate footfalls of a grownup.

Had they fallen heir to two ghosts? The thought seemed farfetched even to ESP-prone Carole, but it could not be dismissed entirely. What was going on, she wondered. Evidently she was not losing her mind, for others had also heard these things.

Once she had gone out for the evening and when she returned around ten P.M., she dismissed the babysitter. After the girl had left, she was alone with the baby. Suddenly she heard the water running in the bathroom upstairs. She raced up the stairs and found the bathroom door shut tight. Opening it, she noticed that the water was on and there was some water in the sink.

On January 27 of the next year, Carole had guests for lunch, two neighbors named Pauline J. and Joyce S., both young women about the same age as Carole. The children were all sleeping in the same upstairs front bedroom, the two older girls sharing the bed while the baby girl occupied the crib. The baby had her nap between eleven and two P.M. At noon, however, the baby woke up crying, and, being barely able to talk at age two, kept saying "Baby scared, Mommy!"

The three ladies had earlier been upstairs together, preparing the baby for her crib. At that time, they had also put the entire room carefully in order, paying particular attention to making the covers and spread on the large bed very smooth, and setting up the dolls and toys on the chest in the corner.

When the baby cried at noon, all three women went upstairs and found the bed had wrinkles and an imprint as though someone had been sitting on it. The baby, of course, was still in her crib.

They picked up the child and went downstairs with her. Just as they got to the stairway, all three heard an invisible child falling down the stairs about three steps ahead of where they were standing.

It was after this experience that Mrs. Trausch wondered why the ghost child never touched any of the dolls. You see, the footsteps they kept hearing upstairs always went from the closet to the toy chest where the dolls are kept. But none of the dolls was ever disturbed. It occurred to her that the invisible child was a boy, and there were no boy's toys around.

The sounds of a child running around in the room upstairs became more and more frequent; she knew it was not one of her children, having accounted for her own in other ways. The whole situation began to press on her nerves, and even her husband—who had until now tended to shrug off what he could not understand—became concerned. Feelers were put out to have me come to the house as soon as possible, but I could not make it right away and they would have to cope with their unseen visitors for the time being, or until I arrived on the scene.

All during February the phenomena continued, so much so that Mrs. Trausch began to take them as part of her routine. But she kept as much to the downstairs portion of the house as she could. For some unknown reason, the phenomena never intruded on that part of the house.

She called in the lady who managed the development for the owners and cautiously told her of their problem. But the manager knew nothing whatever about the place, except that it was new and to her knowledge no great tragedies had occurred there in her time.

When the pitter-patter of the little feet continued, Carole Trausch decided she just had to know. On March 16, she decided to place some white flour on the linoleum-covered portion of the upstairs floor to trap the unseen child. This was the spot where the footsteps were most often heard, and for the past two days the ghost child had indeed "come out" there to run and play.

In addition, she took a glass of water with some measuring spoons of graduated sizes in it, and set it all down in a small pan and put it into her baby's crib with a cracker in the pan beside the glass. This was the sort of thing a little child might want—that is, a living child.

She then retired to the downstairs portion of the house and called in a neighbor. Together the two women kept watch, waiting for the early afternoon hours when the ghost child usually became active upstairs.

As the minutes ticked off, Carole began to wonder how she would look if nothing happened. The neighbor probably would consider her neurotic, and accuse her of making up the whole story as an attention-getter in this rather quiet community.

But she did not have to worry long. Sure enough, there were the footsteps again upstairs. The two women waited a few moments to give the ghost a chance to leave an impression, then they rushed upstairs.

They saw no child, but the white flour had indeed been touched. There were footmarks in the flour, little feet that seemed unusually small and slender. Next to the prints there was the picture of a flower, as if the child had bent down and finger-painted the flower as a sign of continuing presence. From the footprints, they took the child to be between three and four years of age. The water and pan in the crib had not been touched, and as they stood next to the footprints, there was utter silence around them.

Mrs. Trausch now addressed the unseen child gently and softly, promising the child they would not hurt it. Then she placed some boys' toys, which she had obtained for this occasion, around the children's room and withdrew.

There was no immediate reaction to all this, but two days later the eight-year-old daughter came running down the stairs to report that she had seen the shadow of a little boy in front of the linen closet in the hall. He wore a striped shirt and pants, and was shorter than she.

When I heard of the footprints by telephone, I set the week of June 2 aside for a visit to the house. Meanwhile I instructed the Trausches to continue observing whatever they could.

But the Trausches had already resolved to leave the house, even if I should be able to resolve their "problem." No matter what, they could never be quite sure. And living with a ghost—or perhaps two ghosts—was not what they wanted to do, what with three living children to keep them on their toes.

Across from the Trausch apartment, and separated from it by a narrow lane, is another house just like it and built about the same time, on what was before only open farmland—as far as everyone there knows. A few years before, the area was flooded and was condemned, but it dried out later. There is and always has been plenty of water in the area, a lowland studded with ponds and fishing holes.

The neighbor's name was Bonnie Swanson and she too was plagued by footsteps that had no human causing them. The curious thing is that these phenomena were heard only in the upstairs portion of her house, where the bedrooms are, just as in the Trausch house.

Twice the Swansons called in police, only to be told that there was no one about causing the footsteps. In April, the Swansons had gone away for a weekend, taking their child with them. When they returned, the husband opened the door and was first to step into the house. At this moment he distinctly heard footsteps running very fast from front to rear of the rooms, as if someone had been surprised by their return. Mrs. Swanson, who had also heard this, joined her husband in looking the house over, but there was no stranger about and no one could have left.

Suddenly they became aware of the fact that a light upstairs was burning. They knew they had turned it off when they left. Moreover, in the kitchen they almost fell over a child's tricycle. Last time they saw this tricycle, it had stood in the corner of their living room. It could not have gotten to the kitchen by itself, and there was no sign of anyone breaking and entering in their absence. Nothing was missing.

It seemed as if my approaching visit was somehow getting through to the ghost or ghosts, for as the month of June came closer, the phenomena seemed to mount in intensity and frequency.

On the morning of May 10, at nine-thirty, Mrs. Trausch was at her front bedroom window, opening it to let in the air. From her window she could see directly into the Swanson house, since both houses were on the same level with the windows parallel to each other. As she reached her window and casually looked out across to the Swanson's rooms, which she knew to be empty at this time of day (Mr. Swanson was at work, and Mrs. Swanson and a houseguest were out for the morning) she saw to her horror the arm of a woman pushing back the curtain of Mrs. Swanson's window.

There was a curiously stiff quality about this arm and the way it moved the curtain back. Then she saw clearly a woman with a deathlike white mask of a face staring at her. The woman's eyes were particuarly odd. Despite her excitement, Mrs. Trausch noticed that the woman had wet hair and was dressed in something filmy, like a white nylon negligee with pink flowers on it.

For the moment, Mrs. Trausch assumed that the houseguest must somehow have stayed behind, and so she smiled at the woman across from her. Then the curtain dropped and the woman disappeared. Carole Trausch could barely wait to question her neighbor about the incident, and found that there hadn't been anyone at the house when she saw the woman with the wet hair.

Now Mrs. Trausch was sure that there were two unseen visitors, a child and a woman, which would account for the different quality of the footsteps they had been hearing.

She decided to try and find out more about the land on which the house stood.

A neighbor living a few blocks away on Chestnut Street, who had been in her house for over twenty years, managed to supply some additional information. Long before the development had been built, there had been a farm there.

In the exact place where the Trausches now lived there had been a barn. When the house was built, a large trench was dug and the barn was pushed into it and burned. The people who lived there at the time were a Mexican family named Felix. They had a house nearby but sold the area of the farm to the builders.

But because of the flooded condition of the area, the houses stood vacant for a few years. Only after extensive drainage had taken place did the houses become inhabitable. At this time the Trausches were able to move into theirs.

The area was predominantly Mexican and the development was a kind of Anglo-Saxon island in their midst.

All this information was brought out only after our visit, incidentally, and neither Sybil Leek, who acted as my medium, nor I had any knowledge of it at the time.

Mrs. Trausch was not the only adult member of the family to witness the phenomena. Her husband finally confessed that on several occasions he had been puzzled by footsteps upstairs when he came home late at night. That was around one A.M., and when he checked see if any of the children had gotten out of bed, he found them fast asleep. Mr. Trausch is a very realistic man. His business is manufacturing industrial tools, and he does not believe in ghosts. But he heard the footsteps too.

The Trausches also realized that the shuffling footsteps of what appeared to be a small child always started up as soon as the two older girls had left for school. It was as if the invisible boy wanted to play with their toys when they weren't watching.

Also, the ghost evidently liked the bathroom and water, for the steps resounded most often in that area. On one occasion Mrs. Trausch was actually using the bathroom when the steps resounded next to her. Needless to say, she left the bathroom in a hurry.

Finally the big day had arrived. Mr. Trausch drove his Volkswagen all the way to Hollywood to pick up Mrs. Leek and myself, and while he did not believe in ghosts, he didn't scoff at them either.

After a pleasant ride of about two hours, we arrived at Westminster. It was a hot day in June, and the Santa Ana area is known for its warm

climate. Mr. Trausch parked the car, and we went into the house where
the rest of the family was already awaiting our visit.

I asked Sybil to scout around for any clairvoyant impressions she
might get of the situation, and as she did so, I followed her around the
house with my faithful tape recorder so that not a word might be lost.

As soon as Sybil had set foot in the house, she pointed to the
staircase and intoned ominously, "It's upstairs."

Then, with me trailing, she walked up the stairs as gingerly as a
trapeze artist while I puffed after her.

"Gooseflesh," she announced and held out her arm. Now whenever
we are in a haunted area Sybil does get gooseflesh—not because she
is scared but because it is a natural, instant reaction to whatever presence
might be there.

We were in the parents' room now, and Sybil looked around with
the expectant smile of a well-trained bird dog casing the moors.

"Two conflicting types," she then announced. "There's anger and
resentfulness toward someone. There's something here. Has to do with
the land. Two people."

She felt it centered in the children's room, and that there was a
vicious element surrounding it, an element of destruction. We walked
into the children's room and immediately she made for the big closet
in the rear. Behind that wall there was another apartment, but the
Trausches did not know anything about it except that the people in it
had just recently moved in.

"It's that side," Sybil announced and waved toward the backyard
of the house where numerous children of various ages were playing
with the customary racket.

"Vincent," Sybil added, out of the blue. "Maybe I don't have the
accent right, but it is Vincent. But it is connected with all this. Incidentally,
it is the land that's causing the trouble, not the house itself."

The area Sybil had pointed out just a moment before as being the
center of the activities was the exact spot where the old barn had once
stood.

"It's nothing against this house," Sybil said to Mrs. Trausch, "but
something out of the past. I'd say 1925. The name Vincent is important.
There's fire involved. I don't feel a person here but an influence . . .
a thing. This is different from our usual work. It's the upper part of
the building where the evil was."

I then eased Sybil into a chair in the children's room and we
grouped ourselves silently around her, waiting for some form of manifestation to take place.

Mrs. Trausch was nervously biting her lips, but otherwise bearing
up under what must have been the culmination of a long and great
strain for her. Sybil was relaxing now, but she was still awake.

"There's some connection with a child," she said now, "a lost child . . . 1925 . . . the child was found here, dead."

"Whose child is it?" I pressed.

"Connected with Vincent . . . dark child . . . nine years old . . a boy . . . the children here have to be careful . . ."

"Does this child have any connection with the house?"

"He is lost."

"Can you see him; can he see you?"

"I see him. Corner . . . the barn. He broke his neck. Two men . . . hit the child, they didn't like children, you see . . . they left him . . . until he was found . . . woman . . . Fairley . . . name . . . Pete Fairley . . ."

By now Sybil had glided into a semi-trance and I kept up the barrage of questions to reconstruct the drama in the barn.

"Do they live here?" I inquired.

"Nobody lives here. Woman walked from the water to find the boy. He's dead. She has connection with the two men who killed him. Maniacs, against children."

"What is her connection with the boy?"

"She had him, then she lost him. She looked after him."

"Who were the boy's parents then?"

"Fairley. Peter Fairley. 1925."

Sybil sounded almost like a robot now, giving the requested information.

"What happened to the woman?" I wanted to know.

"Mad . . . she found the boy dead, went to the men . . . there was a fight . . . she fell in the water . . . men are here . . . there's a fire . . ."

"Who were these men?"

"Vincent . . . brothers . . . nobody is very healthy in this farm . . . don't like women . . ."

"Where did the child come from?"

"Lost . . . from the riverside . . ."

"Can you see the woman?"

"A little . . . the boy I can see clearly."

It occurred to me how remarkable it was for Sybil to speak of a woman who had fallen into the water when the apparition Mrs. Trausch had seen had had wet hair. No one had discussed anything about the house in front of Sybil, of course. So she had no way of knowing that the area had once been a farm, or that a barn had stood there where she felt the disturbances centered. No one had told her that it was a child the people in the house kept hearing upstairs.

"The woman is out of tempo," Sybil explained. "That makes it difficult to see her. The boy is frightened."

Sybil turned her attention to the little one now and, with my prodding, started to send him away from there.

"Peter go out and play with the children . . . outside," she pleaded.

"And his parents . . . they are looking for him," I added.

"He wants the children here to go with him," Sybil came back.

Mrs. Trausch started to swallow nervously.

"Tell him he is to go first," I instructed.

"He wants to have the fair woman come with him," Sybil explained and I suggested that the two of them go.

"She understands," Sybil explained, "and is willing, but he is difficult. He wants the children."

I kept pleading with the ghost boy. Nothing is harder than dealing with a lost one so young.

"Join the other children. They are already outside," I said.

There was a moment of silence, interrupted only by the muffled sounds of living children playing outside.

"Are they still here?" I cautiously inquired a little later.

"Can't see them now, but I can see the building. Two floors. Nobody there now."

I decided it was time to break the trance which had gradually deepened and at this point was a full trance. A moment later Sybil Leek "was back."

Now we discussed the matter freely and I researched the information just obtained.

As I understood it, there had been this boy, age nine, Peter Fairley by name, who had somehow gotten away from his nanny, a fair woman. He had run into a farm and gone up to the upper story of a barn where two brothers named Vincent had killed him. When the woman found him, she went mad. Then she looked for the men whom she knew, and there was a fight during which she was drowned. The two of them are ghosts because they are lost; the boy lost in a strange place and the woman lost in guilt for having lost the boy.

Mrs. Kunze and Mrs. Trausch volunteered to go through the local register to check out the names and to see if anything bearing on this tragedy could be found in print.

Unfortunately the death records for the year 1925 were incomplete, as Mrs. Trausch discovered at the Santa Ana *Register;* and this was true even at the local Hall of Records in the Court House. The County Sheriff's Office was of no help either. But they found an interesting item in the *Register* of January 1, 1925:

Deputies probe tale of "burial" **in orange grove.** Several Deputy Sheriffs, in a hurried call to **Stanton late last** night, failed to find any trace of several men who were **reported to be** "burying

something" in an isolated orange grove near that town, as reported
to them at the Sheriff's office here.

Officers rushing to the scene were working under the impression
that a murder had been committed and that the body was being
interred, but a thorough search in that vicinity failed to reveal
anything unusual, according to a report made by Chief Criminal
Deputy Ed McClellan, on their return. Deputy Sheriffs Joe Scott
and Joe Ryan accompanied McClellan.

Mrs. Kunze, a long-time resident of the area and quite familiar
with its peculiarities, commented that such a burial in an isolated orange
grove could easily have been covered up by men familiar with the
irrigating system, who could have flooded that section, thus erasing all
evidence of a newly made grave.

I wondered about the name Peter Fairley. Of course I did not
expect to find the boy listed somewhere, but was there a Fairley family
in these parts in 1925?

There was.

In the Santa Ana County Directories, S.W. Section, for the year
1925, there is a listing for a Frank Fairley, carpenter, at 930 W. Bishop,
Santa Ana. The listing continues at the same address the following year
also. It was not in the 1924 edition of the directory, however, so perhaps
the Fairleys were new to the area then.

At the outset of the visit Mrs. Leek had mentioned a Felix connected
with the area. Again consulting the County Directories for 1925, we
found several members of the Felix family listed. Andres Felix, rancher,
at Golden West Avenue and Bolsa Chica Road, post office Westminster,
Adolph and Miguel Felix, laborers, at the same address—perhaps
brothers— and Florentino Felix, also a rancher, at a short distance
from the farm of Andres Felix. The listing also appears in 1926.

No Vincent or Vincente, however. But of course not all members
of the family need to have been listed. The directories generally list
only principals, i.e., those gainfully employed or owners of business
or property. Then again, there may have been two hired hands by that
name, if Vincente was a given name rather than a Christian name.

The 1911 *History of Orange County,* by Samuel Armor, described
the area as consisting of a store, church, school, and a few residences
only. It was then called Bolsa, and the main area was used as ranch
and stock land. The area abounds in fish hatcheries also, which started
around 1921 by a Japanese named Akiyama. Thus was explained the
existence of water holes in the area along with fish tanks, as well as
natural lakes.

With the help of Mrs. Kunze, I came across still another interesting
record.

According to the Los Angeles *Times* of January 22, 1956, "an ancient residence at 14611 Golden West Street, Westminster, built 85 years ago, was razed for subdivision.''

This was undoubtedly the farm residence and land on which the development we had been investigating was later built.

And there we have the evidence. Three names were given by our psychic friend: Felix, Vincent, and Peter Fairley. Two of them are found in the printed record, with some difficulty, and with the help of local researchers familiar with the source material, which neither Mrs. Leek nor I was prior to the visit to the haunted house. The body of the woman could easily have been disposed of without leaving a trace by dumping it into one of the fish tanks or other water holes in the area, or perhaps in the nearby Santa Ana River.

About a month after our investigation, the Trausch family moved back to Huntington Beach, leaving the Westminster house to someone else who might some day appear on the scene.

But Carole Trausch informed me that from the moment of our investigation onward, not a single incident had marred the peace of their house.

So I can only assume that Sybil and I were able to help the two unfortunate ghosts out into the open, the boy to find his parents, no doubt also on his side of the veil, and the woman to find peace and forgiveness for her negligence in allowing the boy to be killed.

It is not always possible for the psychic investigator to leave a haunted house free of its unseen inhabitants, and when it does happen, then the success is its own reward.

chapter 7

A Haunted House Is Not a Home

A LOT OF PEOPLE are particular about the privacy of their home. They like it fine when nobody bothers them, except for their own kinfolk. Some do not even mind if a relative or friend stays over or comes to visit them, because, after all, they will leave again in time. But when a ghost overstays his welcome, and stays on and on and on, the matter can become upsetting, to say the least. This becomes even more of a problem when the guest is not aware of the passage of time, or when he thinks that your home is actually his home. When that happens, the owner of the house or apartment is faced with a difficult choice: fight the intruder and do everything at one's command to get rid of him, or accept the invasion of privacy and consider it a natural component of daily living.

When the ghost comes with the house—that is, if he or she lived there before you did—there is a certain sentimentality involved; after all, the previous owner has earlier rights to the place, even if he is dead and you paid for the house, and an attempt to chase him away may create a sense of guilt in some sensitive souls. However, as often as not, the spectral personality has nothing to do with the house itself. The ghost may have lived in a previous dwelling standing on the spot prior to the building of the present one, or he may have come with the land and thus go back even further. This is entirely possible, because a ghost lives in his own environment, meaning that the past is the only world he knows. In some of these cases, telling the ghost to pack up and leave to join the regular spirits on the Other Side of Life will meet resistance: after all, to the ghost you are the invader, the usurper. He was there first. But whatever the status of the phantom in the house or place, panic will not help much.

The more the current tenant of a house or apartment becomes frightened, the more the ghost derives benefit from it, because the negative nervous energy generated by the present-day inhabitants of a house can be utilized by the ghost to create physical phenomena—the so-called poltergeist disturbances, where objects move seemingly of their own volition. The best thing to do is to consider the ghost a fellow human being, albeit in trouble, and perhaps not in his right mind. Ghosts have to be dealt with compassionately and with understanding; they have to be *persuaded* to leave, not forcefully ejected.

Mrs. Sally S. lived in what was then a nice section of Brooklyn, half an hour from Manhattan and, at the time of the happenings I am about to report, was semi-retired, working two days a week at her old trade of being a secretary. A year after the first phenomena occurred, she moved away to Long Island, not because of her ghostly experiences, but because the neighborhood had become too noisy for her: ghosts she could stand, human disturbances were too much.

Miss S. moved into her Brooklyn apartment in May of the same year. At first, it seemed nice and quiet. Then, on August 3, she had an unusual experience. It must have been around three A.M. when she awoke with an uncanny feeling that she was not alone. In the semi-darkness of her apartment, she looked around and had the distinct impression that there was an intruder in her place. She looked out into the room, and in the semi-darkness saw what appeared to be a dark figure. It was a man, and though she could not make out any features, he seemed tall and as lifelike as any human intruder might be.

Thinking that it was best for her to play possum, she lay still and waited for the intruder to leave. Picture her shock and surprise when the figure approached her and started to touch her quilt cover. About fifteen minutes prior to this experience, she had herself awakened because she was cold, and had pulled the cover over herself. Thus she was very much awake when the "intruder" appeared to her. She lay still, trembling, watching his every move. Suddenly he vanished into thin air, and it was only then that Miss S. realized she wasn't dealing with any flesh and blood person, but a ghost.

A month later, again around three A.M., Miss S. awoke to see a white figure gliding back and forth in her room. This time, however, she was somewhat sleepy, so she did not feel like doing much about it. However, when the figure came close to her bed, she stuck our her arm to touch it, and at that moment it dissolved into thin air. Wondering who the ghost might be, Miss S. had had another opportunity to observe it in November, when around six A.M. she went into her kitchen to see the dark outline of a six-foot-tall man standing in the archway between the kitchen and dinette. She looked away for a moment, and then returned her gaze to the spot. The apparition was still there. Once more Miss S. closed her eyes and looked away, and when she returned her eyes to the spot, he was gone.

She decided to speak to her landlady about the incidents. No one had died in the house, nor had there been any tragedy to the best of her knowledge, the owner of the house assured her. As for a previous owner, she wouldn't know. Miss S. realized that it was her peculiar psychic talent that made the phenomena possible. For some time now she had been able to predict the results of horse races with uncanny accuracy, getting somewhat of a reputation in this area. Even during her school days, she came up with answers she had not yet been taught. In April of the next year, Miss S. visited her sister and her husband in New Jersey. They had bought a house the year before, and knew nothing of its history. Sally was assigned a finished room in the attic. Shortly after two A.M., a ghost appeared to her in that room. But before she could make out any details, the figure vanished. By now Miss S. knew that she had a talent for such things, and preferred not to talk about them with her sister, a somewhat nervous individual. But she kept wondering who the ghost at *her* house was.

Fourteen years earlier, a close friend named John had passed away. A year before, he had given her two nice fountain pens as gifts, and Miss S. had kept one at home, and used the other at her office. A year after her friend's death, she was using one of the pens in the office when the point broke. Because she couldn't use it anymore, she put the pen into her desk drawer. Then she left the office for a few minutes. When she returned, she found a lovely, streamlined black pen on top of her desk. She immediately inquired whether any of the girls had left it there, but no one had, nor had anyone been near her desk. The pen was a rather expensive Mont Blanc, just the thing she needed. It made her wonder whether her late friend John had not presented her with it even from the Beyond.

This belief was reinforced by an experience she had had on the first anniversary of his passing, when she heard his voice loud and clear calling her "sweetheart"—the name he had always used to address her, rather than her given name, Sally.

All this ran through her head fourteen years later, when she tried to come to terms with her ghostly experiences. Was the ghost someone who came with the house, someone who had been there before, or was it someone who somehow linked up with her? Then Sally began to put two and two together. She was in the habit of leaving her feet outside her quilt cover because the room was rather warm with the heat on. However, in the course of the night, the temperature in the room fell, and frequently her feet became almost frostbitten as a result. One Saturday night in March, the same year she visited her sister, she was still awake, lying in bed around eleven P.M. Her feet were sticking out of the quilt, as the temperature was still tolerable. Suddenly she felt a terrific tug on her quilt; it was first raised from above her ankles, and then pulled down to cover her feet. Yet, she saw no one actually doing it.

Suddenly she remembered how her late friend John had been in the habit of covering her feet when she had fallen asleep after one of his visits with her. Evidently he was still concerned that Sally should not get cold feet or worse, and had decided to watch over her in this manner.

Mrs. I.B. was a recently married young wife, expecting a baby some months later. She and her husband were looking for a furnished apartment. They had picked their favorite neighborhood, and decided to just look around until they saw a sign saying "Apartment for Rent." At the time, this was still possible. They stopped into a candy store in the area and asked the owner if he knew of a vacant apartment. As they were speaking to the owner of the store, a young soldier who had been standing in the rear of the store, and had overheard the conversation, came over to them. He informed them that he had an apartment across the street from the store. When they inquired why he offered them the apartment, the soldier very quietly explained that he had come home to bury his wife. In his absence abroad, she had gone on a diet and, because of a weakened condition, had suddenly passed away. It had been the soldier's intention to live with her in the apartment after he returned from service. Under the circumstances, Mr. and Mrs. B. could have it until he returned, for he still wanted to live in it eventually.

This was agreeable to the young couple, especially as the apartment was handsomely furnished. A deal was quickly made, and that very night Mr. and Mrs. B. went to sleep in the bedroom of the apartment, with nothing special on their minds.

At four-thirty A.M., Mr. B. got up to go to work while his wife was still fast asleep. It was around five when she heard someone running around in the room, in what sounded like bare feet. The noise awoke her, and as she looked up, Mrs. B. saw at the foot of her bed the figure of a very pretty young woman wearing a nightgown.

Mrs. B. had no idea who the stranger might be, but thought that the young woman had somehow wandered into the apartment and asked her what she wanted. Instead of answering her, however, the young girl simply disappeared into thin air.

Mrs. B. flew into a panic. Dressing in haste, she left the apartment while it was still dark outside and took refuge in her mother's home. Nobody would believe her story, not her mother, not her husband, and, because Mrs. B. was pregnant at the time, her condition was blamed for the "hallucination." Reluctantly, Mrs. B. went back to the apartment the following evening. Shortly after her husband left for work, again early in the morning, Mrs. B. was awakened by the same apparition. This time Mrs. B. did not run out of the house, but instead closed her eyes; eventually the figure faded.

As soon as she was fully awake the next day, Mrs. B. determined to try and find out who the ghost might have been. Going through the various drawers in the apartment, she came across some photo albums belonging to the soldier. Leafing through them, she gave out a startled cry when her eyes fell on a photograph of the soldier, wearing plain clothes, with the very woman next to him whom she had seen early in the morning! Now Mrs. B. knew that she hadn't imagined the experiences. She showed the album to her husband, feeling that she had been visited by the soldier's dead wife. This time her husband was somewhat more impressed, and it was decided to obtain the "services" of a dog Mrs. B. had grown up with.

That night, the dog slept at the foot of her bed, as she had done many times before Mrs. B. was married. This made Mrs. B feel a lot safer, but early in the morning she was awakened by her dog. The animal was standing on the foot of her bed, growling at the same spot where Mrs. B. had seen the apparition. The dog's fur was bristling on her back, and it was obvious that the animal was thoroughly scared.

But Mrs. B. did not see the ghost this time. It occurred to her that the ghost might resent her sleeping in what was once the bride's bed, so she and her husband exchanged beds the following night. From that moment on, the apparition did not return in the early mornings, and gradually, Mrs. B. got over her fear. A few weeks passed; then she noticed that in the kitchen some cups would fall off the shelf of their own volition whenever she tried to cook a meal. Then the clock fell off the wall by itself, and it became clear to her that objects were moved about by unseen hands. Some of this happened in the presence of her husband, who was no longer skeptical about it.

He decided it was time for them to move on. He wrote to the soldier, informing him that he was turning the apartment back to the landlord so that he could have it for himself again upon his return. Undoubtedly, that was exactly what the ghostly woman had wanted in the first place. . . .

Not all ghostly visitors are necessarily frightening or negative influences. Take the case of Mrs. M. N. One October, she signed a lease for a lovely old house on Commerce Street in New York's Greenwich Village. Legend had it that the house had been built by Washington Irving, although nothing was offered to substantiate this claim. It was a charming small white house, with three stories and a basement. It had five steps leading up from the street, and was guarded by wrought iron rails. On the first floor there was a narrow hallway, with stairs to the right; then came the living room, to the left, running the full depth of the house. The second story contained the master bedroom, with a bath and a small room, possibly used as a dressing room originally. On the third floor were three small bedrooms with dormer windows and a bathroom.

Mrs. N. loved the house like a friend; and because she was then going through a personal crisis in her life, a group of friends had gathered around her and moved into the house with her. These were people much younger than she, who had decided to share the old house with her. Before actually moving into the house, Mrs. N. made the acquaintance of a neighbor, who was astonished at her having taken this particular house.

"For goodness' sake," the neighbor said, "why are you moving in *there?* Don't you know that place is haunted?"

Mrs. N. and her friends laughed at the thought, having not the slightest belief in the supernatural. Several days before the furniture was to be moved into the house, the little group gathered in the bare living room, lit their first fire in the fireplace, and dedicated the house with prayers. It so happened that they were all followers of the Baha'i faith, and they felt that this was the best way to create a harmonious atmosphere in what was to be their home.

They had been in the empty living room for perhaps an hour, praying and discussing the future, when suddenly there was a knock on the door. Dick, one of the young people who was nearest the door, went to answer the knock. There was no one there. It was a brilliant, moonlit night, and the whole of little Commerce Street was empty. Shaking his head, Dick went back into the room, but fifteen minutes later somebody knocked again. Again, there was no one outside, and the knocking sounded once more that night. Just the same, they moved in and almost immediately heard the footsteps of an unseen person. There were six in the house at the time: Kay sleeping on the couch in the basement dining room, Dick on a huge divan in the living room, Mrs. N. in the master bedroom on the second floor, and her fifteen-year-old daughter Barbara in one of the dormer bedrooms; Evie was in the second room and Bruce in the third. The first time they heard the steps, they were all at dinner in the basement dining room. The front door, which was locked, opened and closed by itself, and footsteps went into the living room where they seemed to circle the room, pausing now and again, and then continuing.

Immediately Dick went upstairs to investigate, and found there was no one about. Despite this, they felt no sense of alarm. Somehow they knew that their ghost was benign. From that moment on, the footsteps of an unseen person became part of their lives. They were heard going upstairs and downstairs, prowling the living room, but somehow they never entered one of the bedrooms. Once in awhile they heard the opening and then a loud slamming of the front door. They checked, but there was nobody to be seen, and eventually they realized that whoever it was who was sharing the house with them preferred to remain unseen.

Since there were no other uncanny phenomena, the group accepted the presence of a ghost in their midst without undue alarm. One night, however, they had invited a group of Baha'i Youth to stay with them, and as a result, Mrs. N. had to sleep on the couch in the basement dining room. It turned into a night of sheer terror for her; she didn't see anything, but somehow the terror was all about her like a thick fog. She didn't sleep a moment that night. The following morning, Mrs. N. queried Kay, who ordinarily slept on the basement couch, as to whether she had had a similar experience. She had not. However, a few days later, Kay reported a strange dream she had had while occupying the same couch.

She had been awakened by the opening of the area-way door. Startled, she had sat up in bed and watched fascinated as a band of Indians came through the door, moved along the end of the dining room, went through the kitchen and out the back door again, where she could hear their feet softly scuffing the dead leaves! They paid no attention to her at all, but she was able to observe that they were in full war paint.

Since Kay had a lively imagination, Mrs. N. was inclined to dismiss the story. As there were no further disturbances, the matter of the ghost receded into the back of their minds. About a year after they had moved into the house, some of the little group were leaving town and the household was being broken up. It was a week before they were to part when Mrs. N. had an early morning train to catch and, not having an alarm clock herself, had asked Dick to set his for six A.M. and wake her.

Promptly at six A.M. there was a knock at her door, to which Mrs. N. responded with thanks and just as promptly went back to sleep. A few minutes later, there was a second knock on the door, and this time Mrs. N. replied that she was already getting up. Later she thanked her friend for waking her, and he looked at her somewhat sheepishly, asking her not to rub it in, for he hadn't heard the alarm at all. It appears that he had slept through the appointed hour and not awakened Mrs. N. as promised.

However, the friendly ghost had seen to it that she didn't miss her morning train. Was it the same benign spectre who had shielded them from the hostile Indians during their occupancy? That is, if the "dream" of Indians in war paint belonged to the past of the house, and was not merely an expression of a young girl's fancy.

Adriana Victoria is a spunky, adventurous lady of Mexican ancestry, of whom I have written before. At one time she worked as a housekeeper in a Hollywood mansion that was once the property of the noted actress Carole Lombard. One night, Adriana awoke to see the blood-stained body of the actress standing by her bed, as if begging for attention. . . . By then Adriana knew that she was psychic, she knew that her mother was psychic also, and that this particular talent ran in the family. She accepted it as something perfectly natural and learned to live with it, although at times she underwent frightening experiences that were not easily forgotten.

Miss Victoria now lived in an apartment in New York City, which consisted of two-and-a-half rooms. In view of the small size of the apartment, it was something of a problem to put up her mother and her two children who were then living with her; but Adriana managed somehow, when they came for a visit to New York in the summer of that year. They were on their way from Florida to Europe, and were staying for only a few days.

Since there was little room for everybody, they put a mattress on the living room floor. One night Miss Victoria, sleeping on the mattress, was awakened by two invisible hands that she saw only in her mind's eye. At the same time, she was shaken strongly by the ankles and opened her eyes wide. She couldn't see any intruder, and didn't dare wake the others in the apartment. But nothing further happened until the end of the summer, when her mother left with her granddaughter, leaving Miss Victoria's nine-year-old son at home.

About two months later, Miss Victoria was doing the dishes after dinner, and a girlfriend from an apartment in the same building was watching television while waiting for her to finish with the dishes. Suddenly her son came running in and locked himself into the bathroom next to the kitchen, as if he were frightened by something. Before she could figure out what was happening, Miss Victoria heard heavy footsteps coming from the living room in the direction of the kitchen, and stopping right behind her. Quickly, she turned around, but her friend was still sitting on the living room couch watching TV. Obviously she hadn't heard the footsteps.

With her friend in the living room on the couch, and her nine-year-old son in the bathroom, there was no one present who could have caused the footsteps. Besides, they were heavy, like those of a man. That same night, Adriana entered her bedroom. Her bed stood against the wall with a night table on either side of it. Suddenly she saw the figure of a woman standing next to her bed, moving her hands as if she were trying to get some papers or letters in a hurry.

As Adriana watched in fascinated horror, the apparition was putting imaginary things down from the night table onto the bed. There were some real books on the night table, but they did not move. Standing at the entrance to the room, Adriana looked at the apparition: she could see right through her, but was able to make out that the woman had brown hair down to her shoulders, stood about five feet two or three, and seemed to be about thirty years old. When Adriana made a move towards the bed, the figure looked up and straight at her—then vanished before her very eyes. A little later, Adriana's little boy came to sleep with her, and of course she did not tell him about the apparition. Evidently, the child had heard the footsteps too, and there was no need to frighten him further. The following evening around nine o'clock, the boy complained about being frightened by footsteps again. It was difficult for Adriana to explain them to her son, but she tried to calm his fears. The ghost reappeared from time to time, always in the same spot, always looking for some papers or seeming so, and not necessarily at night: there were times when Adriana saw her standing by her bed in plain daylight.

In July of the following year, Adriana had to go into the hospital for a minor operation. She asked a Spanish-speaking lady, a neighbor, to stay with her son for the four days Adriana was to be in the hospital. The babysitter left the bedroom to the boy and slept on the couch herself.

When Adriana returned from the hospital on the fifth day, the babysitter grabbed her by the hand and rushed her into the bedroom, for she didn't want to talk in front of the boy. She was absolutely terrified. It seems that the previous night, she was awakened toward three in the morning by heavy footsteps right next to her. She was sure that it was a man, and heard him bump into a chair! Frightened, she screamed and called out, "Who's there?" but there was no answer. Through all this the boy had slept soundly.

She turned on the lights, and noticed that the chair had been moved a little from where it had stood before. That was enough for her! She crawled into bed with the little boy—and decided never to stay in the apartment overnight again, unless Adriana was there also.

Adriana decided to make some inquiries about the past occupants of her apartment, but all she could ascertain was that two nurses had lived there for about eight years. The building is very old and has a long history, so it may well be that one or more tragedies had taken place in what is now Adriana's apartment.

Adriana found herself invited to a Christmas party, and somehow the conversation drifted to ghosts. Her host did not believe in such things, and doubted Adriana's experiences. When they brought her back to her apartment, Adriana invited them in. She was just bending down trying to open a bottle of soda when she suddenly heard those heavy footsteps again, coming from the bedroom and stopping right at the entrance to the living room. At the same time, the thought crossed her mind that it was like a husband, waking from sleep to greet his wife returning from a party. Somehow this terrified her, and she let out a loud scream. That night she stayed with friends.

After her son left in July of the following year, things seemed to quiet down a little. One night, shortly afterward, around six P.M., Adriana returned home from work. As soon as she opened the door, she could smell burned papers. Immediately she checked the kitchen, where everything seemed in order. Suddenly she realized that she could smell the strange smell better in her mind than with her nose. At the same time a thought crossed her mind, "My lady ghost finally found the papers and burned them." Adriana knew that they were love letters, and that all was right now with her ghost. There were no further disturbances after that.

Some ghostly invasions have a way of snowballing from seemingly quiet beginnings into veritable torrents of terror. Mrs. C. of North Dakota is a housewife with an eight-year-old daughter, a husband who does not believe in ghosts or anything of that nature. They live in an old house that would be a comfortable, roomy house if it weren't for—*them*. Mrs. C. and her family moved into the house in 1970. Whether it was because both she and her husband worked at different times, thus being absent from the house a great deal of the time, or whether the unseen forces had not yet gathered enough strength to manifest, nothing of an uncanny nature occurred until January, 1973.

One day during January, Mrs. C. was working in the basement, washing some clothes. All of a sudden she heard someone whistle; no definite tune, just one long whistle repeated several times. Immediately her dog, Pud, ran around the basement to see where the noise came from, but neither Mrs. C. nor her dog could find the origin of the whistle.

The whistling continued on several occasions during the month, and while it seemed puzzling, it did not upset her greatly. At the time she was working nights, returning home between midnight and one A.M. One night night during February, she returned home, and as soon as she had entered the house, had a very strange feeling of being watched by someone. At the same time it became freezing cold, and the hair on her arms stood up. She looked all over the house but found no intruder, nothing human that could account for the strange feeling.

Mrs. C. decided to prepare for bed, and changed clothes in the kitchen as was her custom, in order not to wake her husband who was already asleep. She then went toward the bedroom in semi-darkness, with the lights off but sufficiently illuminated to make out the details of the room. All of a sudden, about a foot and a half in front of her face and a little over her head, she noticed a smoky, whitish-gray haze. To her horror, she saw that in the middle of it there was a human face without either body or neck. It was the head of a bald man, very white,

with distinctive black eyes and a very ugly face. All through it and
around it was this strange white fog. Mrs. C. had never seen anything
like it and became very frightened. She dashed into the bedroom, not
sure whether the whole thing had been her imagination, and eventually
fell asleep. The next day, the whistling returned and continued all
month long. This was followed by a mumbling human voice, at first
one person, then later two people speaking. Both she and her seven-
year-old daughter heard it. At first the mumbling was heard only in the
daytime; later it switched to nighttime as well.

At the time, Mrs. C.'s husband left for work at four o'clock in the
morning, and she was in the habit of sleeping on till about eight. But
now she could not; as soon as her husband had left for work the
mumbling would start, always in the bedroom and seemingly coming
from the foot of the bed. It then moved to the side of the bed opposite
where she slept, then back to the foot of the bed again, directly in front
of her feet. She tried hard not to pay any attention to it, and after
listening to it for awhile, managed to fall asleep. Soon it sounded as if
several women and one man were speaking, perhaps as many as four
individuals. This continued every morning until April of that year. Then
something new was added to the torment: something that sounded like
a faint growling noise.

The growling was the last straw. Mrs. C. became very frightened
and decided to do something to protect herself. She recalled a small
cross her husband had given her the previous Christmas. Now she put
the cross and chain around her neck, never taking it off again.

Mrs. C. loves animals. At the time of the haunting, the family
owned two parakeets, six guinea pigs, two dogs and two cats. Since
the uncanny events had started in her house, she had kept a day-to-
day diary of strange happenings, not because she hoped to convince
her husband of the reality of the phenomena, but to keep her own
sanity and counsel. On May 5, 1973, Mrs. C. awoke and found her
blue parakeet dead, horribly disfigured in its cage; the green parakeet
next to it acted as if it were insane, running back and forth all day,
screaming. The following day, May 6, Mrs. C. awoke to find the green
bird dead, destroyed in exactly the same way as the first parakeet had
been.

Four days later, as she was washing her hair, Mrs. C. felt the chain
with the cross being lifted up from the back of her neck by an unseen
hand and unclasped, then dropped to the floor. When she turned around,
there was no one in back of her. Still shaken, she left her house at
nine-thirty to do some errands. When she returned at eleven o'clock,
she found one of her guinea pigs lying on the living room floor, flopping
its head in a most pitiful fashion. A short time later the animal died.
Its neck had been broken by an unseen force. No one had been in the
house at the time, as her daughter and a friend who had slept over had

accompanied Mrs. C. on her errands. What made the incident even more grisly was the fact that the guinea pig had been kept in a cage, that the cage was locked, and that the key rested safely in Mrs. C.'s cigarette case that she took when she went out of the house.

Two weeks passed. On May 25, while taking a bath, Mrs. C. felt the necklace with the cross being lifted up into the air from the back of her neck and pulled so hard that it snapped and fell into the tub. This was the beginning of a day of terror. During the night, the two children heard frightening noises down in the basement, which kept them from sleeping. Mrs. C., exhausted from the earlier encounters, had slept so deeply she had not heard them. The children reported that the dogs had growled all night and that they had heard the meowing of the cats as well.

Mrs. C. went downstairs to check on things. The dogs lay asleep as if exhausted; the cats were not there, but were upstairs by now; on the floor, scattered all over the basement, lay the remaining guinea pigs except for one. That one was alive and well in its cage, but two others lay dead inside their cage, which was still locked and intact. Their bodies were bloody and presented a horrible sight—fur all torn off, eyes gone and bodies torn apart. At first, Mrs. C. thought that the dogs might have attacked them, but soon realized that they could not have done so inside the animals' cages.

For a few days, things quieted down somewhat. One morning, the ominous growling started again while Mrs. C. was still in bed. Gradually, the growling noise became louder and louder, as if it were getting closer. This particular morning the growling had started quietly, but when it reached a deafening crescendo, Mrs. C. heard over it a girl's voice speak quite plainly, "No, don't hurt her! Don't hurt her!" The growling continued, nevertheless. Then, as Mrs. C. looked on in horror, someone unseen sat down in front of her feet on the bed, for the bed sank down appreciably from the weight of the unseen person.

Then the spectral visitor moved up closer and closer in the bed towards her, while the growling became louder. Accompanying it was the girl's voice, "No, no! Don't do it!" That was enough for Mrs. C. Like lightning, she jumped out of bed and ran into the kitchen and sat down trembling. But the growling followed her from the bedroom, started into the living room across from the kitchen, then went back to the bedroom—and suddenly stopped.

That was the last time Mrs. C. slept on in the morning after her husband left for work. From that moment on she got up with him, got dressed, and sat in the kitchen until the children got up, between seven-thirty and nine A.M.

About that time they heard the sound of water running, both at night and in the morning upon arising. Even her husband heard it now and asked her to find out where it was coming from. On checking the bathroom, kitchen, upstairs sink, basement bathroom and laundry room, Mr. and Mrs. C. concluded that the source of the running water was invisible.

From time to time they heard the sound of dishes being broken and crashing, and furniture being moved with accompanying loud noise. Yet when they looked for the damage, nothing had been touched, nothing broken.

At the beginning of the summer of 1973, Mrs. C. had a sudden cold feeling and suddenly felt a hand on her neck coming around from behind her, and she could actually feel fingers around her throat! She tried to swallow and felt as if she were being choked. The sensation lasted just long enough to cause her great anxiety, then it went away as quickly as it had come.

Some of the phenomena were now accompanied by rapping on the walls, with the knocks taking on an intelligent pattern, as if someone were trying to communicate with them. Doorknobs would rattle by themselves or turn themselves, even though there was no one on the other side of them. All over the house footsteps were heard. One particular day, when Mrs. C. was sitting in the kitchen with her daughter, all the doors in the house began to rattle. This was followed by doors all over the house opening and slamming shut by themselves, and the drapes in the living room opening wide and closing quickly, as if someone were pulling them back and forth. Then the window shades in the kitchen went up and down again, and windows opened by themselves, going up, down, up, down in all the rooms, crashing as they fell down without breaking.

It sounded as if all hell had broken loose in the house. At the height of this nightmare, the growling started up again in the bedroom. Mrs. C. and her little daughter sat on the bed and stared towards where they thought the growling came from. Suddenly Mrs. C. could no longer talk, no matter how she tried; not a word came from her mouth. It was clear to her that something extraordinary was taking place. Just as the phenomena reached the height of fury, everything stopped dead silent, and the house was quiet again.

Thus far only Mrs. C. and her little daughter shared the experiences, for her husband was not only a skeptic but prided himself on being an atheist. No matter how pressing the problem was, Mrs. C. could not unburden herself to him.

One night, when the couple returned from a local stock car race and had gone to bed, the mumbling voices started up again. Mrs. C. said nothing in order not to upset her husband, but the voices became louder. All of a sudden Mr. C. asked, "What is that?" and when she informed him that those were the ghostly voices she had been hearing all along, he chided her for being so silly. But *he* had heard them *also*. A few days later Mr. C. told his wife he wanted a cross similar to the one she was wearing. Since his birthday was coming up, she bought one for him as a gift. From that moment on, Mr. C. also always wore a necklace with a cross on it.

In despair Mrs. C. turned to her brother, who had an interest in occult matters. Together with him and her young brother-in-law, Mrs. C. went downstairs one night in August to try and lay the ghosts to rest. In a halting voice, her brother spoke to the unseen entities, asking them to speak up or forever hold their peace. There was no immediate response. The request to make their presence felt was repeated several times.

All of a sudden, all hell broke loose again. Rattling and banging in the walls started up around them, and the sound of walking on the basement steps was clearly heard by the three of them. Mrs. C.'s brother started up the stairs and, as he did so, he had the chill impression of a man standing there.

Perhaps the formula of calling out the ghosts worked, because the house has been quiet since then. Sometimes Mrs. C. looks back on those terrible days and nights, and wishes it had happened to someone else, and not her. But the empty cages where her pet animals had been kept are a grim reminder that it had all been only too true.

Mrs. J.H. is a housewife living in Maryland. At the time of the incidents I am about to report, her son Richard was seven and her daughter Cheryl, six. Hers was a conventional marriage, until the tragic death of her husband Frank. On September 3, he was locking up a restaurant where he was employed near Washington, D.C. Suddenly, two men entered by the rear door and shot him while attempting a robbery. For more than a year after the murder, no clue as to the murderers' identities was found by the police.

Mrs. H. was still grieving over the sudden loss of her husband when something extraordinary took place in her home. Exactly one month to the day of his death, she happened to be in her living room when she saw a "wall of light" and something floated across the living room towards her. From it stepped the person of her late husband Frank. He seemed quite real to her, but somewhat transparent. Frightened, the widow turned on the lights and the apparition faded.

From that moment on, the house seemed to be alive with strange phenomena: knocks at the door which disclosed no one who could have caused them, the dog barking for no good reason in the middle of the night, or the cats staring as if they were looking at a definite person in the room. Then one day the two children went into the bathroom and saw their dead father taking a shower! Needless to say, Mrs. H. was at a loss to explain that to them. The widow had placed all of her late husband's clothes into an unused closet that was kept locked. She was the last one to go to bed at night and the first one to arise in the morning, and one morning she awoke to find Frank's shoes in the hallway; nobody could have placed them there.

One day Mrs. H.'s mother, Mrs. D. who lives nearby, was washing clothes in her daughter's basement. When she approached the washer, she noticed that it was spotted with what appeared to be fresh blood. Immediately she and the widow searched the basement, looking for a possible leak in the ceiling to account for the blood, but they found nothing. Shortly afterwards, a sister of the widow arrived to have lunch at the house. A fresh tablecloth was placed on the table. When the women started to clear the table after lunch, they noticed that under each dish there was a blood spot the size of a fifty-cent piece. Nothing they had eaten at lunch could possibly have accounted for such a stain.

But the widow's home was not the only place where manifestations took place. Her mother's home was close by, and one night a clock radio alarm went off by itself in a room that had not been entered by anyone for months. It was the room belonging to Mrs. H.'s grandmother, who had been in the hospital for some time before.

It became clear to Mrs. H. that her husband was trying to get in touch with her, since the phenomena continued at an unabated pace. Three years after his death, two alarm clocks in the house went off at the same time, although they had not been set, and all the kitchen cabinets flew open by themselves. The late Frank H. appeared to his widow punctually on the third of each month, the day he was murdered, but the widow could not bring herself to address him and ask him what he wanted. Frightened, she turned on the light, which caused him to fade away. In the middle of the night Mrs. H. would feel someone shake her shoulder, as if to wake her up. She recognized this touch as that of her late husband, for it had been his habit to wake her in just that manner.

Meanwhile the murderers were caught. Unfortunately, by one of those strange quirks of justice, they got off very lightly, one of the murderers with three years in prison, the other with ten. It seemed like a very light sentence for having taken a man's life so deliberately.

Time went on, and the children were ten and eleven years of age, respectively. Mrs. H. could no longer take the phenomena in the house and moved out. The house was rented to strangers who are still living in it. They have had no experiences of an uncanny nature since, after all, Franks wants nothing from *them*.

As for the new house where Mrs. H. and her children live now, Frank has not put in an appearance as of yet. But there are occasional tappings on the wall, as if he still wanted to communicate with his wife. Mrs. H. wishes she could sleep in peace in the new home, but then she remembers how her late husband, who had been a believer in scientology, had assured her that when he died, he would be back. . . .

Alice H. is sixty-nine years old, and lives in a five-room bungalow flat in the Middle West. She still works part-time as a saleswoman, but lives alone. Throughout her long life she never had any real interest in psychic phenomena. She even went to a spiritualist meeting with a friend and was not impressed one way or another. She was sixty-two when she had her first personal encounter with the unknown.

One night she went to bed and awoke because something was pressing against her back. Since she knew herself to be alone in the apartment, it frightened her. Nevertheless, she turned around to look— and to her horror she saw the upper part of her late husband's body. As she stared at him, he glided over the bed, turned to look at her once more with a mischievous look in his eye, and disappeared on the other side of the bed. Mrs. H. could not figure out why he had appeared to her, because she had not been thinking of him at that time. But evidently he was to instigate her further psychic experiences.

Not much later, she had another manifestation that shook her up a great deal. She had been sound asleep when she was awakened by the whimpering of her dog. The dog, a puppy, was sleeping on top of the covers of the bed. Mrs. H. was fully awake now and looked over her shoulder where stood a young girl of about ten years, in the most beautiful shade of blue tailored pajamas that had a T-pattern. She was looking at the dog. As Mrs. H. looked closer, she noticed that the child had neither face nor hands nor feet showing. Shaken, she jumped out of bed and went toward the spirit. The little girl moved back toward the wall, and Mrs. H. followed her. As the little girl in the blue pajamas neared the wall, it somehow changed into a beautiful flower garden with a wide path!

She walked down the path in a mechanical sort of way, with the wide cuffs of her pajamas showing, but still with no feet. Nevertheless, it was a happy walk, then it all disappeared.

The experience bothered Mrs. H. so she moved into another room. But her little dog stayed on in the room where the experience had taken place, sleeping on the floor under the bed. That first experience took place on a Sunday in October, at four A.M. The following Sunday, again at four o'clock, Mrs. H. heard the dog whimper, as if he were conscious of a presence. By the time she reached the other room, however, she could not see anything. These experiences continued for some time, always on Sunday at four in the morning. It then became clear to Mrs. H. that the little girl hadn't come for her in particular—but only to visit her little dog.

Mrs. S.F. works in an assembly plant, putting together electronic parts. She is a middle-aged woman of average educational background, is divorced, and is living in a house in central Pennsylvania. A native

of Pittsburgh, she went to public school in that city where her father
worked for a steel company, and she has several brothers and sisters.

When she was fourteen years of age, she had her first remembered
psychic experience. In the old house her parents then lived in, she saw
a column of white smoke in front of her, but since she didn't understand
it, it didn't bother her, and she went off to sleep anyway.

Many times she would get impressions of future events and foretell
things long before they happened, but she paid little attention to her
special gift. It was only when she moved into her present house that
the matter took on new dimensions.

The house Mrs. F. moved into is a small house, two stories high,
connected to two similar houses by what is locally called a party wall,
in which two houses share the same wall. Two rooms are downstairs
and two rooms are upstairs. Her house has its bathroom down in the
cellar, and when you first enter it, you are in the living room, then the
kitchen. Upstairs there are two bedrooms, with the stairs going up from
the kitchen. There is no attic; the house is small and compact, and it
was just the thing Mrs. F. needed since she was going to live in it
alone. The house next door was similar to hers, and it belonged to a
woman whose husband had passed away some time previously. Next
to that was another similar house in which some of the widowed woman's
family lived at the time Mrs. F. moved in. There were four houses in
all, all identical and connected by "party walls." The four houses share
a common ground, and seemed rather old to her when she first saw
them.

When Mrs. F. moved into the house, she decided to sleep in the
bedroom in back of the upper story and she put her double bed into
it. But after she had moved into the house, she discovered that the
back room was too cold in the winter and too hot in the summer, so
she decided to sleep in the front room, which had twin beds in it.
Depending upon the temperature, she would switch from one bedroom
to the other. Nothing much out of the ordinary happened to her at first,
or perhaps she was too busy to notice.

Then one spring night, when she was asleep in the back bedroom,
she woke from her sound sleep around four o'clock in the morning.
Her eyes were open, and as she looked up, she saw a man bending
over her, close to her face. She could see that he had a ruddy complexion,
a high forehead, and was partly bald with white hair around his ears.

When he noticed that she was looking at him, he gave her a cold
stare and then slowly drifted back away from her until he disappeared.
She could not see the rest of his body, but had the vague impression
of some sort of robe. Immediately Mrs. F. thought she had had a
hallucination or had dreamt the whole thing, so she went back to sleep.

Not much later Mrs. F. was in bed, reading. It was around two-
thirty in the morning. The reading lamp was on, as was the light in the

hall, when she suddenly heard a swish-like sound followed by a thump. At the same time something punched her bed, and then hit her in the head. She clearly felt a human hand in the area of her eye, but could not see anything. Immediately, she wondered, what could have hit her? There was no one in the room but her. After a while, she dismissed the matter from her mind and went back to reading.

A few days later, when she was reading again in the late hours of the night, she noticed that the bed would go down as if someone had sat on it. It clearly showed the indentation of a human body, yet she could not see anything. This disturbed her, but she decided to pay it no attention—until one night she also heard a man's voice coming to her as if from an echo chamber. It sounded as if someone were trying to talk to her but couldn't get the words out properly, like a muffled "hello."

Mrs. F. never felt comfortable in the back bedroom, so she decided to move into the front room. One night she was in bed in that room, when her eyes apparently opened by themselves and rested on a cupboard door across from the bed. This time she clearly saw the figure of a man, but she couldn't make out legs or feet. It was a dark silhouette of a man, but she could clearly see his rather pointed ears. His most outstanding features were his burning eyes and those strangely pointed ears. When he saw her looking at him, he moved back into the door and disappeared.

Again, Mrs. F. refused to acknowledge that she had a ghost, but thought it was all a hallucination since she had been awakened from a deep sleep. Not much later, she happened to be watching television a little after midnight because her work ended at twelve. She felt like getting some potato chips from a cupboard in the corner, and as she got up to get the potato chips and rounded the bend of the hall, she happened to glance at the wall in the hallway. There was the same man again. She could clearly make out his face and the pointed ears, but again he had neither legs nor feet. As soon as the ghost realized that she had discovered him, he quickly moved back into the wall and disappeared. Now Mrs. F.'s composure was gone; clearly, the apparition was not a hallucination, since she was fully awake now and could not blame her dreams for it.

While she was still debating within herself what this all meant, she had another experience. She happened to be in bed reading when she thought she heard something move in the kitchen. It sounded like indistinct movements, so she tried to listen, but after awhile she didn't hear anything further and went back to reading. A little while later she decided to go down to get a fruit drink out of the refrigerator. The hall lights were on, so the kitchen wasn't too dark. Just the same, when she reached the kitchen, Mrs. F. turned on the fluorescent lights. As soon as the lights came on, she saw the same ghostly apparition standing there in the kitchen, only this time there was a whole view of him, with feet, legs, and even shoes with rounded toes. He wore pants and a shirt, and she could see his color; she could see that he had curly hair, a straight nose, and full lips. She particularly noticed the full lips, and, of course, the pointed ears.

At first the apparition must have been startled by her, perhaps because he had thought that it was the cat coming down the stairs into the kitchen. He turned towards her and Mrs. F. could see his profile. As soon as he noticed her, he ran into the wall and disappeared. But she noticed that his legs started to shake when the lights went on, as if he were trying to get going and didn't quite know how. Then he hunched over a little, and shot into the wall.

Mrs. F. was shocked. She shut off the light and went back to bed. For a long time she just lay there, with the eeriest, chilliest feeling. Eventually she drifted off to sleep again. The entire incident puzzled her, for she had no idea who the ghost might be. One day she was leaving her house, and as she passed her neighbor's house, there was a young man sitting on the steps looking out into the street. She saw his profile, and like a flash it went through her mind that it was the same profile as that of the man she had seen in her kitchen! She looked again, and noticed the same full lips and the same pointed ears she had seen in the face of the ghost!

Immediately she decided to discuss the matter with a neighbor, a Mrs. J.M. Mrs. M. lived at the end of the street, and she was a good person to talk to because she understood about such matters. In fact, Mrs. F. had spent a night at her house at one time when she was particularly upset by the goings-on in her *own* house. The neighbor assured her that the widow's son, the one she had seen sitting on the steps, was the spit and image of his father. The reason Mrs. F. had not seen him before was that he was married and lived somewhere else, and had just been visiting on that particular day.

Well, Mrs. F. put two and two together, and realized that the ghost she had seen was her late neighbor. On making further inquiries, she discovered that the man had suffered from rheumatic fever, and had been in the habit of lying on a couch to watch television. One day his family had awakened him so he wouldn't miss his favorite program. At that moment he had a heart attack, and died right there on the couch. He was only middle-aged.

With this information in her hands, Mrs. F. wondered what she could do about ridding herself of the unwelcome visitor from next door. In August a niece was visiting her with some friends and other relatives. One of the people in the group was an amateur medium, who suggested that they try their hand at a seance. There were about seven in the group, and they sat down and tried to make contact with the late neighbor. The seance was held in the upstairs bedroom, and they used a card table borrowed from Mrs. M. from the other end of the street.

They all put their hands on the table, and immediately felt that the table was rising up. Nothing much happened beyond that, however, and eventually the amateur medium had to leave. But Mrs. F. wanted an answer to her problem, so she continued with those who were still visiting with her. They moved the table down into the kitchen, turned out all the lights but one, and waited. Mrs. F. asked the ghost questions: who he was, what he wanted, etc. Sure enough, her questions were answered by knocks. Everybody could hear them, and after awhile they managed to get a conversation going. From this communication, Mrs. F. learned that her neighbor had been forty-three years old when he died, that his name was Bill, and that he wasn't very happy being dead! But apparently he appreciated the fact that they had tried to get through to him because he never appeared to Mrs. F. again after that.

Only a small fraction of ghosts are "fortunate" enough to be relieved of their status by an investigation in which they are freed from their surroundings and allowed to go into the greater reaches of the World Beyond. The majority have no choice but to cling to the environment in which their tragedy has occurred. But what about those who are in an environment that suddenly ceases to exist? As far as houses are concerned, tearing down one house and building another on the spot doesn't alter the situation much. Frequently, ghosts continue to exist in the new house, even more confused than they were in the old one. But if the environment is radically changed and no new dwelling is erected on the spot, what is there to occupy the ghost in his search for identity?

Mrs. Robert B. is a housewife and mother of four children, leading a busy life in Pittsburgh. Because of her interest in parapsychology, she was able to assist her parents in a most unusual case. In a small town north of Pittsburgh on the Ohio River, her parents occupied a house built approximately seventy-five years ago. They were the second owners, the house having been planned and partially built by the original owner, a certain Daniel W.

Mr. W. had lived in the house with his brother and sister for many years, and had died a bachelor at the age of ninety-four. His last illness was a long one, and his funeral was held in what later became the living room of Mrs. B.'s parents. Thus, Mr. W. not only "gave birth" to the little house, but he lived in it for such a long period that he must have become very attached to it, and formed one of those rare bonds that frequently lead to what I have called "Stay-Behinds," people who live and die in their houses and just don't feel like leaving them.

One spring, Mrs. B.'s parents decided to remodel the house somewhat. In particular, they tore through the wall connecting her mother's bedroom with that of her father, which was next to it. Each room had a cupboard in it, but instead they decided to build a new closet with sliding doors. Although they had occupied the house for fourteen years, this was the first change they had made in it.

One week after the alteration had been completed, Mrs. B.'s mother found it difficult to fall asleep. It was toward one o'clock in the morning and she had been tossing for hours. Suddenly, from the direction of the cupboard in the left-hand corner of the room, came the sound of heavy breathing. This startled her, as she could also hear her husband's breathing from the room next to hers. The mysterious breathing was husky, labored, and sounded as though it came from an echo chamber. Frightened, she lay still and listened. To her horror, the breathing sound moved across the room and stopped in front of the bureau against the far wall. Then, as she concentrated on that spot, she saw a mist starting to form above the chest. At this point, she managed to switch on the light and call out, "Who is there?" Immediately, the breathing stopped.

Mrs. B.'s mother then called Mrs. B., knowing of her interest in the occult, and reported the incident to her. Her daughter advised her not to be alarmed, but to watch out for further occurrences, which were bound to happen. Sure enough, a few days later a curtain was pulled back in full view of her mother, as if by an unseen hand, yet no window was open that would have accounted for it. Shortly thereafter, a chair in the living room sagged as if someone were sitting in it, yet no one was visible. That was enough for one day! A few days later, a window was lowered in the hall while Mrs. B.'s mother was talking to her on the telephone and there was no one else in the house. Shadow-like streaks began to appear on the dining room and living room floors; a Japanese print hanging in the living room, two-by-four feet in size and very heavy, moved of its own volition on the wall. Mrs. B.'s father began to hear the heavy breathing on his side of the dividing wall, but as soon as he had taken notice of it, it moved to the foot of his bed.

By now it was clear to both parents that they had a ghost in the house; they suspected the original owner. Evidently he was displeased with the alterations in the house, and this was his way of letting them know. Mr. W.'s continued presence in the house also shook up their dog. Frequently she would stand in the hall downstairs and bark in the direction of the stairs, with the hair on her back bristled, unable to move up those stairs. At times she would run through the house as if someone were chasing her—someone unseen, that is.

It looked as if Mrs. B.'s parents would have to get used to the continued presence of the original owner of the house, when the authorities decided to run a six-lane state highway through the area, eliminating about half of the little town in which they lived, including their house. This has since been done, and the house exists no more. But what about Mr. W.? If he couldn't stand the idea of minor alterations in his house, what about the six-lane highway eliminating it altogether?

Ghosts, as a rule, do not move around much. They may be seen in one part of the house or another, not necessarily in the room in which they died as people, but there are no cases on record in which ghosts have traveled any kind of distance to manifest.

chapter 8

Yankee Phantoms and Dixie Ghosts

THERE ARE TWO AREAS of the United States that the average person frequently connects with hauntings: New England and the South. Perhaps it is because these two regions are more likely to inspire romantic notions; perhaps it's because their physical appearance is more conducive to unusual phenomena than, let us say, the Plains States or the Rocky Mountains.

But it is not only the unusual and varied geographical appearance of New England and the South that is seemingly conducive to the occurrence of hauntings, but the people who live there as well. Both regions have one thing in common: they were settled at an early stage in American history, mainly from western European roots, and they share a fierce loyalty to basic nationalistic values. In New England, Yankeeland, the traditions of the mother country, England, are continued and the cultural backgrounds of the old country extended into the new. In the South, the traditions of Great Britain have been largely over-shadowed by native-grown values inherent to the region, such as plantation life, the horse country appeal of the wide-open spaces, and the gentility of a closely-knit society going back several hundred years. While the "aristocracy" of New England is likely to be of the middle-class, perhaps even the lower-class such as fishermen and hereditary homesteaders, it is more often on the higher social scale in the South. This Southern Aristocracy is frequently an extension of European nobility concepts, to the point where land grants dating back to pre-Colonial days are still considered important documents, and where the changes of history are not quite able to wipe out firmly-rooted concepts of a feudal past.

The ghosts of an area are likely to reflect the people of that region;

frequently, they *are* people who once lived in the region. Thus the appearances of spectres may differ greatly in New England and the South, but the degree of their involvement with the land, with traditions, and with strongly parochial points of view is very similar. For that reason I have grouped the following cases together, rather than to try to reconcile the erstwhile Civil War foes.

Mrs. Geraldine W. is a graduate of Boston City Hospital and works as a registered nurse; her husband is a teacher, and they have four children. Neither Mr. nor Mrs. W. ever had the slightest interest in the occult; in fact, Mrs. W. remembers hearing some chilling stories about ghosts as a child and considering them just so many fairy tales.

One July, the W.'s decided to acquire a house about twenty miles from Boston, as the conditions in the city seemed inappropriate for bringing up their four children. Their choice fell upon a Victorian home sitting on a large rock that overlooked a golf course in this little town. Actually, there are two houses built next door to each other by two brothers. The one to the left had originally been used as a winter residence, while the other, upon which their choice fell, was used as a summer home. It presented a remarkable sight, high above the other houses in the area. The house so impressed the W.'s that they immediately expressed their interest in buying it. They were told that it had once formed part of the H. estate, and had remained in the same family until nine years prior to their visit. Originally built by a certain Ephraim Hamblin, it had been sold to the H. family and remained a family property until it passed into the hands of a family initialed P. It remained in their possession until the W.'s acquired it that spring.

Prior to obtaining possession of the house, Mrs. W. had a strange dream in which she saw herself standing in the driveway, looking up at the house. In the dream she had a terrible feeling of foreboding, as if something dreadful had happened in the house. On awakening the next morning, however, she thought no more about it and later put it out of her mind.

Shortly after they moved in on July 15, Mrs. W. awoke in the middle of the night for some reason. Her eyes fell upon the ceiling and she saw what looked to her like a sparkler-type of light. It swirled about in a circular movement, then disappeared. On checking, Mrs. W. found that all the shades were drawn in the room, so it perplexed her how such a light could have occurred on her ceiling. But the matter quickly slipped from her mind.

Several days later, she happened to be sitting in the living room one evening with the television on very low since her husband was asleep on the couch. Everything was very quiet. On the arm of a wide-armed couch there were three packages of cigarettes side by side. As she looked at them, the middle package suddenly flipped over by itself and fell to the floor. Since Mrs. W. had no interest in psychic phenomena, she dismissed this as probably due to some natural cause. A short time thereafter, she happened to be sleeping in her daughter's room, facing directly alongside the front hall staircase. The large hall light was burning since the lamp near the children's rooms had burned out. As she lay in the room, she became aware of heavy, slow, plodding footsteps coming across the hallway.

Terrified, she kept her eyes closed tight because she thought there was a prowler in the house. Since everyone was accounted for, only a stranger could have made the noises. She started to pray over and over in order to calm herself, but the footsteps continued on the stairs, progressing down the staircase and around into the living room where they faded away. Mrs. W. was thankful that her prayers had been answered and that the prowler had left.

Just as she started to doze off again the footsteps returned. Although she was still scared, she decided to brave the intruder, whoever he might be. As she got up and approached the area where she heard the steps, they resounded directly in front of her—yet she could see absolutely no one. The next morning she checked all the doors and windows and found them securely locked, just as she had left them the night before. She mentioned the matter to her husband, who ascribed it to nerves. A few nights later, Mrs. W. was again awakened in the middle of the night, this time in her own bedroom. As she woke and sat up in bed, she heard a woman's voice from somewhere in the room. It tried to form words, but Mrs. W. could not make them out. The voice was of a hollow nature and resembled something from an echo chamber. It seemed to her that the voice had come from an area near the ceiling over her husband's bureau, but the matter did not prevent her from going back to sleep, perplexing though it was.

By now Mrs. W. was convinced that they had a ghost in the house. She was standing in her kitchen, contemplating where she could find a priest to have the house exorcised, when all of a sudden a trash bag, which had been resting quietly on the floor, burst and crashed with its contents spilling all over the floor. The disturbances had become so frequent that Mrs. W. took every opportunity possible to leave the house early in the morning with her children, and not go home until she had to. She did not bring in a priest to exorcise the house, but managed to obtain a bottle of blessed water from Lourdes. She went through each room, sprinkling it and praying for the soul of whoever was haunting the house.

About that time, her husband came home from work one evening around six o'clock and went upstairs to change his clothes while Mrs. W. was busy setting the table for dinner. Suddenly Mr. W. called his wife and asked her to open and close the door to the back hall stairs.

Puzzled by his request, she did so five times, each time more strenuously. Finally she asked her husband the purpose of this exercise. He admitted that he wanted to test the effect of the door being opened and closed in this manner, because he had just observed the back gate to the stairs opening and closing by itself!

This was as good a time as any to have a discussion of what was going on in the house, so Mrs. W. went up the stairs to join Mr. W. in the bedroom where he was standing. As she did so, her eye caught a dim, circular light that seemed to skip across the ceiling in two strokes; at the same time, the shade at the other end of the room suddenly snapped up, flipping over vigorously a number of times. Both Mr. and Mrs. W. started to run from the room; then, catching themselves, they returned to the bedroom.

On looking over these strange incidents, Mrs. W. admitted that there had been some occurrences that could not be explained by natural means. Shortly after they had moved to the house, he had started to paint the interior, at the same time thinking about making some structural changes in the house because there were certain things in it he did not like. As he did so, two cans of paint were knocked out of his hands, flipping over and covering a good portion of the living room and hall floors.

Then there was that Saturday afternoon when Mr. W. had helped his wife vacuum the hall stairs. Again he started to talk about the bad shape the house was in, in his opinion, and as he condemned the house, the vacuum cleaner suddenly left the upper landing and traveled over the staircase all by itself, finally hitting him on the head with a solid thud!

But their discussion did not solve the matter; they had to brace themselves against further incidents, even though they did not know why and who caused them.

One evening Mrs. W. was feeding her baby in the living room near the fireplace, when she heard footsteps overhead and dragging the movement of something very heavy across the floor. This was followed by a crashing sound on the staircase, as if something very heavy had fallen against the railing. Her husband was asleep, but Mrs. W. woke him up and together they investigated, only to find the children asleep and no stanger in the house.

It was now virtually impossible to spend a quiet evening in the living room without hearing some uncanny noises. There was scratching along the tops of the doors inside the house, a rubbing sound along the door tops, and once in awhile the front doorknob would turn by itself, as if an unseen hand were twisting it. No one could have done this physically, because the enclosed porch leading to the door was locked and the locks were intact when Mrs. W. examined them.

The ghost, whoever he or she was, roamed the entire house. One night, Mrs. W. was reading in her bedroom at around midnight, when she heard a knocking sound halfway up the wall of her room. It seemed to move along the wall and then stop dead beside her night table. Needless to say, it did not contribute to a peaceful night. By now the older children were also aware of the disturbances. They, too, heard knocking on doors with no one outside, and twice Mrs. W.'s little girl, then seven years old, was awakened in the middle of the night because she heard someone walking about the house. At the time, both her parents were fast asleep.

That year, coming home on Christmas night to an empty house, or what they *presumed* to be an empty house, the W.'s noticed that a Christmas light was on in the bedroom window. Under the circumstances, the family stayed outside while Mr. W. went upstairs to check the house. He found everything locked and no one inside. The rest of the family then moved into the lower hall, waiting for Mr. W. to come down from upstairs. As he reached the bottom of the stairs, coming from what he assured his family was an empty upper story, they all heard footsteps overhead from the area he had just examined.

On the eve of St. Valentine's Day, Mrs. W. was readying the house for a party the next evening. She had waxed the floors and spruced up the entire house, and it had gotten late. Just before going to bed, she decided to sit down for awhile in her rocking chair. Suddenly she perceived a moaning and groaning sound coming across the living room from left to right. It lasted perhaps ten to fifteen seconds, then ended as abruptly as it had begun.

During the party the next evening, the conversation drifted to ghosts, and somehow Mrs. W. confided in her sister-in-law about what they had been through since moving to the house. It was only then that Mrs. W. found out from her sister-in-law that her husband's mother had had an experience in the house while staying over one night during the summer. She, too, had heard loud footsteps coming up the hall stairs; she had heard voices, and a crackling sound as if there had been a fire someplace. On investigating these strange noises, she had found nothing that could have caused them. However, she had decided not to tell Mrs. W. about it, in order not to frighten her.

Because of her background and position, and since her husband had a respected position as a teacher, the W.'s were reluctant to discuss their experiences with anyone who might construe them as imaginary, or think the family silly. Eventually, however, a sympathetic neighbor gave her one of my books, and Mrs. W. contacted me for advice. She realized, of course, that her letter would not be read immediately, and that in any event, I might not be able to do anything about it for some time. Frightening though the experiences had been, she was reconciled to living with them, hoping only that her children would not be hurt or frightened.

On March 3, she had put her three young boys to bed for a nap, and decided to check if they were properly covered. As she went up over the stairway, she thought she saw movement out of the corner of her eye. Her first thought was that her little boy, then four years old, had gotten up instead of taking his nap. But, on checking, she found him fast asleep. Exactly one week later, Mrs. W. was in bed trying to go to sleep when she heard a progressively louder tapping on the wooden mantle at the foot of the bed. She turned over to see where the noise was coming from or what was causing it when immediately it stopped. She turned back to the side, trying to go back to sleep, when suddenly she felt something or someone shake her foot as though trying to get her attention. She looked down at her foot and saw absolutely nothing.

Finally, on March 26, she received my letter explaining some of the phenomena to her and advising her what to do. As she was reading my letter, she heard the sound of someone moving about upstairs, directly over her head. Since she knew that the children were sleeping soundly, Mrs. W. realized that her unseen visitor was not in the least bit put off by the advice dispensed her by the Ghost Hunter. Even a dog the W.'s had acquired around Christmas had its difficulty with the unseen forces loose in the house.

At first, he had slept upstairs on the rug beside Mrs. W.'s bed. But a short time after, he began to growl and bark at night, especially in the direction of the stairs. Eventually he took to sleeping on the enclosed porch and refused to enter the house, no matter how one would try to entice him. Mrs. W. decided to make some inquiries in the neighborhood, in order to find out who the ghost might be or what he might want.

She discovered that a paper-hanger, who had come to do some work in the house just before they had purchased it, had encountered considerable difficulties. He had been hired to do some paper-hanging in the house, changing the decor from what it had been. He had papered a room in the house as he had been told to, but on returning the next day found that some of his papers were on upside down, as if moved around by unseen hands. He, too, heard strange noises and would have nothing further to do with the house. Mrs. W. then called upon the people who had preceded them in the house, the P. family, but the daughter of the late owner said that during their stay in the house they had not experienced anything unusual. Perhaps she did not care to discuss such matters; at any rate, Mrs. W. discovered that the former owner, Mr. P., had actually died in the house three years prior to their acquisition of it. Apparently, he had been working on the house, which he loved very much, and had sustained a fracture. He recovered from it, but sustained another fracture in the same area of his leg. During the recovery, he died of a heart attack in the living room.

It is conceivable that Mr. P. did not like the rearrangements made by the new owners, and resented the need for repapering or repainting, having done so much of that himself while in the flesh. But if it is he who is walking up and down the stairs at night, turning doorknobs, and appearing as luminous balls of light—who, then, is the woman whose voice has also been heard?

So it appears that the house overlooking the golf course for the past hundred and twenty-two years has more than one spectral inhabitant in it. Perhaps Mr. P. is only a johnny-come-lately, joining the earlier shades staying on in what used to be their home. As far as the W.'s are concerned, the house is big enough for all of them; so long as they know their place!

Peter Q. comes from a devout Catholic family, part Scottish, part Irish. One June, Peter Q. was married, and his brother Tom, with whom he had always maintained a close and cordial relationship, came to the wedding. That was the last time the two brothers were happy together. Two weeks later Tom and a friend spent a weekend on Cape Cod. During that weekend, Tom lost his prize possession, his collection of record albums worth several hundred dollars. Being somewhat superstitious, he feared that his luck had turned against him and, sure enough, his car was struck by a hit-and-run driver shortly afterwards.

Then, in August of the same year, Tom and his father caught a very big fish on a fishing trip and won a prize consisting of a free trip during the season. As he was cleaning the fish to present it to the jury, the line broke and Tom lost the prize fish. But his streak of bad luck was to take on ominous proportions soon after. Two weeks later, Tom Q. and the same friend who had been with him when his record collection had been stolen were planning another trip together. Tom was very happy the night before because he was looking forward to the trip. He was joyful, and in the course of conversation said, "When I die, I want a good send-off," meaning a good traditional Irish wake. His friend, David, on the other hand, was quiet and withdrawn, not quite himself that evening.

The following morning, the two young men set out on their trip. Before the day was out, they were involved in an automobile accident. Tom Q. died instantly and David died the next day.

Even before the bad news was brought home to Peter Q. and the family, an extraordinary thing happened at their house. The clock in the bedroom stopped suddenly. When Peter checked it and wound it again, he found nothing wrong with it. By then, word of Tom's death had come, and on checking out the time, Peter found that the clock had stopped at the very instant of his brother's death.

During the following days, drawers in their bedroom would open by themselves when there was no one about. This continued for about four weeks, then it stopped again. On the anniversary of Tom's death, Peter, who was then a junior at the university, was doing some studying and using a fountain pen to highlight certain parts in the books. Just then, his mother called him and asked him to help his father with his car. Peter placed the pen inside the book to mark the page and went to help his father. On returning an hour later, he discovered that a picture of his late brother and their family had been placed where Peter had left the pen, and the pen was lying outside the book next to it. No one had been in the house at the time, since Peter's wife was out working.

Under the influence of Tom's untimely death and the phenomena taking place at his house, Peter Q. became very interested in life after death and read almost everything he could, talking with many of his friends about the subject, and becoming all the time more and more convinced that man does in some mysterious way survive death. But his wife disagreed with him and did not wish to discuss the matter.

One night, while her husband was away from the house, Peter's wife received a telepathic impression concerning continuance of life, and as she did so, a glowing object about the size of a softball appeared next to her in her bed. It was not a dream, for she could see the headlights from passing cars shining on the wall of the room, yet the shining object was still there next to her pillow, stationary and glowing. It eventually disappeared.

Many times since, Peter Q. has felt the presence of his brother, a warm, wonderful feeling; yet it gives him goose bumps all over. As for the real big send-off Tom had wanted from this life, he truly received it. The morning after his accident, a number of friends called the house without realizing that anything had happened to Tom. They had felt a strong urge to call, as if someone had communicated with them telepathically to do so.

Tom Q. was a collector of phonograph records and owned many, even though a large part of his collection had been stolen. The night before his fatal accident, he had played some of these records. When Peter later checked the record player, he discovered that the last song his brother had played was entitled, "Just One More Day." Of the many Otis Redding recordings his brother owned, why had he chosen that one?

Mr. Harold B. is a professional horse trainer who travels a good deal of the time. When he does stay at home, he lives in an old home in W., a small town in Massachusetts. Prior to moving to New England, he and his wife lived in Ohio, but he was attracted by the old world atmosphere of New England and decided to settle down in the East. They found a house that was more than two hundred years old, but unfortunately it was in dire need of repair. There was neither electricity nor central heating, and all the rooms were dirty, neglected, and badly in need of renovating. Nevertheless, they liked the general feeling of the house and decided to take it.

The house was in a sad state, mostly because it had been lived in for fifty-five years by a somewhat eccentric couple who had shut themselves off from the world. They would hardly admit anyone to their home, and it was known in town that three of their dogs had died of starvation. Mr. and Mrs. B. moved into the house on Walnut Road in October. Shortly after their arrival, Mrs. B. fractured a leg, which kept her housebound for a considerable amount of time. This was unfortunate, since the house needed so much work. Nevertheless, they managed. With professional help, they did the house over from top to bottom, putting in a considerable amount of work and money to make it livable, until it became a truly beautiful house.

Although Mrs. B. is not particularly interested in the occult, she has had a number of psychic experiences in the past, especially of a precognitive nature, and has accepted her psychic powers as a matter of course. Shortly after the couple had moved into the house on Walnut Road, they noticed that there *was* something peculiar about their home.

One night, Mrs. B. was sleeping alone in a downstairs front room off the center entrance hall. Suddenly she was awakened by the sensation of a presence in the room, and as she looked up she saw the figure of a small woman before her bed, looking right at her. She could make out all the details of the woman's face and stature, and noticed that she was wearing a veil, as widows sometimes did in the past. When the apparition became aware of Mrs. B.'s attention, she lifted the veil and spoke to her, assuring her that she was not there to harm her, but that she came as a friend. Mrs. B. was too overcome by it all to reply, and before she could gather her wits, the apparition drifted away.

Immediately, Mrs. B made inquiries in town, and since she was able to give a detailed description of the apparition, it was not long until she knew who the ghost was. The description fit the former owner of the house, Mrs. C., to a tee. Mrs. C. died at age eighty-six, shortly before the B.'s moved into what was her former home. Armed with this information, Mrs. B. braced herself for the presence of an unwanted inhabitant in the house. A short time afterwards, she saw the shadowy outline of what appeared to be a heavy-set person moving along the hall from her bedroom. At first she thought it was her husband so she called out to him, but she soon discovered that her husband was actually upstairs. She then examined her room and discovered that the shades were drawn, so there was no possibility that light from traffic on the road outside could have cast a shadow onto the adjoining hall. The shadowy figure she had seen did not, however, look like the outline of the ghost she had earlier encountered in the front bedroom.

While she was still wondering about this, she heard the sound of a dog running across the floor. Yet there was no dog to be seen. Evidently her own dog also heard or sensed the ghostly dog's doings, because he reacted with visible terror.

Mrs. B. was still wondering about the second apparition when her small grandson came and stayed overnight. He had never been to the house before, and had not been told of the stories connected with it. As he was preparing to go to sleep, but still fully conscious, he saw a heavy-set man wearing a red shirt standing before him in his bedroom. This upset him greatly, especially when the man suddenly disappeared without benefit of a door. He described the apparition to his grandparents, who reassured him by telling him a white lie: namely, that he had been dreaming. To this the boy indignantly replied that he had not been dreaming, but in fact had been fully awake. The description given by the boy not only fitted the shadowy outline of the figure Mrs. B. had seen along the corridor, but was a faithful description of the late Mr. C., the former owner of the house.

Although the ghost of Mrs. C. had originally assured the B.'s that they meant no harm and that she had, in fact, come as a friend, Mrs. B. had her doubts. A number of small items of no particular value disappeared from time to time, and were never found again. This was at times when intruders were completely out of the question.

Then Mrs. B. heard the pages of a wallpaper sampler lying on the dining room table being turned one day. Thinking her husband was doing it, she called out to him, only to find that the room was empty. When she located him in another part of the house, he reported having heard the pages being turned also, and this reassured Mrs. B. since she now had her husband's support in the matter of ghosts. It was clear to her that the late owners did not appreciate the many changes they had made in the house. But Mrs. B. also decided that she was not about to be put out of her home by a ghost. The changes had been made for the better, she decided, and the C.'s, even in their present ghostly state, should be grateful for what they had done for the house and not resent them. Perhaps these thoughts somehow reached the two ghosts telepathically; at any rate, the atmosphere in the house became quiet after that.

Not all ghosts have selfish motives, so to speak, in reasserting their previous ownership of a home: some even help later occupants, although the limits of a ghost's rationality are very narrow. For one thing, if a ghost personality is aware of later inhabitants of a house and wants to communicate with them—not in order to get them out but to warn them—such a ghost is still unable to realize that the warning may be entirely unnecessary because time has passed, and the present reality no longer corresponds to the reality he or she knew when his or her own tragedy occurred.

Still, there is the strange case of Rose S., now a resident of New York State, but at one time living in Fort Worth, Texas. Miss S. is a secretary by profession, and during the middle 1960s worked for a well-known social leader. That summer, Miss S. moved into an old house in Fort Worth, renting a room at one end of the house. At the time, she wanted to be near her fiancé, an army pilot who was stationed not far away.

The old house she chanced upon was located on Bryce Avenue, in one of the older sections of Fort Worth. The owner was renting out a furnished room because the house had become too large for her. Her husband, an attorney, had passed away, and their children were all grown and living away from home.

The house seemed pleasant enough, and the room large and suitable, so Miss S. was indeed happy to have found it. Moreover, her landlady did not restirct her to the rented room, but allowed her to use the kitchen and in fact have the freedom of the house, especially as there were no other tenants. The landlady seemed a pleasant enough woman in her middle or late sixties at the time, and except for an occasional habit of talking to herself, there was nothing particularly unusual about her. Miss S. looked forward to a pleasant, if uneventful stay at the house on Bryce Avenue.

Not long after moving in, it happened that the landlady went off to visit a daughter in Houston, leaving the house entirely to Miss S. That night, Rose S. decided to read and then retire early. As soon as she switched off the lights to go to sleep, she began to hear footsteps walking around the house. At the same time, the light in the bathroom, which she had intended to leave on all night, started to grow dimmer and brighter alternately, which puzzled her. Frightened because she thought she had to face an intruder, Miss S. got up to investigate, but found not a living soul anywhere in the house. She then decided that the whole thing was simply her imagination acting up because she had been left alone in the house for the first time, and went to bed. The days passed and the incident was forgotten. A few weeks later, the landlady was again off for Houston, but this time Miss S.'s fiancé was visiting her. It was evening, and the couple was spending the time after dinner relaxing.

Miss S.'s fiance, the pilot, had fallen asleep. Suddenly, in the quiet of the night, Miss S. heard someone whistle loudly and clearly from the next room. It was a marching song, which vaguely reminded her of the well-known melody, the Colonel Bogey March. Neither TV nor radio were playing at the time, and there was no one about. When she realized that the source of the whistling was uncanny, she decided not to tell her fiancé, not wishing to upset him.

Time went on, and another periodical trip by her landlady left Miss S. alone again in the house. This time she was in the TV den, trying to read and write. It was a warm night, and the air cooler was on.

As she was sitting there, Miss S. gradually got the feeling that she was not alone. She had the distinct impression that someone was watching her, and then there came the faint whining voice of a woman above the sound of the air cooler. The voice kept talking, and though Miss S. tried to ignore it, she had to listen. Whether by voice or telepathy, she received the impression that she was not to stay in the house, and that the voice was warning her to move out immediately. After another restless night with very little sleep, Miss S. decided she could take the phenomena no longer.

As soon as the landlady returned, she informed her that she was leaving, and moved in with friends temporarily. Eventually, her experiences at the house on Bryce Avenue aroused her curiosity and she made some quiet inquiries. It was then that she discovered the reasons for the haunting. On the very corner where the house stood, a woman and a girl had been murdered by a man while waiting for a bus. As if that were not enough to upset her, something happened to her fiancé from that moment on. Following the incident with the whistling ghost, of which her fiancé knew nothing, his behavior towards her changed drastically. It was as if he was not quite himself any more, but under the influence of another personality. Shortly afterwards, Miss S. and her pilot broke off their engagement.

Mike L. lives in Tennessee, where his family has been in residence for several generations. Ever since he can remember, he has had psychic ability. At the time when a favorite uncle was in the hospital, he was awakened in the middle of the night to see his uncle standing by his bed. "Goodbye, Michael," the uncle said, and then the image faded away. At that instant, Mike knew that his uncle had passed away, so he went back to sleep. The following morning, his mother awoke him to tell him that his uncle had passed away during the night.

In April, he and his wife moved to a residential section in one of the large cities of Tennessee. They bought a house from a lady well in her seventies, who had the reputation of being somewhat cranky. She was not too well-liked in the neighborhood.

Shortly after they had settled down in the house, they noticed footsteps in the rafters over their bedroom. Regardless of the hour, these footsteps would come across the ceiling from one side of the room to the other. Whenever they checked, there was no one there who could have caused the footsteps.

While they were still puzzled about the matter, though not shocked, and since they had had psychic presences in other houses, something still more remarkable occurred. There were two floor lamps in the living room, on opposite sides of the room. In order to make them work, a switch had to be turned on. One night, Mr. L. awoke and noticed one of the floor lamps lit. Since he clearly remembered having turned it off on going to bed, he was puzzled, but got out of bed and switched it off again. As if to complement this incident, the other floor lamp came on by itself a few nights later, even though it had been turned off by hand a short time before.

This was the beginning of an entire series of lights being turned on in various parts of the house, seemingly by unseen hands. Since it was their practice not to leave any lights on except for a small night light in their daughter's room, there was no way in which this could be explained by negligence or on rational grounds. The house has a basement, including a small space below the wooden front porch. As a result of this hollow space, if anyone were walking on the porch, the steps would reverberate that much more audibly. The L's frequently heard someone come up the porch, approach the door and stop there. Whenever they looked out, they saw no one about. Not much later, they were awakened by the noise of a large number of dishes crashing to the floor of the kitchen, at least so they thought. When they checked everything was in order; no dish had been disturbed.

They were still wondering about this when they caught the movement of something—or someone— out of the corner of their eye in the living room. When they looked closer, there was no one there. Then the dresser in the bedroom *seemed* to be moving across the floor, or so it sounded. By the time they got to the room, nothing had been changed.

One night, just after retiring, Mr. L. was shocked by a great deal of noise in the basement. It sounded as if someone were wrecking his shop. He jumped out of bed, grabbed a gun, opened the basement door, and turned on the light. There was an audible scurrying sound, as if someone were moving about, which was followed by silence.

Immediately Mr. L. thought he had a burglar, but realized he would be unable to go downstairs undetected. Under the circumstances, he called for his wife to telephone the police while he stood at the head of the stairs guarding the basement exit. As soon as he heard the police arrive, he locked the only door to the basement and joined them on the outside of the house. Together they investigated, only to find no one about, no evidence of foul play. Even more inexplicable, nothing in the shop had been touched. About that time, Mr. L. noticed a tendency of the basement door to unlock itself seemingly of its own volition, even though it was Mr. L.'s custom to lock it both at night and when leaving the house. During the daytime, Mrs. L. frequently heard footsteps overhead when she was in the basement, even though she was fully aware of the fact that there was no one in the house but her.

By now, Mr. and Mrs. L. realized that someone was trying to get their attention. They became aware of an unseen presence staring at them in the dining room, or bothering Mrs. L. in one of the other rooms of the house. Finally, Mike L. remembered that a Rosicrucian friend had given them a so-called Hermetic Cross when they had encountered ghostly troubles in another house. He brought the cross to the dining room and nailed it to the wall. This seemed to relieve the pressure somewhat, until they found a calendar hung in front of the cross, as if to downgrade its power.

Mr. L. made some further inquiries in the neighborhood, in order to find out who the unseen intruder might be. Eventually, he managed to piece the story together. The woman from whom they had bought the house had been a widow of about nine years when they had met her. The husband had been extremely unhappy in the house; he was not permitted to smoke, for instance, and had to hide his cigarettes in a neighbor's basement. Nothing he did in his own house met with his wife's approval, it appeared, and he died a very unhappy man. Could it not be that his restless spirit, once freed from the shackles of the body, finally enjoyed his unobstructed power to roam the house and do whatever he pleased? Or perhaps he could now even enjoy the vicarious thrill of frightening the later owners, and for the first time in his long life, become the stronger party in the house.

Finally is the strange case of Dorothy B., a young Pennsylvanian woman in her early thirties, who spent many years living with a maternal uncle and aunt in North Carolina. The house was a two-hundred-year-old farmhouse, surrounded by a medium-sized farm. Her uncle and aunt were people in their late fifties, who continued farming on a reduced scale since they lived alone; their two children had long gone to the city. Dorothy was assigned a pleasant corner room in the upper story of the house, and when she moved into it one April, she thought she had, at last, found a place where she could have peace and quiet.

This was very necessary, you see, because she had just been through a nervous breakdown due to an unhappy love affair, and had decided to withdraw from life in the city. Fortunately, she had saved up some money so she could afford to live quietly by herself for at least a year. When her uncle had heard of her predicament, he had offered the hospitality of the house in return for some light chores she could easily perform for him. The first night after her arrival at the farmhouse, Dorothy slept soundly, due probably to the long journey and the emotional release of entering a new phase of her life. But the following night, and she remembers this clearly because there was a full moon that night, Dorothy went to bed around ten P.M. feeling very relaxed and hopeful for the future. The conversation at the dinnertable had been about art and poetry, two subjects very dear to Dorothy's heart. Nothing about the house or its background had been mentioned by her uncle and aunt, nor had there been any discussion of psychic phenomena. The latter subject was not exactly alien to Dorothy, for she had had a number of ESP experiences over the years, mainly precognitive in nature and not particularly startling.

She extinguished the lights and started to drift off to sleep. Suddenly her attention was focused on a low level noise, seemingly emanating from below the ceiling. It sounded as if someone were tapping on the wall. At first, Dorothy assumed that the pipes were acting up, but then she remembered that it was the middle of spring and the heat was not on.

She decided not to pay any attention, assuming it was just one of those noises you hear in old houses when they settle. Again she tried to drift off to sleep and was almost asleep when she felt a presence close to her bed. There was an intense chill accompanying that feeling, and she sat bolt upright in bed, suddenly terrified. As she opened her eyes and looked toward the corner of her room, she saw that she was not alone. Due to the strong moonlight streaming in from the window, she could make out everything in the room. Perhaps a yard or a yard and a half away from her stood the figure of a young girl, motionless, staring at her with very large, sad eyes!

Despite her terror, Dorothy could make out that the girl was dressed in very old-fashioned clothes, unlike the kind that are worn today. She seemed liked a farm girl; the clothes were simple but clean, and her long brown hair cascaded down over her shoulders. There was a terrible feeling of guilt in her eyes, as if she were desperately seeking help. "What do you want?" Dorothy said, trembling with fear as she spoke. The apparition did not reply, but continued to stare at her. At this moment, Dorothy had the clear impression that the girl wanted her to know how sorry she was. At this point Dorothy's fear got the better of her, and she turned on the light. As she did so, the apparition vanished immediately.

Still shaken, she went back to sleep and managed a somewhat restless night. The following morning she asked her aunt whether there had ever been any psychic experience in the family, in particular whether anyone had ever seen or heard anything unusual in the house. Her aunt gave her a strange look and shook her head. Either there hadn't been anything, or she didn't care to discuss it. Dorothy, as the newcomer, did not feel like pressing her point, so she changed the subject.

That night she went to bed with anticipatory fears, but nothing happened. Relieved that it might all have been her imagination due to the long trip the day before, Dorothy began to forget the incident. Three days later, however, she was again awakened by the feeling of a presence in her room. The cold was as intense as it had been the first time, and when she opened her eyes, there was the same apparition she had seen before. This time she was pleading for help even more, and since Dorothy did not feel the same gripping fear she had experienced the first time, she was able to communicate with the apparition.

"I want to help you; tell me who you are," she said to the spectre, waiting for some sort of reply. After what seemed to her an eternity, but could have been no more than a few seconds, Dorothy received the impression that the girl was in trouble because of a man she had become involved with. To be sure, the ghost did not speak to her; the thoughts came to Dorothy on a telepathic level, haltingly, in bits, picturing the apparition with a tall, good-looking man, also wearing old-fashioned farm clothes. In her mind's eye, Dorothy saw the two lovers, and then she heard what sounded like a tiny infant. At that point, the apparition vanished, leaving Dorothy very much shaken.

The following morning she broached the subject of ghosts to her aunt. But the reaction she got was so cold, she hesitated to go on, and again, she did not relate her experiences. Several weeks passed, without any incident of any kind. That is, except for some strange noises Dorothy ascribed to a settling of the house, or perhaps a squirrel or two in the rafters above her room. It sounded like furtive, light footsteps if one were so inclined to interpret the sounds. Again there was a full moon, and Dorothy realized that she had been at the house for a full month. That night, Dorothy went to bed earlier than usual, hoping to get a good start toward a night's sleep since she had been particularly active during the day helping her aunt clear out a woodshed in the back of the farmhouse.

It had not been an easy chore. Somehow the atmosphere in the woodshed was very depressing, and Dorothy wanted to leave more than once, but hesitated to do so lest her aunt accuse her of being lazy. But the feeling inside the woodshed was heavy with tragedy and unhappiness, even though Dorothy could not pinpoint the reasons for it.

Now she lay in bed, waiting for sleep to come. She had drawn the blinds, but the moonlight kept streaming in through them, bathing the room in a sort of semi-darkness, which allowed Dorothy to see everything in the room in good detail. After a few minutes she became aware of an intense chill toward the left side of her bed. She realized she was not about to drift into peaceful sleep after all, and prepared herself for what she knew would be her nocturnal visitor. In a moment, there was the pale-looking girl again, this time standing by the window as if she did not dare come near Dorothy.

"Very well," Dorothy thought, "let's get to the bottom of this. I've had about enough of it, and if this ghost is going to make my life miserable here, I might as well know why." Somehow the ghost seemed to have read her mind, because she came closer to the bed, looking at Dorothy again with her tearful, large eyes. As if someone had told her to, Dorothy now closed her own eyes, and allowed the apparition to impress her with further details of her story. Again she saw the husky young man and the ghost girl together, and this time there was an infant with them. Next she saw an old woman entering what appeared to be a very run-down shack or room, and something in Dorothy recognized the shack as the woodshed she had been in during the day!

Then something horrible happened: although she could not see it with her mind's eye, Dorothy knew that the child was being *butchered*, and that the old woman was the instigator of it! Quickly, Dorothy opened her eyes and looked at the apparition. For a moment the girl looked at Dorothy again as if to say *now you understand why I am still here*—but then the ghost faded into the woodwork. Somehow Dorothy was able to sleep peacefully that night, as if a burden had been lifted from her.

The following morning, she told her aunt everything that had happened from the very first day on. This time her aunt did not interrupt her, but listened in stony silence, as Dorothy recounted her ghostly experiences. Finally, she said, "I wish you had been left in peace; that is why I did not want to tell you anything about this ghost." She explained that a young girl named Anne, who had been working for them for a number of years prior to Dorothy's arrival, had also slept in the same room. She, too, had seen the apparition, although she was unable to understand the reasons for the ghostly encounter. A few years after taking over the farm, Dorothy's uncle had stumbled across an unmarked grave in back of the woodshed. It was clear to him that it was a grave, even though the headstone had been partially destroyed by time and weather. He had assumed that it belonged to a slave, for there were slaves in the area at the time when the farm was first built.

But the grave seemed unusually small, and Dorothy's aunt wondered whether perhaps it might not be that of a child. As she said this, Dorothy felt a distinct chill and received the clear impression that her aunt had hit on something connected with her ghost. On the spur of the moment, the two women went to the spot where the grave had been discovered. It was barely discernible amid the surrounding rocks and earth, but eventually they located it. Dorothy fetched some flowers from the house and placed them upon what must have been the headstone at one time. Then she fashioned a crude cross from two wooden sticks and placed them in the center. This done, she said a simple prayer, hoping that the soul of whoever was underneath the stones would find an easy passage into the world beyond.

When Dorothy went to bed that night, she had a sense of relief at

having done something constructive about her ghost. She half-expected
the ghostly girl to appear again, but nothing happened that night, or
the following night, or any night thereafter, until Dorothy left the farmhouse to go back to the city about a year later.

chapter 9
The Stay-Behinds

THE AVERAGE PERSON thinks that there is just one kind of ghost, and that spirits and ghosts are all one and the same. Nothing could be further from the truth; ghosts are not spirits, and psychic impressions are not the same as ghosts. Basically, there are three phenomena involved when a person dies under traumatic, tragic circumstances and is unable to adjust to the passing from one state of existence to the next. The most common form of passing is of course the transition from physical human being to spirit being, without difficulty and without the need to stay in the denser physical atmosphere of the Earth. The majority of tragic passings do not present any problems, because the individual accepts the change and becomes a free spirit, capable of communicating freely with those on the Earth plane, and advancing according to his abilities, likes and dislikes, and the help he or she may receive from others already on the other side of life. A small fraction of those who die tragically are unable to recognize the change in their status and become so-called ghosts: that is, parts of human personality hung up.in the physical world, but no longer part of it or able to function in it. These are the only *true* ghosts in the literal sense of the term.

However a large number of sightings of so-called ghosts are not of this nature, but represent imprints left behind in the atmosphere by the individual's actual passing. Anyone possessed of psychic ability will sense the event from the past and, in his or her mind's eye, reconstruct it. The difficulty is that one frequently does not know the difference between a psychic imprint having no life of its own and a true ghost. Both seem very real, subjectively speaking. The only way one can differentiate between the two phenomena is when several sightings are

116

compared for minute details. True ghosts move about somewhat, although not outside the immediate area of their passing. Imprints are always identical, regardless of the observers involved, and the details do not alter at any time. Psychic imprints, then, are very much like photographs or films of an actual event, while true ghosts are events themselves, which are capable of some measure of reaction to the environment. Whenever there are slight differences in detail concerning an apparition, we are dealing with a true ghost-personality; but whenever the description of an apparition or scene from the past appears to be identical from source to source, we are most likely dealing only with a lifeless imprint reflecting the event but in no way suggesting an actual presence at the time of the observation.

However, there is a subdivision of true ghosts that I have called "the Stay-Behinds." The need for such a subdivision came to me several years ago when I looked through numerous cases of reported hauntings that did not fall into the category of tragic, traumatic passings, nor cases of death involving neither violence nor great suffering—the earmarks of true ghosts. To the contrary, many of these sightings involved the peaceful passings of people who had lived in their respective homes for many years and had grown to love them. I realized, by comparing these cases one with the other, that they had certain things in common, the most outstanding of which was this: they were greatly attached to their homes, had lived in them for considerable periods prior to their death, and were strong-willed individuals who had managed to develop a life routine of their own. It appears, therefore, that the Stay-Behinds are spirits who are unable to let go of their former homes, are more or less aware of their passing into the next dimension, but are unwilling to go on. To them, their earthly home is preferable, and the fact that they no longer possess a physical body is no deterrent to their continuing to live in it.

Some of these Stay-Behinds adjust to their limitations with marvelous ingenuity. They are still capable of causing physical phenomena, especially if they can draw on people living in the house. At times, however, they become annoyed at changes undertaken by the residents in their house, and when these changes evoke anger in them they are capable of some mischievous activities, like Poltergeist phenomena, although of a somewhat different nature. Sometimes they are quite satisfied to continue living their former lives, staying out of the way of flesh-and-blood inhabitants of the house, and remaining undiscovered until someone with psychic ability notices them by accident. Sometimes, however, they *want* the flesh-and-blood people to know they are still very much in residence and, in asserting their continuing rights, may come into conflict with the living beings in the house. Some of these manifestations seem frightening or even threatening to people living in houses of this kind, but they should not be, since the Stay-Behinds are, after all, human beings like all others, who have developed a continuing and very strong attachment to their former homes. Of course, not everyone can come to terms with them.

For instance, take the case of Margaret C. A few years ago when she lived in New York state, she decided to spend Christmas with her sister and brother-in-law in Pennsylvania. The husband's mother had recently passed away, so it was going to be a sad Christmas holiday for them. Mrs. C. was given a room on the second floor of the old house, close to a passage which led to the downstairs part of the house. Being tired from her long journey, she went to bed around eleven, but found it difficult to fall asleep. Suddenly she clearly heard the sound of a piano being played in the house. It sound like a very old piano, and the music on it reminded her of music played in church. At first Mrs. C. thought someone had left a radio on, so she checked but found that this was not the case. Somehow she managed to fall asleep, despite the tinkling sound of the piano downstairs. At breakfast, Mrs. C. mentioned her experience to her sister. Her sister gave her an odd look, then took her by the hand and led her down the stairs where she pointed to an old piano. It had been the property of the dead mother who had recently passed away, but it had not been played in many years, since no one else in the house knew how to play it. With mounting excitement, the two women pried the rusty lid open. This took some effort, but eventually they succeeded in opening the keyboard.

Picture their surprise when they found that thick dust had settled on the keys, but etched in the dust were unmistakable human fingerprints. They were thin, bony fingers, like the fingers of a very old woman. Prior to her passing, the deceased had been very thin indeed, and church music had been her favorite. Was the lady of the house still around, playing her beloved piano?

The house on South Sixth Street in Hudson, New York, is one of the many fine old town houses dotting this old town on the Hudson River. It was built between 1829 and 1849, and a succession of owners lived in it to the present day. In 1904 it passed into the hands of the Parker family, who had a daughter, first-named Mabel, a very happy person with a zest for life. In her sixties, she had contracted a tragic illness and suffered very much, until she finally passed away in a nearby hospital. She had been truly house-proud, and hated to leave for the cold and ominous surroundings of the hospital. After she died, the house passed into the hands of Mr. and Mrs. Jay Dietz, who still owned it when I visited them. Mrs. Dietz had been employed by Mabel Parker's father at one time.

The psychic did not particularly interest Mrs. Dietz, although she had had one notable experience the night her step-grandfather died, a man she had loved very much. She had been at home taking care of him throughout the daytime and finally returned to her own house to spend the night. Everybody had gone to bed, and as she lay in hers with her face to the wall, she became aware of an unusual glow in the room. She turned over and opened her eyes, and noticed that on the little nightstand at the head of the bed was a large ball of light, glowing with a soft golden color. As she was still staring at the phenomenon, the telephone rang, and she was told that her step-grandfather had passed away.

Eleven years before, the Dietzes moved into the house on South Sixth Street. At first the house seemed peaceful enough. Previous tenants included a German war bride and her mother. The old lady had refused to sleep upstairs in the room that later became Mrs. Dietz's mother's. There was something uncanny about that room, she explained. So she slept down on the ground floor on a couch instead. The Dietzes paid no attention to these stories, until they began to notice some strange things about their house. There were footsteps heard going up and down the stairs and into the hall, where they stopped. The three of them, Mr. and Mrs. Dietz and her mother, all heard them many times.

One year, just before Christmas, Mrs. Dietz was attending to some sewing in the hall downstairs while her husband was in the bathroom. Suddenly she thought he came down the hall which was odd, since she hadn't heard the toilet being flushed. But as she turned around, no one was there. A few nights later she went upstairs and had the distinct impression that she was not alone in the room. Without knowing what she was doing, she called out to the unseen presence, "Mabel?" There was no reply then, but one night not much later, she was awakened by someone yanking at her blanket from the foot of the bed. She broke out into goose pimples, because the pull was very distinct and there was no mistaking it.

She sat up in her upstairs bedroom, very frightened by now, but there was no one to be seen. As she did this, the pulling ceased abruptly. She went back to sleep with some relief, but several nights later the visitor returned. Mrs. Dietz likes to sleep on her left side with her ear covered up by the blanket. Suddenly she felt the covers being pulled off her ear, but being already half-asleep, she simply yanked them back. There was no further movement after that.

The upstairs bedroom occupied by Mrs. Dietz's mother seemed to be the center of activities, however. More than once after the older lady had turned out the lights to go to sleep, she became aware of someone standing beside her bed, and looking down at her.

Sometimes nothing was heard for several weeks or months, only to resume in full force without warning. In February of the year I visited the Dietzes, Mrs. Dietz happened to wake up at five o'clock one morning. It so happened that her mother was awake too, for Mrs. Dietz heard her stir. A moment later, her mother went back to bed. At that moment, Mrs. Dietz heard, starting at the foot of the stairs, the sound of heavy footsteps coming up very slowly, going down the hall and stopping, but they were different from the footsteps she had heard many times before.

It sounded as if a very sick person were dragging herself up the stairs, trying not to fall, but determined to get there nevertheless. It sounded as if someone very tired was coming home. Was her friend finding a measure of rest, after all, by returning to the house where she had been so happy? Mrs. Dietz does not believe in ghosts, however, but only in memories left behind.

Thanks to a local group of psychic researchers, a bizarre case was brought to my attention not long ago. In the small town of Lafayette, Louisiana, there stands an old bungalow that had been the property of an elderly couple for many years. They were both retired people, and of late the wife had become an invalid confined to a wheelchair. One day a short time ago, she suffered a heart attack and died in that chair. Partially because of her demise, or perhaps because of his own fragile state, the husband also died a month later. Rather, he was found dead and declared to have died of a heart attack.

Under the circumstances the house remained vacant for awhile, since there were no direct heirs. After about nine months, it was rented to four female students from the nearby university. Strangely, however, they stayed only two months—and again the house was rented out. This time it was taken by two women, one a professional microbiologist and the other a medical technician. Both were extremely rational individuals and not the least bit interested in anything supernatural. They moved into the bungalow, using it as it was, furnished with the furniture of the dead couple.

Picture their dismay, however, when they found out that all wasn't as it should be with their house. Shortly after moving in, they were awakened late at night by what appeared to be mumbled conversations and footsteps about the house. At first neither woman wanted to say anything about it to the other, out of fear that they might have dreamt the whole thing or of being ridiculed. Finally, when they talked to each other about their experiences, they realized that they had shared them, detail for detail. They discovered, for instance, that the phenomena always took place between one a.m. and sunrise. A man and a woman were talking, and the subject of their conversation was the new tenants!

"She has her eyes open—I can see her eyes are open now," the invisible voice said, clearly and distinctly. The voices seemed to emanate from the attic area. The two ladies realized the ghosts were talking about *them;* but what were they to do about it? They didn't see the ghostly couple, but felt themselves being watched at all times by invisible presences. What were they to do with their ghosts, the two ladies wondered.

I advised them to talk to them, plain and simple, for a ghost who can tell whether a living person's eyes are open or not is capable of knowing the difference between living in one's own house, and trespassing on someone else's, even if it *was* their former abode.

Mrs. Carolyn K. lives in Chicago, Illinois, with her husband and four children, who are between the ages of eight and thirteen. She has for years been interested in ESP experiences, unlike her husband who held no belief of this kind. The family moved into its present home some years ago. Mrs. K. does not recall any unusual experiences for the first six years, but toward the end of April, six years after they moved in, something odd happened. She and her husband had just gone to bed and her husband, being very tired, fell asleep almost immediately. Mrs. K., however, felt ill at ease and was unable to fall asleep, since she felt a presence in the bedroom.

Within a few minutes she saw, in great detail, a female figure standing beside the bed. The woman seemed about thirty years old, had fair skin and hair, a trim figure, and was rather attractive. Her dress indicated good taste and a degree of wealth, and belonged to the 1870s or 1880s. The young woman just stood there and looked at Mrs. K. and vice versa. She seemed animated enough, but made no sound. Despite this, Mrs. K. had the distinct impression that the ghost wanted her to know something specific. The encounter lasted for ten or fifteen minutes, then the figure slowly disintegrated.

The experience left Mrs. K. frightened and worried. Immediately she reported it to her husband, but he brushed the incident aside with a good deal of skepticism. In the following two weeks. Mrs. K. felt an unseen presence all about the house, without, however, seeing her mysterious visitor again. It seemed that the woman was watching her as she did her daily chores. Mrs. K. had no idea who the ghost might be, but she knew that their house was no more than fifty years old and that there had been swamp land on the spot before that. Could the ghost have some connection with the land itself, or perhaps with some of the antiques Mrs. K. treasured?

About two weeks after the initial experience, Mr. K. was studying in the kitchen, which is located at the far eastern end of the house, while Mrs. K. was watching television in the living room at the other end of the house. Twice she felt the need to go into the kitchen and warn her husband that she felt the ghost moving about the living room, but he insisted it was merely her imagination. So she returned to the living room and curled up in an easy chair to continue watching television. Fifteen minutes later, she heard a loud noise reverberating throughout the house. It made her freeze with fright in the chair, when her husband ran into the living room to ask what the noise had been.

Upon investigation, he noticed a broken string on an antique zither hanging on the dining room wall. It was unlikely that the string could have broken by itself, and if it had, how could it have reverberated so strongly? To test such a possibility, they broke several other strings of the same zither in an effort to duplicate the sound, but without success. A few weeks went by, and the ghost's presence persisted. By now Mrs. K had the distinct impression that the ghost was annoyed at being ignored. Suddenly, a hurricane lamp which hung from a nail on the wall fell to the floor and shattered. It could not have moved of its own volition. Again some time passed, and the ghost was almost forgotten. Mrs. K.'s older daughter, then six years old, asked her mother early one morning who the company was the previous evening. Informed that there had been no guests at the house, she inisted that a lady had entered her bedroom, sat on her bed and looked at her, and then departed. In order to calm the child, Mrs. K. told her she had probaby dreamt the whole thing. But the little girl insisted that she had not, and furthermore, she described the visitor in every detail including the "funny" clothes she had worn. Appalled, Mrs. K. realized that her daughter had seen the same ghostly woman. Apparently, the ghost felt greater urgency to communicate now, for a few days later, after going to bed, the apparition returned to Mrs. K.'s bedroom. This time she wore a different dress than on the first meeting, but it was still from the 1880s. She was wiping her hands on an apron, stayed only for a little while, then slowly disintegrated again. During the following year, her presence was felt only occasionally, but gradually Mrs. K. managed to snatch a few fleeting impressions about her. From this she put together the story of her ghost. She was quite unhappy about a child, and one evening the following winter, when Mrs. K. felt the ghost wandering about in their basement, she actually heard her crying pitifully for two hours. Obviously, the distraught ghost wanted attention, and was determined to get it at all costs.

One day the following summer, when Mrs. K. was alone with the children after her husband had left for work, one of the children complained that the door to the bathroom was locked. Since the door can be locked only from the inside, and since all four children were accounted for, Mrs. K. assumed that her ghost lady was at it again. When the bathroom door remained locked for half an hour and the children's needs became more urgent, Mrs. K. went to the door and demanded in a loud tone of voice that the ghost open the door. There was anger in her voice and it brought quick results. Clearly the click of a *lock being turned* was heard inside the bathroom and, after a moment, Mrs.

K. opened the bathroom door easily. There was no one inside the bathroom, of course. Who, then, had turned the lock—the only way the door could be opened?

For awhile things went smoothly. A few weeks later, Mrs. K. again felt the ghost near her. One of her daughters was sitting at the kitchen table with her, while she was cutting out a dress pattern on the counter. Mrs. K. stepped back to search for something in the refrigerator a few feet away, when all of a sudden she and her daughter saw her box of dressmaking pins rise slightly off the counter and fall to the floor. Neither one of them had been near it, and it took them almost an hour to retrieve all the pins scattered on the floor.

A little later, they clearly heard the basement door connecting the dining room and kitchen fly open and slam shut by itself, as if someone in great anger was trying to call attention to her presence. Immediately they closed the door, and made sure there was no draft from any windows.

An instant later, it flew open again by itself. Now they attached the chain to the latch—but that didn't seem to stop the ghost from fooling around with the door. With enormous force, it flew open again as far as the chain allowed, as if someone were straining at it. Quickly Mrs. K. called a neighbor to come over and watch the strange behavior of the door but the minute the neighbor arrived, the door behaved normally, just as before. The ghost was not about to perform for strangers.

One evening in the summer some years later, Mr. K. was driving some dinner guests home and Mrs. K. was alone in the house with the children. All of a sudden, she felt her ghost following her as she went through her chores of emptying ashtrays and taking empty glasses into the kitchen. Mrs. K. tried bravely to ignore her, although she was frightened by her, and she knew that her ghost knew it, which made it all the more difficult to carry on.

Not much later, the K. family had guests again. One of the arriving guests pointed out to Mrs. K. that their basement light was on. Mrs. K. explained that it was unlikely, since the bulb had burned out the day before. She even recalled being slightly annoyed with her husband for having neglected to replace the bulb. But the guest insisted, and so the K.'s opened the basement door only to find the light off. A moment later another guest arrived. He wanted to know who was working in the basement at such a late hour, since he had seen the basement light on. Moreover, he saw a figure standing at the basement window looking out. Once more, the entire party went downstairs with a flashlight, only to find the light off and no one about.

That was the last the K.'s saw or heard of their ghost. Why had she so suddenly left them? Perhaps it had to do with a Chicago news-paperwoman's call. Having heard of the disturbances, she had telephoned the K.'s to offer her services and that of celebrated psychic Irene

Hughes to investigate the house. Although the K.'s did not want any attention because of the children, Mrs. K. told the reporter what had transpired at the house. To her surprise, the reporter informed her that parallel experiences had been reported at another house not more than seven miles away. In the other case, the mother and one of her children had observed a ghostly figure, and an investigation had taken place with the help of Irene Hughes and various equipment, the result of which was that a presence named Lizzy was ascertained.

From this Mrs. K. concluded that they were sharing a ghost with a neighbor seven miles away, and she, too, began to call the ghostly visitor Lizzy. Now if Lizzy had two homes and was shuttling back and forth between them, it might account for the long stretches of no activity at the K. home. On the other hand, if the ghost at the K.'s was not named Lizzy, she would naturally not want to be confused with some other unknown ghost seven miles away. Be this as it may, Mrs. K. wishes her well, wherever she is.

Mrs. J. P. lives in central Illinois, in an old three-story house with a basement. Prior to her acquiring it, it had stood empty for six months. As soon as she had moved in, she heard some neighborhood gossip that the house was presumed haunted. Although Mrs. P. is not a skeptic, she is level-headed enough not to take rumors at face value.

She looked the house over carefully. It seemed about eighty years old, and was badly in need of repair. Since they had bought it at a bargain price, they did not mind, but as time went on, they wondered how cheap the house had really been. It became obvious to her and her husband that the price had been low for other reasons. Nevertheless, the house was theirs, and together they set out to repaint and remodel it as best they could. For the first two weeks, they were too busy to notice anything out of the ordinary. About three weeks after moving in, however, Mr. and Mrs. P. began hearing things such as doors shutting by themselves, cupboards opening, and particularly, a little girl persistently calling for "Mama, Mama" with a great deal of alarm. As yet, Mr. and Mrs. P. tried to ignore the phenomena.

One evening, however, they were having a family spat over something of little consequence. All of a sudden a frying pan standing on the stove lifted off by itself, hung suspended in mid-air for a moment, and then was flung back on the stove with full force. Their twelve-year-old son who witnessed it flew into hysterics; Mr. P. turned white, and Mrs. P. was just plain angry. How dare someone invade their privacy? The following week, the ten-year-old daughter was watching television downstairs in what had been turned into Mrs. P.'s office, while Mr. P. and their son were upstairs also watching television. Suddenly, a glass of milk standing on the desk in the office rose up by itself and dashed itself to the floor with full force. The child ran screaming from the room, and it took a long time for her father to calm her down.

As a result of these happenings, the children implored their mother to move from the house, but Mrs. P. would have none of it. She liked the house fine, and was not about to let some unknown ghost displace her. The more she thought about it, the angrier she got. She decided to go from floor to floor, cursing the unknown ghost and telling him or her to get out of the house, even if they used to own it.

But that is how it is with Stay-Behinds: they don't care if you paid for the house. After all, they can't use the money where they are, and would rather stay on in a place they are familiar with.

Strange places can have Stay-Behind ghosts. Take Maryknoll College of Glen Ellyn, Illinois, a Roman Catholic seminary that closed its doors in June of 1972, due to a dwindling interest in what it had to offer. In the fall a few years before, a seminarian named Gary M. was working in the darkroom of the college. This was part of his regular assignments, and photography had been a regular activity for some years, participated in by both faculty and students.

On this particular occasion, Mr. M. felt as though he were being watched while in the darkroom. Chalking it up to an active imagination, he dismissed the matter from his mind. But in the spring a few years later, Mr. M. was going through some old chemicals belonging to a former priest, when he received the strongest impression of a psychic presence. He was loading some film at the time, and as he did so, he had the uncanny feeling that he was not alone in the room. The chemicals he had just handled were once the property of a priest who had died three years before. The following day, while developing film in an open tank, he suddenly felt as though a cold hand had gone down his back. He realized also that the chemicals felt colder than before. After he had turned the lights back on, he took the temperature of the developer. At the start it had been 70° F., while at the end it was down to 64° F. Since the room temperature was 68° F., there was a truly unaccountable decrease in temperature.

The phenomena made him wonder, and he discussed his experiences with other seminarians. It was then learned that a colleague of his had also had experiences in the same place. Someone, a man, had appeared to him, and he had felt the warm touch of a hand at his cheek. Since he was not alone at the time, but in a group of five students, he immediately reported the incident to them. The description of the apparition was detailed and definite. Mr. M. quickly went into past files, and came up with several pictures, so that his fellow student, who had a similar experience, could pick out that of the ghostly apparition he had seen. Without the slightest hesitation, he identified the dead priest as the

man he had seen. This was not too surprising; the students were using
what was once the priest's own equipment and chemicals, and perhaps
he still felt obliged to teach them their proper use.

Mr. and Mrs. E. live in an average home in Florida that was built
about thirteen years ago. They moved into this house in August. Neither
of them had any particular interest in the occult, and Mr. E. could be
classified as a complete skeptic, if anything. For the first few months
of their residence, they were much too busy to notice anything out of
the ordinary, even if there were such occurrences.

It was just before Christmas when they got their first inkling that
something was not as it should be with their house. Mrs. E. was sitting
up late one night, busy with last-minute preparations for the holiday.
All of a sudden the front door, which was secured and locked, flew
open with a violent force, and immediately shut itself again, with the
handle turning by itself and the latch falling into place. Since Mrs. E.
didn't expect any visitors, she was naturally surprised. Quickly walking
over to the door to find out what had happened, she discovered that
the door was locked. It is the kind of lock that can only be unlocked
by turning a knob. Shaking her head in disbelief, she returned to her
chair, but before she could sit down again and resume her chores, the
door to the utility room began to rattle as though a wind were blowing.
Yet there were no open windows that could have caused it. Suddenly,
as she was staring at it, the knob turned and the door opened. Somehow
nonplussed, Mrs. E. thought, rather sarcastically, "While you're at it,
why don't you shake the Christmas tree too?" Before she had completed
the thought, the tree began to shake. For a moment, Mrs. E. stood
still and thought all of this over in her mind. Then she decided that she
was just overtired and had contracted a case of the holiday jitters. It
was probably all due to imagination. She went to bed and didn't say
anything about the incident.

Two weeks later, her fourteen-year-old daughter and Mrs. E. were
up late talking, when all of a sudden every cupboard in the kitchen
opened by itself, one by one. Mrs. E.'s daughter stared at the phenomena
in disbelief. But Mrs. E. simply said, "Now close them." Sure enough,
one by one, they shut with a hard slam by themselves, almost like a
little child whose prank had not succeeded. At this point Mrs. E.
thought it best to tell her daughter of her first encounter with the unseen,
and implored her not to be scared of it, or tell the younger children or
anyone else outside the house. She didn't want to be known as a weird
individual in the neighborhood into which they had just moved. However,
she decided to inform her husband about what had happened. He didn't
say much, but it was clear that he was not convinced. However, as
with so many cases of this kind where the man in the house takes a

lot longer to be convinced than the women, Mr. E.'s time came about two weeks later.

He was watching television when one of the stereo speakers began to tilt back all of a sudden, rocking back and forth without falling over, on its own, as if held by unseen hands. Being of a practical bent, Mr. E. got up to find an explanation, but there was no wind that would have been strong enough to tilt a twenty-pound speaker. At this point, Mr. E. agreed that there was something peculiar about the house. This was the more likely as their dog, an otherwise calm and peaceful animal, went absolutely wild at the moment the speakers tilted, and ran about the house for half an hour afterwards, barking, sniffing, and generally raising Cain.

However, the ghost was out of the bag, so to speak. The two younger children, then nine and ten years old, noticed him—it was assumed to be a man all along. A house guest remarked how strange it was that the door was opening seemingly by itself. Mrs. E. explained this with a remark that the latch was not working properly. "But how did the knob turn, then?" the house guest wanted to know.

Under the circumstances, Mrs. E. owned up to their guest. The ghost doesn't scare Mrs. E., but he makes it somewhat unpleasant for her at times, such as when she is taking a shower and the doors fly open. After all, one doesn't want to be watched by a man while showering, even if he *is* a ghost. The Stay-Behind isn't noticeable all the time, to be sure, but frequently enough to count as an extra inhabitant of the house. Whenever she feels him near, there is a chill in the hall and an echo. This happens at various times of day or night, early or late. To the children he is a source of some concern, and they will not stay home alone.

But to Mrs. E. he is merely an unfortunate human being, caught up in the entanglement of his own emotions from the past, desperately trying to break through the time barrier to communicate with her, but unable to do so because conditions aren't just right. Sometimes she wishes she were more psychic than she is, but in the meantime she has settled down to share the her home with someone she cannot see, but who, it appears, considers himself part of the family.

One of the most amazing stories of recent origin concerns a family of farmers in central Connecticut. Some people have a ghost in the house, a Stay-Behind who likes the place so much he or she doesn't want to leave. But this family had entire *groups* of ghosts staying on, simply because they liked the sprawling farmhouse, and simply because it happened to be their home too. The fact that they had passed across the threshold of death did not deter them in the least. To the contrary, it seemed a natural thing to stay behind and watch what the young ones were doing with the house, to possibly help them here and there, and, at the very least, to have some fun with them by causing so-called "inexplicable" phenomena to happen.

After all, life can be pretty dull in central Connecticut, especially in the winter. It isn't any more fun being a ghost in central Connecticut, so one cannot really hold it against these Stay-Behinds if they amuse themselves as best they can in the afterlife. Today the house shows its age; it isn't in good condition, and needs lots of repairs. The family isn't as large as it was before some of the younger generation moved out to start lives of their own, but it's still a busy house and a friendly one, ghosts or no ghosts. It stands on a quiet country road off the main route, and on a clear day you can see the Massachusetts border in the distance; that is, if you are looking for it. It is hardly noticeable, for in this part of the country, all New England looks the same.

Because of the incredible nature of the many incidents, the family wants no publicity, no curious tourists, no reporters. To defer to their wishes, I changed the family name to help them retain that anonymity, and the peace and quiet of their country house. The house in question was already old when a map of the town, drawn in 1761, showed it. The present owners, the Harveys, have lived in it all their lives, with interruption. Mrs. Harvey's great-great-grandparents bought it from the original builder, and when her great-great-grandfather died in 1858, it happened at the old homestead. Likewise, her great-great-grandmother passed on in 1871, at the age of eighty, and again it happened at home. One of their children died in 1921, at age ninety-one, also at home.

This is important, you see, because it accounts for the events that transpired later in the lives of their descendants. A daughter named Julia married an outsider and moved to another state, but considers herself part of the family just the same, so much so that her second home was still the old homestead in central Connecticut. Another daughter, Martha, was Mrs. Harvey's great-grandmother. Great-grandmother Martha died at age ninety-one, also in the house. Then there was an aunt, a sister of her great-great-grandfather's by the name of Nancy, who came to live with them when she was a widow; she lived to be ninety and died in the house. They still have some of her furniture there. Mrs. Harvey's grandparents had only one child, Viola, who became her mother, but they took in boarders, mostly men working in the nearby sawmills. One of these boarders died in the house too, but his name is unknown. Possibly several others died there too.

Of course the house doesn't look today the way it originally did; additions were built onto the main part, stairs were moved, a well in the cellar was filled in because members of the family going down for cider used to fall into it, and many of the rooms that later became bedrooms originally had other purposes. For instance, daughter Marjorie's bedroom was once called the harness room because horses' harnesses were once made in it, and the room of one of the sons used to be called the cheese room for obvious reasons. What became a sewing room was originally used as a pantry, with shelves running across the south wall.

The fact that stairs were changed throughout the house is important, because in the mind of those who lived in the past, the original stairs would naturally take precedence over later additions or changes. Thus phantoms may appear out of the wall, seemingly without reason, except that they would be walking up staircases that no longer exist.

Mrs. Harvey was born in the house, but at age four her parents moved away from it, and did not return until much later. But even then, Mrs. Harvey recalls an incident which she was never to forget. When she was only four years old, she remembers very clearly an old lady she had never seen before appear at her crib. She cried, but when she told her parents about it, they assured her it was just a dream. But Mrs. Harvey knew she had not dreamt the incident; she remembered every detail of the old lady's dress.

When she was twelve years old, at a time when the family had returned to live in the house, she was in one of the upstairs bedrooms and again the old lady appeared to her. But when she talked about it to their parents, the matter was immediately dropped. As Frances Harvey grew up in the house, she couldn't help but notice some strange goings-on. A lamp moved by itself, without anyone being near it. Many times she could feel a presence walking close behind her in the upstairs part of the house, but when she turned around, she was alone. Nor was she the only one to notice the strange goings-on. Her brothers heard footsteps around their beds, and complained about someone bending over them, yet no one was to be seen. The doors to the bedrooms would open by themselves at night, so much so that the boys tied the door latches together so that they could not open by themselves. Just the same, when morning came, the doors were wide open with the knot still in place.

It was at that time that her father got into the habit of taking an after-dinner walk around the house before retiring. Many times he told the family of seeing a strange light going through the upstairs rooms, a glowing luminosity for which there was no rational explanation. Whenever Frances Harvey had to be alone upstairs she felt uncomfortable, but when she mentioned this to her parents she was told that all old houses made one feel like that and to never mind. One evening, Frances was playing a game with her grandfather when both of them clearly heard footsteps coming up the back stairs. But her grandfather didn't budge. When Frances asked him who this could possibly be, he merely shrugged and said there was plenty of room for *everyone*.

As the years passed, the Harveys would come back to the house from time to time to visit. On these occasions, Frances would wake up in the night because someone was bending over her. At other times there was a heavy depression on the bed as if someone were sitting there! Too terrified to tell anyone about it, she kept her experiences to herself for the time being.

Then, in the early 1940s, Frances married, and with her husband and two children, eventually returned to the house to live there permanently with her grandparents. No sooner had they moved in when the awful feeling came back in the night. Finally she told her husband, who of course scoffed at the idea of ghosts.

The most active area in the house seemed to be upstairs, roughly from her son Don's closet, through her daughter Lolita's room, and especially the front hall and stairs. It felt as if someone were standing on the landing of the front stairs, just watching.

This goes back a long time. Mrs. Harvey's mother frequently complained, when working in the attic, that all of a sudden she would feel someone standing next to her, someone she could not see.

One day Mrs. Harvey and her youngest daughter went grocery shopping. After putting the groceries away, Mrs. Harvey reclined on the living room couch while the girl sat in the dining room reading. Suddenly they heard a noise like thunder, even though the sky outside was clear. It came again, only this time it sounded closer, as if it were upstairs! When it happened the third time, it was accompanied by a sound as if someone were making up the bed in Mrs. Harvey's son's room upstairs.

Now, they had left the bed in disorder because they had been in a hurry to go shopping. No one else could have gone upstairs, and yet when they entered the son's room, the bed was made up as smoothly as possible. As yet, part of the family still scoffed at the idea of having ghosts in the house, and considered the mother's ideas as dreams or hallucinations. They were soon to change their minds, however, when it happened to them as well.

The oldest daughter felt very brave and called up the stairs, "Little ghosties, where are you?" Her mother told her she had better not challenge them, but the others found it amusing. That night she came downstairs a short time after she had gone to bed, complaining that she felt funny in her room, but thought it was just her imagination. The following night, she awoke to the feeling that someone was bending over her. One side of her pillow was pulled away from her head as though a hand had pushed it down. She called out and heard footsteps receding from her room, followed by heavy rumblings in the attic above. Quickly she ran into her sister's room, where both of them lay awake the rest of the night listening to the rumbling and footsteps walking around overhead. The next day she noticed a dusty black footprint on the light-colored scatter rug next to her bed. It was in the exact location where she had felt someone standing and bending over her. Nobody's footprint in the house matched the black footprint, for it was long and very narrow. At this point the girls purchased special night lights and left them on in the hope of sleeping peacefully.

One day Mrs. Harvey felt brave, and started up the stairs in response to footsteps coming from her mother's bedroom. She stopped, and as the footsteps approached the top of the stairs, a loud ticking noise came with them, like a huge pocket watch. Quickly she ran down the stairs and outside to get her son to be a witness to it. Sure enough, he too could hear the ticking noise. This was followed by doors opening and closing by themselves. Finally, they dared go upstairs, and when they entered the front bedroom, they noticed a very strong, sweet smell of perfume. When two of the daughters came home from work that evening, the family compared notes and it was discovered that they, too, had smelled the strange perfume and heard the ticking noise upstairs. They concluded that one of their ghosts, at least, was a man.

About that time, the youngest daughter reported seeing an old woman in her room, standing at a bureau with something shiny in her hand. The ghost handed it to her but she was too frightened to receive it. Since her description of the woman had been very detailed, Mrs. Harvey took out the family album and asked her daughter to look through it in the hope that she might identify the ghostly visitor. When they came to one particular picture, the girl let out a small cry: that was the woman she had seen! It turned out to be Julia, a great-great-aunt of Mrs. Harvey's, the same woman whom Mrs. Harvey herself had seen when she was twelve years old. Evidently, the lady was staying around.

Mrs. Harvey's attention was deflected from the phenomena in the house by her mother's illness. Like a dutiful daughter, she attended her to the very last, but in March of that year her mother passed away. Whether there is any connection with her mother's death or not, the phenomena started to increase greatly, both in volume and intensity, in July of that same year. To be exact, the date was July 20. Mrs. Harvey was hurrying one morning to get ready to take her daughter Lolita to the center of town so she could get a ride to work. Her mind was preoccupied with domestic chores, when a car came down the road, with brakes squealing. Out of habit, she hurried to the living room window to make sure that none of their cats had been hit by the car. This had been a habit of her mother's and hers, whenever there was the sound of sudden brakes outside.

As she did so, for just a fleeting glance, she saw her late mother looking out of her favorite window. It didn't register at first, then Mrs. Harvey realized her mother couldn't possibly have been there. However, since time was of the essence, Mrs. Harvey and her daughter Lolita left for town without saying anything to any of the others in the house. When they returned, her daughter Marjorie was standing outside waiting for them. She complained of hearing someone moving around in the living room just after they had left, and it sounded just like Grandma when she straightened out the couch and chair covers.

It frightened her, so she decided to wait in the dining room for her mother's return. But while there, she heard footsteps coming from the living room and going into the den, then the sound of clothes being folded. This was something Mrs. Harvey's mother was also in the habit of doing there. It was enough for Marjorie to run outside the house and wait there. Together with her sister and mother, she returned to the living room, only to find the chair cover straightened. The sight of the straightened chair cover made the blood freeze in Mrs. Harvey's veins; she recalled vividly how she had asked her late mother not to bother straightening the chair covers during her illness, because it hurt her back. In reply, her mother had said, "Too bad I can't come back and do it after I die."

Daughter Jane was married to a Navy man, who used to spend his leaves at the old house. Even during his courtship days, he and Mrs. Harvey's mother got along real fine, and they used to do crossword puzzles together. He was sleeping at the house some time after the old lady's death, when he awoke to see her standing by his bed with her puzzle book and pencil in hand. It was clear to Mrs. Harvey by now that her late mother had joined the circle of dead relatives to keep a watch on her and the family. Even while she was ill, Mrs. Harvey's mother wanted to help in the house. One day after her death, Mrs. Harvey was baking a custard pie and lay down on the couch for a few minutes while it was baking.

She must have fallen asleep, for she awoke to the voice of her mother saying, "Your pie won't burn, will it?" Mrs. Harvey hurriedly got up and checked; the pie was just right and would have burned if it had been left in any longer. That very evening, something else happened. Mrs. Harvey wanted to watch a certain program that came on television at seven-thirty p.m., but she was tired and fell asleep on the couch in the late afternoon. Suddenly she heard her mother's voice say to her, "It's time for your program, dear." Mrs. Harvey looked at the clock, and it was exactly seventy-thirty p.m. Of course, her mother did exactly the same type of thing when she was living, so it wasn't too surprising that she should continue with her concerned habits after she passed on into the next dimension.

But if Mrs. Harvey's mother had joined the ghostly crew in the house, she was by no means furnishing the bulk of the phenomena—not by a long shot. Lolita's room upstairs seemed to be the center of many activities, with her brother Don's room next to hers also very much involved. Someone was walking from her bureau to her closet, and her brother heard the footsteps too. Lolita looked up and saw a man in a uniform with gold buttons, standing in the back of her closet.

At other times she smelled perfume and heard the sound of someone dressing near her bureau. All the time she heard people going up the front stairs mumbling, then going into her closet where the sound stopped abruptly. Yet, they could not see anyone on such occasions.

Daughter Jane wasn't left out of any of this either. Many nights she would feel someone standing next to her bed, between the bed and the wall. She saw three different people, and felt hands trying to lift her out of bed. To be sure, she could not see their faces; their shapes were like dark shadows. Marjorie, sleeping in the room next to Jane's, also experienced an attempt by some unseen forces to get her out of bed. She grabbed the headboard to stop herself from falling when she noticed the apparition of the same old woman whom Mrs. Harvey had seen the time she heard several people leave her room for the front hall.

One night she awoke to catch a glimpse of someone in a long black coat hurrying through the hall. Mumbling was heard in that direction, so she put her ear against the door to see if she could hear any words, but she couldn't make out any. Marjorie, too, saw the old woman standing at the foot of her bed—the same old woman whom Mrs. Harvey had seen when she was twelve years old. Of course, that isn't too surprising; the room Marjorie slept in used to be Julia's a long time ago. Lolita also had her share of experiences: sounds coming up from the cellar bothering her, footsteps, voices, even the sound of chains. It seemed to her that they came right out of the wall by her head, where there used to be stairs. Finally, it got so bad that Lolita asked her mother to sleep with her. When Mrs. Harvey complied, the two women clearly saw a glow come in from the living room and go to where the shelves used to be. Then there was the sound of dishes, and even the smell of food.

Obviously, the ghostly presences were still keeping house in their own fashion, reliving some happy or at least busy moments from their own past. By now Mr. Harvey was firmly convinced that he shared the house with a number of dead relatives, if not friends. Several times he woke to the sound of bottles being placed on the bureau. One night he awoke because the bottom of the bed was shaking hard; as soon as he was fully awake, it stopped. This was followed by a night in which Mrs. Harvey could see a glow pass through the room at the bottom of the bed. When "they" got to the hall door, which was shut, she could hear it open, but it actually did not move. Yet the sound was that of a door opening. Next she heard several individuals walk up the stairs, mumbling as they went.

The following night a light stopped by their fireplace, and as she looked closely it resembled a figure bending down. It got so that they compared notes almost every morning to see what had happened next in their very busy home. One moonlit night Mrs. Harvey woke to see the covers of her bed folded in half, down the entire length of the bed. Her husband was fully covered, but she was totally uncovered. At the same time, she saw some dark shadows by the side of the bed. She felt someone's hand holding her own, pulling her gently. Terrified, she couldn't move, and just lay there wondering what would happen next. Then the blankets were replaced as before, she felt something cold touch her forehead, and the ghosts left. But the Stay-Behinds were benign, and meant no harm. Some nights, Mrs. Harvey would wake up because of the cold air, and notice that the blankets were standing up straight from the bed as if held by someone. Even after she pushed them back hard, they would not stay in place.

On the other hand, there were times when she accidentally uncovered herself at night and felt someone putting the covers back on her, as if to protect her from the night chills. This was more important, as the house has no central heating. Of course it wasn't always clear what the ghosts wanted from her. On the one hand, they were clearly concerned with her well-being and that of the family; on the other, they seemed to crave attention for themselves also.

Twice they tried to lift Mrs. Harvey out of her bed. She felt herself raised several inches above it by unseen hands, and tried to call out to her husband but somehow couldn't utter a single word. This was followed by a strange, dreamlike state, in which she remembered being taken to the attic and shown something. Unfortunately she could not remember it afterwards, except that she had been to the attic and how the floorboards looked there; she also recalled that the attic was covered with black dust. When morning came, she took a look at her feet: they were dusty, and the bottom of her bed was grayish as if from dust. Just as she was contemplating these undeniable facts, her husband asked her what had been the matter with her during the night. Evidently he had awakened to find her gone from the bed.

One night daughter Marjorie was out on a date. Mrs. Harvey awoke to the sound of a car pulling into the driveway, bringing Marjorie home. From her bed she could clearly see four steps of the back stairs. As she lay there, she saw the shape of a woman coming down without any sound, sort of floating down the stairs. She was dressed in a white chiffon dress. At the same moment, her daughter Marjorie entered the living room. She too saw the girl in the chiffon dress come down the stairs into the living room and disappear through a door to the other bedroom. Even though the door was open wide and there was plenty of room to go through the opening, evidently the ghostly lady preferred to walk through the door.

The miscellaneous Stay-Behinds tried hard to take part in the daily lives of the flesh-and-blood people in the house. Many times the plants in the living room would be rearranged and attended to by unseen hands. The Harveys could clearly see the plants move, yet no one was near them; no one, that is, visible to the human eye. There was a lot of mumbling about now, and eventually they could make out some words. One day daughter Marjorie heard her late grandmother say to her that "they" would be back in three weeks. Sure enough, not a single incident of a ghostly nature occurred for three weeks. To the day, after the three weeks were up, the phenomena began again. Where had the ghosts gone in the meantime? On another occasion, Marjorie heard someone say, "That is Jane on that side of the bed, but who is that on the other side? The bed looks so smooth." The remark made sense to Mrs. Harvey. Her late mother sometimes slept with Jane, when she was still in good health. On the other hand, daughter Marjorie likes to sleep perfectly flat, so her bed does look rather smooth.

Average people believe ghosts only walk at night. Nothing could be further from the truth, as Mrs. Harvey will testify. Frequently, when she was alone in the house during the daytime, she would hear doors upstairs bang shut and open again. One particular day, she heard the sound of someone putting things on Jane's bureau, so she tried to go up and see what it was. Carefully tiptoeing up the stairs to peek into her door to see if she could actually trap a ghost, she found herself halfway along the hall when she heard footsteps coming along the foot of son Don's bed, in her direction. Quickly, she hurried back down the stairs and stopped halfway down. The footsteps sounded like a woman's, and suddenly there was the rustle of a taffeta gown. With a *whooshing* sound, the ghost passed Mrs. Harvey and went into Jane's room. Mrs. Harvey waited, rooted to the spot on the stairs.

A moment later the woman's footsteps came back, only this time someone walked with her, someone heavier. They went back through Don's room, and ended up in Lolita's closet—the place where Lolita had seen the man in the uniform with the shining gold buttons. Mrs. Harvey did not follow immediately, but that night she decided to go up to Lolita's room and have another look at the closet. As she approached the door to the room it opened, which wasn't unusual since it was in the habit of opening at the slightest vibration. But before Mrs. Harvey could close it, it shut itself tight and the latch moved into place of its own accord. Mrs. Harvey didn't wait around for anything further that night.

For awhile there was peace. But in October the phenomena resumed. One night Mrs. Harvey woke up when she saw a shadow blocking the light coming from the dining room. She looked towards the door and saw a lady dressed all in black come into her bedroom and stand close to her side of the bed. This time she clearly heard her speak.

"Are you ready? It is almost time to go."

With that, the apparition turned and started up the stairs. The stairs looked unusually light, as if moonlight were illuminating them. When the woman in black got to the top step, all was quiet and the stairs were dark again, as before. Mrs. Harvey could see her clothes plainly enough, but not her face. She noticed that the apparition had carried a pouch-style pocketbook, which she had put over her arm so that her hands would be free to lift up her skirts as she went up the stairs. The next morning, Mrs. Harvey told her husband of the visitation. He assured her she must have dreamt it all. But before she could answer, her daughter Marjorie came in and said that she had heard someone talking in the night, something about coming, and it being almost time. She saw a figure at the foot of her bed, which she described as similar to what Mrs. Harvey had seen.

The night before that Thanksgiving, Marjorie heard footsteps come down the stairs. She was in bed and tried to get up to see who it was, but somehow couldn't move at all, except to open her eyes to see five people standing at the foot of her bed! Two of them were women, the others seemed just outlines or shadows. One of the two women wore an old-fashioned shaped hat, and she looked very stern. As Marjorie was watching the group, she managed to roll over a little in her bed and felt someone next to her. She felt relieved at the thought that it was her mother, but then whoever it was got up and left with the others in the group. All the time they kept talking among themselves, but Marjorie could not understand what was being said. Still talking, the ghostly visitors went back up the stairs.

Nothing much happened until Christmastime. Again the footsteps running up and down the stairs resumed, yet no one was seen. Christmas night, Jane and her mother heard walking in the room above the living room, where Mrs. Harvey's mother used to sleep. At that time, Mr. Harvey was quite ill and was sleeping in what used to be the sewing room so as not to awaken when his wife got up early.

On two different occasions Mrs. Harvey had "visitors." The first time someone lifted her a few inches off the bed. Evidently someone else was next to her in bed, for when she extended her hand that person got up and left. Next she heard footsteps going up the stairs and someone laughing, then all was quiet again. About a week later, she woke one night to feel someone pulling hard on her elbow and ankle. She hung onto the top of her bed with her other hand. But the unseen entities pushed, forcing her to brace herself against the wall.

Suddenly it all stopped, yet there were no sounds of anyone leaving. Mrs. Harvey jumped out of bed and tried to turn the light on. It wouldn't go on. She went back to bed when she heard a voice telling her not to worry, that her husband would be all right. She felt relieved at the thought, when the voice added, "But you won't be." Then the unseen voice calmly informed her that she would die in an accident caused by a piece of bark from some sort of tree. That was all the voice chose to tell her, but it was enough to start her worrying. Under the circumstances, and in order not to upset her family, she kept quiet about it, eventually thinking that she had dreamed the whole incident. After all, if it were just a dream, there was no point in telling anyone, and if it were true, there was nothing she could do anyway, so there was no point in worrying her family. She had almost forgotten the incident when she did have an accident about a week later. She hurt her head rather badly in the woodshed, requiring medical attention. While she was still wondering whether that was the incident referred to by the ghostly voice, she had a second accident: a heavy fork fell on her and knocked her unconscious.

But the voice had said that she would die in an accident, so Mrs. Harvey wasn't at all sure that the two incidents, painful though they had been, were what the voice had referred to. Evidently, ghosts get a vicarious thrill out of making people worry, because Mrs. Harvey is alive and well, years after the unseen voice had told her she would die in an accident.

But if it were not enough to cope with ghost people, Mrs. Harvey also had the company of a ghost dog. Their favorite pet, Lucy, passed into eternal dogdom the previous March. Having been treated as a member of the family, she had been permitted to sleep in the master bedroom, but as she became older she started wetting the rug, so eventually she had to be kept out.

After the dog's death, Marjorie offered her mother another dog, but Mrs. Harvey didn't want a replacement for Lucy; no other dog could take her place. Shortly after the offer and its refusal, Lolita heard a familiar scratch at the bathroom door. It sounded exactly as Lucy had always sounded when Lolita came home late at night. At first, Mrs. Harvey thought her daughter had just imagined it, but then the familiar wet spot reappeared on the bedroom rug. They tried to look for a possible leak in the ceiling, but could find no rational cause for the rug to be wet. The wet spot remained for about a month. During that time, several of the girls heard a noise that reminded them of Lucy walking about. Finally the rug dried out and Lucy's ghost stopped walking.

For several years the house has been quiet now. Have the ghosts gone on to their just rewards, been reincarnated, or have they simply tired of living with flesh-and-blood relatives? Stay-Behinds generally stay indefinitely; unless, of course, they feel they are really not wanted. Or perhaps they just got bored with it all.

Several years ago, a tragic event took place at a major university campus in Kansas. A member of one of the smaller fraternities, TKE, was killed in a head-on automobile accident on September 21. His sudden death at so young an age—he was an undergraduate—brought

home a sense of tragedy to the other members of the fraternity, and it
was decided that they would attend his funeral in New York *en masse*.

Not quite a year after the tragic accident, several members of the
fraternity were at their headquarters. Eventually, one of the brothers
and his date were left behind alone, studying in the basement of the
house. Upon completion of their schoolwork, they left. When they had
reached the outside, the girl remembered she had left her purse in the
basement and returned to get it. When she entered the basement, she
noticed a man sitting at the poker table, playing with chips. She said
something to him, explaining herself, then grabbed her purse and returned
upstairs. There she asked her date who the man in the basement was,
since she hadn't noticed him before. He laughed and said that no one
had been down there but the two of them. At that point, one of the
other brothers went into the basement and was surprised to see a man
get up from his chair and walk away. That man was none other than
the young man who had been killed in the automobile crash a year
before.

One of the other members of the fraternity had also been in the
same accident, but had only been injured, and survived. Several days
after the incident in the fraternity house basement, this young man saw
the dead boy walking up the steps to the second floor of the house. By
now the fraternity realized that their dead brother was still very much
with them, drawn back to what was to him his true home—and so they
accepted him as one of the crowd, even if he was invisible at times.

On January 7, Mr. and Mrs. S. moved into an older house on South
Fourth Street, a rented, fully-furnished two-bedroom house in a medium-
sized city in Oklahoma. Mrs. S.'s husband was a career service man
in the Army, stationed at a nearby Army camp. They have a small boy,
and looked forward to a pleasant stay in which the boy could play with
neighborhood kids, while Mrs. S. tried to make friends in what to her
was a new environment.

She is a determined lady, not easily frightened off by anything she
cannot explain, and the occult was the last thing on her mind. They
had lived in the house for about two weeks, when she noticed light
footsteps walking in the hall at night. When she checked on them, there
was no one there. Her ten-year-old son was sleeping across the hall,
and she wondered if perhaps he was walking in his sleep. But each
time she heard the footsteps and would check on her son, she found
him sound asleep. The footsteps continued on and off, for a period of
four months.

Then, one Sunday afternoon at about two o'clock, when her husband
was at his post and her son in the back yard playing, she found herself
in the kitchen. Suddenly she heard a child crying very softly and mutedly,

as if the child were afraid to cry aloud. At once she ran into the back yard to see if her son was hurt. There was nothing wrong with him, and she found him playing happily with a neighborhood boy. It then dawned on her that she could not hear the child crying outside the house, but immediately upon re-entering the house, the faint sobs were clearly audible again.

She traced the sound to her bedroom, and when she entered the room, it ceased to be noticeable. This puzzled her to no end, since she had no idea what could cause the sounds. Added to this were strange thumping sounds, which frequently awakened her in the middle of the night. It sounded as if someone had fallen out of bed.

On these occasions, she would get out of bed quickly and rush into her son's room, only to find him fast asleep. A thorough check of the entire house revealed no source for the strange noises. But Mrs. S. noticed that their Siamese cat, who slept at the foot of her bed when these things happened, also reacted to them: his hair would bristle, his ears would fly back, and he would growl and stare into space at something or someone she could not see.

About that time, her mother decided to visit them. Since her mother was an invalid, Mrs. S. decided not to tell her about the strange phenomena in order to avoid upsetting her. She stayed at the house for three days, when one morning she wanted to know why Mrs. S. was up at two o'clock in the morning making coffee. Since the house had only two bedrooms, they had put a half-bed into the kitchen for her mother, especially as the kitchen was very large and she could see the television from where she was sleeping. Her mother insisted she had heard footsteps coming down the hall into the kitchen. She called out to what she assumed was her daughter, and when there was no answer, she assumed that her daughter and her son-in-law had had some sort of disagreement and she had gotten up to make some coffee.

From her bed she could not reach the light switch, but she could see the time by the illuminated clock and realized it was two o'clock in the morning. Someone came down the hall, entered the kitchen, put water into the coffee pot, plugged it in, and then walked out of the kitchen and down the hall. She could hear the sound of coffee perking and could actually smell it. However, when she didn't hear anyone coming back, she assumed that her daughter and son-in-law had made up and gone back to sleep.

She did likewise, and decided to question her daughter about it in the morning. Mrs. S. immediately checked the kitchen, but there was no trace of the coffee to be found, which did not help her state of mind. A little later she heard some commotion outside the house, and on stepping outside noticed that the dogcatcher was trying to take a neighbor's dog with him. She decided to try and talk him out of it, and the conversation led to her husband being in the service, a statement which seemed to provoke a negative reaction on the part of the dogcatcher. He informed Mrs. S. that the last GI to live in the house was a murderer. When she wanted to know more about it, he clammed up immediately. But Mrs. S. became highly agitated. She called the local newspaper and asked for any and all information concerning her house. It was then that she learned the bitter truth.

In October two years before, a soldier stationed at the same base as her husband had beaten his two-year-old daughter to death. The murder took place in what had now become Mrs. S.'s bedroom. Mrs. S., shocked by the news, sent up a silent prayer, hoping that the restless soul of the child might find peace and not have to haunt a house where she had suffered nothing but unhappiness in her short life. . . .

chapter 10

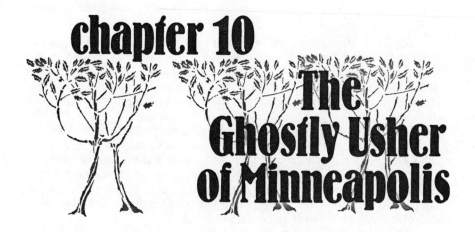

The Ghostly Usher of Minneapolis

FOR THIS ACCOUNT, I am indebted to a twenty-two-year-old creative production assistant in a Minneapolis advertising agency, by the name of Deborah Turner. Miss Turner got hooked on some of my books, and started to look around in the Twin Cities for cases that might whet my appetite for ghost hunting. Being also musically inclined with an interest in theater, it was natural that she should gravitate toward the famed Guthrie Theater, named after the famous director, which is justly known as the pride of Minneapolis. At the theater she met some other young people, also in their early twenties, and shared her interest in psychic phenomena with them. Imagine her surprise when she discovered that she had stumbled upon a most interesting case.

Richard Miller was born in Manhattan, Kansas in 1951. Until age ten, he lived there with his father, a chemist in government service. Then his father was transferred to England, and Richard spent several years going to school in that country. After that, he and his family returned to the United States and moved to Edina. This left Richard not only with a vivid recollection of England, but also somewhat of an accent which, together with his childhood in Kansas, gave him a somewhat unusual personality.

His strange accent became the subject of ridicule by other students at Edina Morningside High School where he went to school, and it did not go down well with the shy, introspective young man. In the tenth grade at this school, he made friends with another young man, Fred Koivumaki, and a good and close relationship sprang up between the two boys. It gave Fred a chance to get to know Richard better than most of the other fellows in school.

As if the strange accent were not enough to make him stand out from the other boys in the area, Richard was given to sudden, jerky movements, which made him a good target for sly remarks and jokes of his fellow students. The Millers did not have much of a social life, since they also did not quite fit into the pattern of life in the small town of Edina.

During the years spent in an English school, Richard had known corporal punishment, since it is still part of the system in some English schools. This terrified him, and perhaps contributed towards his inability to express himself fully and freely. Somehow he never acquired a girlfriend as the other students did, and this, too, bothered him a lot. He couldn't for the world understand why people didn't like him more, and often talked about it to his friend Fred.

When both young men reached the age of sixteen, they went to the Guthrie Theater where they got jobs as ushers. They worked at it for two years. Richard Miller got along well with the other ushers, but developed a close friendship only with Fred Koivumaki and another fellow, Barry Peterson. It is perhaps a strange quirk of fate that both Richard Miller and Barry Peterson never reached manhood, but died violently long before their time.

However, Richard's parents decided he should go to the university, and quit his job. In order to oblige his parents, Richard Miller gave up the job as usher and moved into Territorial Hall for his first year at the university.

However, the change did not increase his ability to express himself or to have a good social life. Also, he seemed to have felt that he was catering to his parents' wishes, and became more antagonistic toward them. Then, too, it appears that these students also made him the butt of their jokes. Coincidentally, he developed a vision problem, with cells breaking off his retinas and floating in the inner humor of the eye. This causing him to see spots before his eyes, a condition for which there is no cure. However, he enjoyed skiing because he knew how to do it well, and joined the university ski club.

But Richard's bad luck somehow was still with him. On a trip to Colorado, he ran into a tree, luckily breaking only his skis. When summer came to the area, Richard rode his bike down a large dirt hill into rough ground and tall weeds at the bottom, injuring himself in the process. Fortunately, a motorcyclist came by just then, and got Richard to the emergency ward of a nearby hospital. All this may have contributed towards an ultimate breakdown; or, as the students would call it, Richard just "flipped out."

He was hospitalized at the university hospital and was allowed home only on weekends. During that time he was on strong medication, but when the medication did not improve his condition, the doctor took him off it and sent him home.

The following February 4, he decided to try skiing again, and asked his father to take him out to Buck Hill, one of the skiing areas not far from town. But to his dismay Richard discovered that he couldn't ski anymore, and this really depressed him. When he got home, there was a form letter waiting for him from the university, advising him that because he had skipped all the final exams due to his emotional problems at the time, he had received F's in all his classes and was on probation.

All this seemed too much for him. He asked his mother for forty dollars, ostensibly to buy himself new ski boots. Then he drove down to Sears on Lake Street, where he bought a high-powered pistol and shells. That was on Saturday, and he killed himself in the car. He wasn't found until Monday morning, when the lot clearing crew found him with most of his head shot off.

Richard Miller was given a quiet burial in Fort Snelling National Cemetery. His parents, Dr. and Mrs. Byron S. Miller, requested that memorials to the Minnesota Association for Mental Health be sent instead of flowers. Richard's mother had always felt that her son's best years had been spent as an usher at the Guthrie Theater; consequently he was cremated wearing his Guthrie Theater blazer. The date was February 7, and soon enough the shock of the young man's untimely death wore off, and only his immediate family and the few friends he had made remembered Richard Miller.

A few weeks after the death of the young usher, a woman seated in the theater in an aisle seat came up to the usher in charge of this aisle and asked him to stop the other usher from walking up and down during the play. The usher in charge was shocked, since he had been at the top of the aisle and had seen no one walk up and down. All the other ushers were busy in their respective aisles. However, the lady insisted that she had seen this young man walk up and down the aisle during the play. The usher in charge asked her to describe what she had seen. She described Richard Miller, even to the mole on his cheek. The incident is on record with the Guthrie Theater. Minneapolis Tribune columnist Robert T. Smith interviewed Craig Scherfenberg, director of audience development at the theater, concerning the incident. "There was no one in our employ at the time who fit the description," the director said, "but it fit the dead young man perfectly."

In the summer several years later, two ushers were asked to spend the night in the theater to make sure some troublesome air conditioning equipment was fully repaired. The Guthrie Theater has a thrust stage with openings onto the stage on all three sides; these openings lead to an actors' waiting area, which in turn has a door opening onto an area used as a lounge during intermissions.

The two young men were sitting in this waiting area with both doors open, and they were the only people in the building. At one o'clock in the morning, they suddenly heard the piano onstage begin to play. Stunned by this, they watched in silence when they saw a cloud-like form floating through the lounge door and hovering in the center of the room. One of the ushers thought the form was staring at him. As quickly as they could gather their wits they left the room.

One of Deborah Turner's friends had worked late one evening shortly after this incident, repairing costumes needed for the next day's performance. She and a friend were relaxing in the stage area while waiting for a ride home. As she glanced into the house, she noticed that the lights on the aisle that had been the dead usher's were going on and off, as if someone were walking slowly up and down. She went to the Ladies' Room a little later, and suddenly she heard pounding on one wall, eventually circling the room and causing her great anxiety, since she knew that she and her friend were the only people in the house.

When the Guthrie Theater put on a performance of *Julius Caesar,* one of the extras was an older woman by the name of Mary Parez. She freely admitted that she was psychic and had been able to communicate with her dead sister. She told her fellow actors that she could sense Richard Miller's presence in the auditorium. Somehow she thought that the ghost would make himself known during Mark Antony's famous speech to the Romans after Caesar's death.

The scene was lit primarily by torches when the body of Julius Caesar was brought upon the stage. Jason Harlen, a young usher, and one of his colleagues, were watching the performance from different vantage points in the theater. One boy was in one of the tunnels leading to the stage, the other in the audience. Both had been told of Mary Parez's prediction, but were disappointed when nothing happened at that time. In boredom, they began to look around the theater. Independently of each other, they saw smoke rising to the ceiling, and shaping itself into a human form. Both young men said that the form had human eyes.

The aisle that the late Richard Miller worked was number eighteen. Two women in the acting company of *Julius Caesar,* named Terry and Gigi, complained that they had much trouble with the door at the top of aisle eighteen for no apparent reason. Bruce Benson, who now worked aisle eighteen, told that people complained of an usher walking up and down the aisle during performances. Bruce Margolis, who works the stage door, leaves the building after everyone else. When he was there one night all alone, the elevator began running on its own.

All this talk about a ghost induced some of the young ushers to try and make contact with him via the Ouija board. Dan Burg, head usher, took a board with him to the stage, and along with colleagues Bruce Benson and Scott Hurner, tried to communicate with the ghost. For awhile nothing happened. Then, all of a sudden the board spelled, "Tiptoe to the tech room." When they asked why, the board spelled the word ghost. They wanted to know which tech room the ghost was referring to: downstairs? "No," the communicator informed them, "upstairs." Then the board signed off with the initials MIL. At that, one of the men tipped over the board and wanted nothing further to do with it.

In November of the next year, an usher working at the theater told columnist Robert Smith, "It was after a night performance. Everyone had left the theater but me. I had forgotten my gloves and returned to retrieve them. I glanced into the theater and saw an usher standing in one of the aisles. It was him. He saw me and left. I went around to that aisle and couldn't find anything."

There is also an opera company connected with the Guthrie Theater. One night not long ago, one of the ladies working for the opera company was driving home from the Guthrie Theater. Suddenly she felt a presence beside her in the car. Terrified, she looked around, and became aware of a young man with dark curly hair, glasses, and a mole on his face. He wore a blue coat with something red on the pocket—the Guthrie Theater blazer. With a sinking feeling, she realized that she was looking at the ghost of Richard Miller.

For the past two years, however, no new reports have come in concerning the unfortunate young man. Could it be that he has finally realized that there await him greater opportunities in the next dimension, and though his life on earth was not very successful, his passing into the spiritual life might give him most of the opportunities his life on earth had denied him? At any rate, things have now quieted down in aisle eighteen at the Guthrie Theater, in Minneapolis, Minnesota.

chapter 11

The Ghostly Adventures of a North Carolina Family

TONI S. is a young woman of good educational background, a psychologist by profession, who works for a large business concern. She is not given to daydreaming or fantasizing. She is the daughter of Mrs. Elizabeth K., or rather the daughter of Mrs. K.'s second marriage. The thrice-married Mrs. K. is a North Carolina lady of upper middle-class background, a socially prominent woman who has traveled extensively.

Neither was the kind of person who pulls out a Ouija board to while away the time, or to imagine that every shadow cast upon the wall is necessarily a ghost. Far from it; but both ladies were taken aback by what transpired in their old house at the town of East La Porte, built on very old ground.

Originally built about fifty years ago, it was to be a home for Mrs. K.'s father who then owned a large lumber company, and the tract of timber surrounding the house extended all the way across the Blue Ridge Parkway. Undoubtedly an older dwelling had stood on the same spot, for Mrs. K. has unearthed what appears to be the remains of a much older structure. The house was renovated and a second story was built on about thirty-five years ago. At that time, her father had lost one leg as the result of an automobile accident, and retired from his lumber mill activities to East La Porte, where he intended to spend his remaining years in peace and quiet. He had liked the climate to begin with, and there was a sawmill nearby, which he could oversee. The house is a doubleboxed frame house, perhaps fifty-by-fifty square, containing around fifteen rooms.

Mrs. K.'s family refer to it as the summer cottage, even though it was a full-sized house; but they had other houses that they visited from time to time, and the house in East La Porte was merely one of their lesser properties. Downstairs there is a thirty-by-fifteen-foot reception room, richly carpeted with chestnut from Furnace Creek, one of the sawmills owned by the family. It was in this room that Mrs. K.'s father eventually passed on.

The house itself is built entirely from lumber originating in one of the family's sawmills. There was a center hall downstairs and two thirty-foot rooms, then there were three smaller rooms, a bath, a card room, and what the family referred to as a sleeping porch. On the other side of the center hall was a lounge, a kitchen, and a laundry porch. Running alongside the south and east walls of the house is a veranda. Upstairs is reached by a very gentle climb up the stairs in the middle of the floor, and as one climbs the steps, there is a bedroom at the head of the stairs. In back of the stairs, there are two more bedrooms, then a bathroom, and finally a storage room; to the left of the stairs are three bedrooms.

The attic is merely a structure to hold up the roof, and does not contain any rooms. There is a cellar, but it contains only a furnace. Although the acreage surrounding the house runs to about sixty acres, only three acres belong to the house proper. All around the house, even today, there is nothing but wilderness, and to get to the nearest town, East La Porte, one needs a car.

Mrs. K. enjoyed traveling, and didn't mind living in so many residences; in fact, she considered the house at East La Porte merely a way-station in her life. She was born in Alaska, where the family also had a sawmill. Her early years were spent traveling from one sawmill to another, accompanying her parents on business trips.

Under the circumstances, they were never very long in residence at the house in East La Porte. Any attempt to find out about the background of the land on which the house stood proved frutiless. This was Cherokee territory, but there is little written history concerning the time before the Cherokees. Anything remotely connected with psychic phenomena was simply not discussed in the circles in which Mrs. K. grew up.

The first time Mrs. K. noticed anything peculiar about the house was after her father had passed away. She and her father had been particularly close, since her mother had died when she was still a small child. That particular day, she was sitting at her late father's desk in the part of the house where her father had died. The furniture had been rearranged in the room, and the desk stood where her father's bed had previously been. Her father was on her mind, and so she thought it was all her imagination when she became aware of a distinctive sound like someone walking on crutches down the hall.

Since Mrs. K. knew for a fact that she was the only person in the house at the time, she realized that something out of the ordinary was happening. As the footsteps came closer, she recognized her father's tread. Then she heard her father's familiar voice say, "Baby:" it came from the direction of the door. This gave her a feeling of great peace, for she had been troubled by emotional turmoil in her life. She felt that her late father was trying to console her, and give her spiritual strength.

Nothing happened until about a year later. It was August, and she had been in New York for awhile. As she was coming down the stairs of the house, she found herself completely enveloped with the fragrance of lilacs. She had not put any perfume on, and there were no lilacs blooming in August. No one was seen, and yet Mrs. K. felt a presence, although she was sure it was benign and loving.

A short time later, she was sitting at a desk in what used to be her father's study upstairs, thinking about nothing in particular. Again she was startled by the sound of footsteps, but this time they were light steps, and certainly not her father's. Without thinking, she called out to her daughter, "Oh, Toni, is that you?" telling her daughter that she was upstairs.

But then the steps stopped, and no one came. Puzzled, Mrs. K. went to the head of the stairs, called out again, but when she saw no one, she realized that it was not a person of flesh and blood who had walked upon the stairs.

During the same month, Mrs. K.'s daughter Toni was also at the house. Her first experience with the unseen happened that month, in an upstairs bedroom.

She was asleep one night when someone shook her hard and said, "Hey, you!" Frightened, she did not open her eyes, yet with her inner eyes, she "saw" a man of about fifty years of age. She was much too frightened to actually look, so instead she dove underneath the covers and lay there with her eyes shut. There was nothing further that night.

In the fall of the same year, Toni decided to have a pajama party and spent the night with a group of friends. Her mother had gone to bed because of a cold. Toni and her friends returned to the house from bowling at around eleven-thirty. They were downstairs, talking about various things, when all of a sudden one of Toni's girlfriends said, "Your mother is calling you."

Toni went out into the hallway, turning on the lights as she approached the stairs. Footsteps were coming down the stairs, audible not only to her but to her two girlfriends who had followed her into the house. And then they heard a voice out of nowhere calling out, "Toni, it is time to go to bed." It was a voice Toni had never heard before.

She went up the stairs and into her mother's room, but her mother was fast asleep, and had not been out of bed. The voice had been a woman's, but it had sounded strangely empty, as if someone were speaking to her from far away.

The following year, Toni was married and left the house. Under the circumstances, Mrs. K. decided to sublease part of the house to a tenant. This turned out to be a pleasant woman by the name of Alice H. and her husband. The lady had been injured and was unable to go far up the mountain where she and her husband were building a summer home at the time. Although Mrs. K. and her new tenants were not associated in any way except that they were sharing the same house, she and Alice H. became friendly after a while. One afternoon, Alice H. came to Mrs. K.'s apartment in order to invite her to have supper with her and her husband that night. She knew that Mrs. K. was in her apartment at the time because she heard her light footsteps inside the apartment. When there was no reply from inside the apartment Alice was puzzled, so she descended to the ground floor, thinking that perhaps Mrs. K. was downstairs.

Sure enough, as she arrived downstairs, she saw a shadow of what she assumed to be Mrs. K.'s figure walking along the hallway. She followed this shadowy woman all the way from the ground floor guest room, through the bath into Mrs. K.'s bedroom, and then through another hallway and back to the bedroom. All the time she saw the shadowy figure, she also heard light footsteps. But when she came to the bedroom again, it suddenly got very cold and she felt all the blood rush to her head. She ran back to her husband in their own apartment, and informed him that there was a stranger in Mrs. K.'s rooms.

But there was no one in the house at the time except themselves, for Mrs. K. had gone off to Asheville for the day. The experience shook Alice H. to the point where she could no longer stand the house, and shortly afterward she and her husband left for another cottage.

In August of the same year, Toni S. returned to her mother's house. By now she was a married lady, and she was coming for a visit only. Her husband was a car dealer, in business with his father. At the time of the incident, he was not in the house. It was raining outside, and Toni was cleaning the woodwork in the house.

Suddenly her Pekinese dog came running down the stairs, nearly out of her mind with terror, and barking at the top of her lungs. Toni thought the dog had been frightened by a mouse, so she picked her up and proceeded up the stairs. But the dog broke away from her and ran behind the door. All of a sudden, Toni felt very cold. She kept walking down the hall and into the room, where there was a desk standing near the window. Someone was going through papers on her desk as if looking for a certain piece of paper, putting papers aside and continuing to move them! But there was no one there. No one, that is, who could be seen. Yet the papers were moving as if someone were actually shuffling them. It was two o'clock in the afternoon, and the light was fairly good.

Suddenly, one letter was pulled out of the piles of papers on the desk, as if to catch her attention. Toni picked it up and read it. It was a letter her father had sent her in February, at the time she got married, warning her that the marriage would not work out after all, and to make sure to call him if anything went wrong. Things *had* gone wrong since, and Toni understood the significance of what she had just witnessed.

At that very moment, the room got warm again, and everything returned to normal. But who was it standing at her desk, pulling out her father's letter? The one person who had been close to her while he was in the flesh was her grandfather.

During Toni's visit at the house, her husband, now her ex-husband, also had some uncanny experiences. Somebody would wake him in the middle of the night by calling out, "Wake up!" or "Hey you!" This went on night after night, until both Toni and her husband awoke around two in the morning because of the sound of loud laughing, as if a big party were going on downstairs.

Toni thought that the neighbors were having a party, and decided to go down and tell them to shut up. She looked out the window, and realized that the neighbors were also fast asleep. So she picked up her dog and went downstairs, and as she arrived at the bottom of the stairs, she saw a strange light, and the laughing kept going on and on. There were voices, as if many people were talking all at once, having a social. In anger, Toni called out to them to shut up, she wanted to sleep, and all of a sudden the house was quiet, quiet as the grave. Evidently, Southern ghosts have good manners!

After her daughter left, Mrs. K. decided to sublease part of the house to a group of young men from a national fraternity who were students at a nearby university. One of the students, Mitchell, was sleeping in a double bed, and he was all alone in the house. Because the heat wasn't turned up, it being rather costly, he decided to sleep in a sleeping bag, keeping warm in this manner. He went to sleep with his pillow at the head of the bed, which meant due east, and his feet going due west. When he awoke, he found himself facing in the opposite direction, with his head where his feet should have been, and vice versa. It didn't surprise the young man though, because from the very first day his fraternity brothers had moved into the house, they had heard the sounds of an unseen person walking up and down the stairs.

One of their teachers, a pilot who had been a colonel in the Korean War, also had an experience at the house. One day while he was staying there, he was walking up the stairs, and when he reached about the halfway mark, someone picked him up by the scruff of his neck and pushed him up the rest of the way to the landing.

But the night to remember was Hallowe'en Eve. Mrs. K. was in the house, and the night was living up to its reputation: it sounded as if someone wearing manacles were moving about. Mrs. K. was downstairs, sleeping in one of the bunk beds, and a noise came from an upstairs hall. This went on for about two hours straight. It sounded as if someone with a limp were pulling himself along, dragging a heavy chain. Mrs. K. was puzzled about this, since the noise did not sound anything like her father. She looked into the background of the area, and discovered that in the pre-colonial period, there had been some Spanish settlers in the area, most of whom kept slaves.

Toni S. takes her involvement with hauntings in stride. She has had psychic experiences ever since she can remember; nothing frightening, you understand, only such things as events before they actually happen—if someone is going to be sick in the family, for instance, or who might be calling. Entering old houses is always a risky business for her: she picks up vibrations from the past, and sometimes she simply can't stand what she feels and must leave at once.

But she thought she had left the more uncanny aspects of the hauntings behind when she came to New York to work. Somehow she wound up residing in a house that is 110 years old.

After a while, she became aware of an old man who liked sitting down on her bed. She couldn't actually see him, but he appeared to her more like a shadow. So she asked some questions, but nobody ever died in the apartment and it was difficult for Toni to accept the reality of the phenomena under the circumstances. As a trained psychologist, she had to approach all this on a skeptical level, and yet there did not seem to be any logical answers.

Soon afterward, she became aware of footsteps where no one was walking, and of doors closing by by themselves, which were accompanied by the definite feeling of another personality present in the rooms.

On checking with former neighbors upstairs, who had lived in the house for seventeen years, Toni discovered that they too had heard the steps and doors closing by themselves. However, they had put no faith in ghosts, and dismissed the matter as simply an old structure settling. Toni tried her innate psychic powers, and hoped that the resident ghost would communicate with her. She began to sense that it was a woman with a very strong personality. By a process of elimination, Toni came to the conclusion that the last of the original owners of the house, a Mrs. A., who had been a student of the occult, was the only person who could be the presence she was feeling in the rooms.

Toni doesn't mind sharing her rooms with a ghost, except for the fact that appliances in the house have a way of breaking down without reason. Then, too, she has a problem with some of her friends; they complain of feelings extremely uncomfortable and cold, and of being watched by someone they cannot see. What was she to do? But then Toni recalled how she had lived through the frightening experiences at

East La Porte, North Carolina, and somehow come to terms with the haunts there. No ordinary Long Island ghost was going to dispossess her!

With that resolve, Toni decided to ignore the presence as much as she could, and go about her business—the business of the living.

chapter 12

Reba's Ghosts

REBA B. is a sensitive, fragile-looking lady with two grown children. She was born in Kentucky, and hails from an old family in which the name Reba has occurred several times before. She works as a medical secretary and doctor's assistant, and nowadays shares her home with three cats, her children having moved away. Mrs. B., who is divorced, wondered whether perhaps she had a particular affinity for ghosts, seeing that she has encountered denizens of the Other World so many times, in so many houses. It wasn't that it bothered her to any extent, but she had gotten used to living by herself except for her cats, and the idea of having to share her home with individuals who could pop in and out at will, and who might hang around her at times when she could not see them, did not contribute to her comfort.

Her psychic ability goes back to age three, when she was living with her grandparents in Kentucky. Even then she had a vivid feeling of presences all around her, not that she actually saw them with her eyes. It was more a sensitivity to unseen forces surrounding her—an awareness that she was never quite alone. As soon as she would go to bed as a child, she would see the figure of a man bending over her, a man she did not know. After a long period of this she wondered if she was dreaming, but in her heart she knew she was not. However, she was much too young to worry about such things, and as she grew up, her ability became part of her character, and she began to accept it as "normal."

This incident begins when she happened to be living in Cincinnati, already divorced. Her mother shared an old house with her, a house that was built around 1900; it had all the earmarks of the post-Victorian era: brass door knobs, little doorbells that were to be turned by hand,

and the various trimmings of that age. The house consisted of three floors; the ground floor contained an apartment, and the two ladies took the second and third floor of the house. Reba had her bedroom on the third floor; it was the only bedroom up there situated in the middle of the floor.

One day she was coming up those stairs, and was approaching the window when she saw a man standing by it. He vanished as she came closer, and she gave this no more thought until a few days later. At that time she happened to be lying in bed, propped up and reading a book.

She happened to look up and saw a man who had apparently come up the stairs. She noticed his features fully: his eyes were brown, and he also had brown hair. Immediately she could sense that he was very unhappy, even angry. It wasn't that she heard his voice, but somehow his thoughts communicated themselves to her, mind to mind.

From her bed she could see him approach, walking out to a small landing and standing in front of her door. Next to her room was a storage room. He looked straight at Reba, and at that moment she received the impression that he was very angry because she and her mother were in the house, because they had moved into *his* house.

Although Reba B. was fully conscious and aware of what was going on, she rejected the notion that she was hearing the thoughts of a ghost. But it did her no good; over and over she heard him say or think, "Out, out, I want you out, I don't want you here." At that moment he raised his arm and pointed outward, as if to emphasize his point. The next moment he was gone. Reba thought for a moment, whether she should tell her mother whose bedroom was downstairs. She decided against it, since her mother had a heart condition and because she herself wasn't too sure the incident had been quite real. Also, she was a little frightened and did not want to recall the incident any more than she had to. After a while, she went off to sleep.

Not too long after that her daughter, who was then fourteen, and her eleven-year-old son were home with her from school. It was a weekend, and she wanted the children to enjoy it. Consequently, she did not tell them anything about her ghostly experience. She had gone into the front storage room, when she thought she saw someone sitting on the boxes stacked in the storage area.

At first she refused to acknowledge it, and tried to look away, but when her gaze returned to the area, the man was still sitting there, quietly staring at her. Again she turned her head, and when she looked back, he was gone. The following weekend, her children were with her again. They had hardly arrived when her daughter returned from the same storage room and asked, "Mother, is there someone sitting in there?" and all Reba could do was nod, and acknowledge that there was. Her daughter then described the stranger and the description matched what her mother had seen. Under the circumstances, Reba B. freely discussed the matter with her children. But nothing further was done concerning the matter, and no inquiries were made as to the background of the house.

Summer came, and another spring and another summer, and they got into the habit of using the entrance at the side of the house. There were some shrubs in that area, and in order to enter the apartment in which they lived, they had to come up the stairs where they would have a choice of either walking into the living room on the second floor, or continuing on to the third floor where Reba's bedroom was. The tenant who had the ground floor apartment also had his own entrance.

One warm summer evening, she suddenly felt the stranger come into the downstairs door and walk up the stairs. When she went to check, she saw nothing. Still, she *knew* he was in the house. A few days passed, and again she sensed the ghost nearby. She looked, and as her eyes peered down into the hall, she saw him walking down the hall towards her. While she was thinking, "I am imagining this, there is no such thing as a ghost," she slowly walked toward him. As he kept approaching her, she walked right through him! It was an eerie sensation: for a moment she could not see, and then he was gone. The encounter did not help Reba to keep her composure, but there was little she could do about it.

Many times she sensed his presence in the house without seeing him, but early one evening, on a Sunday, just as it got dark, she found herself in the living room on the second floor of the house. She had turned on the television set, which was facing her, and she kept the volume down so as not to disturb her mother, whose room was on the same floor. She had altered the furniture in the room somewhat, in order to be closer to the television set, and there were two lounge chairs, one of which she used, and the other one close by, near the television set, so that another person could sit in it and also view the screen. She was just watching television, when she sensed the stranger come up the stairs again and walk into the living room. Next he sat down in the empty chair close to Reba, but this time the atmosphere was different from that first encounter near the door of her room. He seemed more relaxed and comfortable, and Reba was almost glad that he was there keeping her company. Somehow she felt that he was glad to be in the room with her, and that he was less lonely because of her. He was no longer angry; he just wanted to visit.

Reba looked at the stranger's face and noticed his rather high-bridged nose. She also had a chance to study his clothes; also he was wearing a brown suit, rather modern in style. Even though the house was quite old, this man was not from the early years, but his clothes seemed to indicate a comparatively recent period. As she sat there, quietly studying the ghost, she got the feeling that he had owned the house at one time, and that their living room had been the sitting room where the ghost and his wife had received people.

Reba somehow knew that his wife had been very pretty—a fair-complexioned blonde, and she was shown a fire-place in the living room with a small love seat of the French Provincial type next to it, drawn up quite close to the fireplace. She saw this in her mind's eye, as if the man were showing her something from his past. At the same time, Reba knew that some tragedy had occurred between the ghost and his wife.

Suddenly, panic rose in Reba, as she realized she was sharing the evening with a ghost. Somehow her fears communicated themselves to her phantom visitor, for as she looked close, he had vanished.

As much as she had tried to keep these things from her mother, she could not. Her mother owned an antique covered casserole made of silver, which she kept at the head of her bed. The bed was a bookcase bed, and she used to lift the cover and put in receipts, tickets, and papers whenever she wanted.

One day, Reba and her mother found themselves at the far end of her bedroom on the second floor. Her bed was up against the wall, without any space between it and the wall. As the two ladies were looking in the direction of the bed, they suddenly saw the silver casserole being picked up, put down on the bed, turned upside down and everything spilled out of it. It didn't fly through the air, but moved rather slowly, as if some unseen force were holding it. Although her mother had seen it, she did not say anything because she felt it would be unwise to alarm her daughter; but later on she admitted having seen the whole thing. It was ironic how the two women were trying to spare each other's feelings—yet both knew that what they had witnessed was real.

The ghost did not put in any further appearances after the dramatic encounter in the living room. About a year later, the two ladies moved away into another old house far from this one. But shortly before they did, Reba's mother was accosted on the street by a strange middle-aged lady, who asked her whether she was living in the house just up the street. When Reba's mother acknowledged it, the lady informed her the house had once belonged to her parents. Were they happy in it, Reba's mother wanted to know. "Very happy," the stranger assured her, "Especially my father." It occurred to Reba that it might have been he who she had encountered in the house; someone so attached to his home that he did not want to share it with anyone else, especially flesh and blood people like her mother and herself.

The new home the ladies moved into proved "alive" with unseen vibrations also, but by now they didn't care. Reba realized that she had a special gift. If ghosts wanted her company, there was little she could do about it.

She had a friend who worked as a motorcycle patrolman, by the

Three transparent monks in cowls are seen on the left side of the picture, which was taken by the author using a double-exposure-proof camera at Winchester Cathedral. The monks were cruelly driven out by Henry VIII four hundred years ago, but have been seen by many over the years. Copyright © 1966, by Hans Holzer.

Ringwood Manor, in Ringwood, New Jersey, is haunted by the unhappy spirit of a servant, as well as by the Victorian lady/owner who mistreated him! Copyright © 1982, by Hans Holzer.

Rita Atlanta, in front of her haunted trailer at Peabody, Massachusetts. Nearby, a man was run over by a car. Copyright © 1982, by Hans Holzer.

A poltergeist, *or noisy ghost, in Rye, New York, plagued the owners of this Victorian house until the author, with the help of psychics Ethel Meyers and Sybil Leek, made contact with the wraith. The owners have seen a carving knife rise in the air by itself, then fling itself to the floor in plain sight; they have seen doors open and shut by themselves, and have observed the figure of a woman dissolve into thin air. Copyright © 1982, by Hans Holzer.*

This Victorian mansion at 3517 Cornell Place, in Cincinnati, is now an apartment house. One of the tenants, Mrs. S. H. Stenten, has an interest in the psychic world and will talk to an occasional sincere visitor. A man once committed suicide here; now voices are heard out of nowhere, and footsteps resound when no one can be seen. Did a doctor's daughter fall victim to foul play on the stairs? The walls still whisper of yesterday's passions. Copyright © 1982, by Hans Holzer.

A ghostly image at Ross House, in County Mayo, Ireland. A servant girl still appears there, long after her death. Copyright © 1982, by Hans Holzer.

The U.S. Frigate Constellation, now safely at anchor in Baltimore harbor, boasts of the ghost of a sailor who fell asleep at watch, and of a cabin boy who died in battle. **Copyright** © *1982, by Hans Holzer.*

Haunted Ocean-born Mary's house at Henneker, N.H. still has the original owner, Mary Wallace, walk the corridors at times . . . there is also Don Pedro, the pirate, who lies buried somewhere on the grounds. Copyright © 1982, by Hans Holzer.

name of John H. He was a young man and well-liked on the force. One day he chased a speeder—and was killed in the process. At the time, Reba was still married, but she had known John for quite a few years before. They were friends, although not really close ones, and she had been out of touch with him for some time. One morning, she suddenly sensed his presence in the room with her; it made no sense, yet she was positive it was John H. After a while, the presence left her. She remarked on this to her mother and got a blank stare in return. The young man had been killed on the previous night, but Reba could not have known this. The news had come on the radio just that morning, but apparently Reba had had advance news of a more direct kind.

Reba B. shared her interest in the occult with an acquaintance, newscaster Bill G. In his position as a journalist, he had to be particularly careful in expressing an opinion on so touchy a subject as extrasensory perception. They had met at a local restaurant one evening, and somehow the conversation had gotten around to ghosts.

When Mr. G. noticed her apprehension at being one of the "selected" ones who could see ghosts, he told her about another friend, a young medium who had an apartment not far away. One evening she walked out onto her patio, and saw a man in old-fashioned clothes approach her. The man tried to talk to her, but she could not hear anything. Suddenly he disapeared before her eyes. The young lady thought she was having a nervous breakdown, and consulted a psychiatrist; she even went into a hospital to have herself examined, but there was nothing wrong with her. When she returned to her home and went out onto the patio again, she saw the same ghostly apparition once more. This time she did not panic, but instead studied him closely. When he disappeared she went back into her apartment, and decided to make some inquiries about the place. It was then that she discovered that a long time ago, a man of that description had been hanged from a tree in her garden.

"These things *do* happen," Bill G. assured Reba, and asked her not to be ashamed or afraid of them. After all, ghosts are people too. Since then, Reba had come to terms with her ghostly encounters. She has even had an experience with a ghost cat—but that is another story.

chapter 13

Henny from Brooklyn

CLINTON STREET, BROOKLYN is one of the oldest sections of that borough, pleasantly middle-class at one time, and still amongst Brooklyn's best neighborhoods, as neighborhoods go. The house in question is in the 300 block, and consists of four stories. There was a basement floor, then a parlor floor a few steps up, as is the usual custom with brownstone houses, with a third and fourth floor above it. If one preferred, one could call the third floor the fourth floor, in which case the basement becomes the first floor; but no matter how one called it, there were four levels in this brownstone, all capable of serving as apartments for those who wished to live there. The house was more than 100 years old at the time of the events herein described, and the records are somewhat dim beyond a certain point.

In the 1960s, the house was owned by some off-beat people, about whom little was known. Even the Hall of Records isn't of much help, as the owners didn't always live in the house, and the people who lived in it were not necessarily the owners, not to mention tenants, although sharing a part of the house with people legitimately entitled to live there. However, for the purpose of my story, we need only concern ourselves with the two top floors; the third floor contained two bedrooms and a bath, while the fourth or top floor consisted of a living room, dining room, kitchen, and second bath.

At the time my account begins, the first two floors were rented to an architect and his wife, and only the two top floors were available for new tenants.

It was in the summer when two young ladies in their early 20s, who had been living at the Brooklyn YWCA, decided to find a place of their own. Somehow they heard of the two vacant floors in the house on Clinton Street and immediately fell in love with it, renting the two top floors without much hesitation. Both Barbara and Sharon were 23 years old at the time, still going to college, and trying to make ends meet on what money they could manage between them. Two years later, Barbara was living in San Francisco with a business of her own, independently merchandising clothing. Brooklyn was only a hazy memory by then, but on August 1 of the year she and Sharon moved in, it was very much her world.

Immediately after moving in, they decided to clean up the house, which needed it, indeed. The stairway to the top floor was carpeted all the way up, and it was quite a job to vacuum clean it because there were a lot of outlets along the way, and one had to look out for extension cords. Sharon got to the top floor and was cleaning it when she removed the extension cord to plug it in further up. Instead, she just used the regular cord of the vacuum cleaner, which was about 12 feet long, using perhaps 3 feet of it, which left 9 feet of cord lying on the floor.

All of a sudden, the plug just pulled out of the wall. Sharon couldn't believe her eyes; the plug actually pulled itself out of the socket, and flew out onto the floor. She shook her head and put it back in, and turned the vacuum cleaner on again. Only then did she realize that she had turned the switch on the cleaner back on, when she had never actually turned it off in the first place! She couldn't figure out how that was possible. But she had a lot more work to do, so she continued with it. Later she came downstairs and described the incident to her roommate who thought she was out of her mind. "Wait till something happens to you," Sharon said, "there is something strange about this house."

During the next five months, the girls heard strange noises all over the house, but they attributed it to an old house settling, or the people living downstairs in the building. Five months of "peace" were rudely shattered when Sharon's younger brother came to visit from New Jersey.

He was still in high school, and liked to listen to music at night, especially when it was played as loud as possible. The young people were sitting in the living room, listening to music and talking. It was a nice, relaxed evening. All of a sudden the stereo went off. The music had been rather loud rock and roll, and at first they thought the volume had perhaps damaged the set. Then the hallway light went out, followed by the kitchen light. So they thought a fuse had blown. Barbara ran down four flights of stairs into the basement to check. No fuse had blown. To be on the safe side, she checked them anyway, and switched them around to make sure everything was fine. Then she went back upstairs and asked the others how the electricity was behaving.

But everything was still off. At this point, Sharon's brother decided to go into the kitchen and try the lights there. Possibly there was something wrong with the switches. He went into the hallway where there was an old Tiffany-type lamp hanging at the top of the stairway. It had gone off, too, and he tried to turn it on and nothing happened. He pulled again, and suddenly it went on. In other words, he turned it off first, then turned it on, so it had been on in the first place.

This rather bothered the young man, and he announced he was going into the kitchen to get something to eat. He proceeded into the kitchen, and when he came back to join the others he was as white as the wall. He reported that the kitchen was as cold as an icebox, but as soon as one left the kitchen, the temperature was normal in the rest of the house. The others then got up to see for themselves, and sure enough, it was icy cold in the kitchen. This was despite the fact that there were four or five radiators going, and all the windows were closed.

That night they knew that had a ghost, and for want of a better name they called her Hendrix—it happened to have been the anniversary of Jimi Hendrix's death, and they had been playing some of his records.

Shortly afterward, Toby joined the other two girls in the house. Toby moved in on April 1. It had been relatively quiet between the incident in the kitchen and that day, but somehow Toby's arrival was also the beginning of a new aspect of the haunting.

About a week after Toby moved in, the girls were in the living room talking. It was about 11 o'clock at night, and they had dimmers on in the living room. Toby was sitting on the couch, and Barbara and some friends were sitting on the other side of the room, when all of a sudden she felt a chilly breeze pass by her. It didn't touch her, but she felt it nonetheless, and just then the lights started to dim back and forth, back and forth, and when she looked up, she actually saw the dial on the dimmer moving by itself. As yet, Toby knew nothing about the haunting, so she decided to say nothing to the others, having just moved in, and not wishing to have her new roommates think her weird.

But things kept happening night after night, usually after 11 o'clock when the two girls and their friends sat around talking. After a couple of weeks, she could not stand it any longer, and finally asked the others whether they could feel anything strange in the room. Barbara looked at Sharon, and a strange look passed between them; finally they decided to tell Toby about the haunting, and brought her up to date from the beginning of their tenancy in the house.

Almost every day there was something new to report: cooking equipment would be missing, clothing would disappear, windows were opened by themselves, garbage cans would be turned over by unseen hands. Throughout that period, there was the continued walking of an unseen person in the living room located directly over the third-floor bedroom. And the girls heard it at any hour of the night, and once in a while even during the day. Someone was walking back and forth, back and forth. They were loud, stomping footsteps, more like a woman's, but they sounded as if someone were very angry. Each time one of them went upstairs to check they found absolutely nothing.

The girls held a conference, and decided that they had a ghost, make no mistake about it. Toby offered to look into the matter, and perhaps find out what might have occurred at the house at an earlier age. Barbara kept hearing an obscure whistling, not a real tune or song that could be recognized, but a human whistle nevertheless. Meanwhile, Toby heard of a course on witchcraft and the occult being given at New York University, and started to take an interest in books on the subject. But whenever there were people over to visit them and they stayed in the living room upstairs past eleven o'clock at night, the ghost would simply run them out of the room with all the tricks in her ghostly trade.

"She" would turn the stereo on and off, or make the lights go on and off. By now they were convinced it was a woman. There were heavy shutters from the floor to the ceiling, and frequently it appeared as if a wind were coming through them and they would clap together, as if the breeze were agitating them. Immediately after that, they heard footsteps walking away from them, and there was an uncomfortable feeling in the room, making it imperative to leave and go somewhere else, usually downstairs into one of the bedrooms.

As yet, no one had actually seen her. That June, Bruce, Toby's boyfriend, moved into the house with her. They had the master bedroom, and off the bedroom was a bathroom. Since Barbara would frequently walk through in the middle of the night, they left the light on in the bathroom all night so that she would not trip over anything. That particular night in June, Toby and her boyfriend were in bed and she was looking up, not at the ceiling, but at the wall, when suddenly she saw a girl looking at her.

It was just like an outline, like a shadow on the wall, but Toby could tell that she had long hair arranged in braids. Somehow she had the impression that she was an Indian, perhaps because of the braids. Toby looked up at her and called the apparition to her boyfriend's attention, but by the time he had focused on it she had disappeared.

He simply did not believe her. Instead, he asked Toby to go upstairs to the kitchen and make him a sandwich. She wasn't up there for more than five or ten minutes when she returned to the bedroom and found her boyfriend hidden under the covers of the bed. When she asked him what was wrong, he would shake his head, and so she looked around the room, but could find nothing unusual. The only thing she noticed was that the bathroom door was now wide open. She assumed that her boyfriend had gone to the bathroom, but he shook his head and told her that he had not.

He had just been lying there smoking a cigarette, when all of a sudden he saw the handle on the door turn by itself, and the door open.

When he saw that, he simply dove under the covers until Toby returned. From that moment on, he no longer laughed at her stories about a house ghost. The following night, her boyfriend was asleep when Toby woke up at two o'clock in the morning. The television set had been left on and she went to shut it off, and when she got back into bed, she happened to glance at the same place on the wall where she had seen the apparition the night before. For a moment or two she saw the same outline of a girl, only this time she had the impression that the girl was smiling at her.

Two weeks after that, Toby and her boyfriend broke up, and this rather shook her. She had come back home one day and didn't know that he had left, then she found a note in which he explained his reasons for leaving, and that he would get in touch with her later. This very much upset her, so much so that her two roommates had to calm her down. Finally, the two other girls went upstairs and Toby was lying on the bed trying to compose herself.

In the quiet of the room, she suddenly heard someone sob a little and then a voice said, "Toby." Toby got up from bed and went to the bottom of the stairs and called up, demanding to know what Barbara wanted. But no one had called her. She went back to the room and lay down on the bed again. Just then she heard a voice saying "Toby" again and again. On checking, she found that no one had called out to her—no one of flesh and blood, that is.

Toby then realized who had been calling her, and she decided to talk to "Henny," her nickname for Hendrix, which was the name given by the others to the ghost since that night when they were playing Jimi Hendrix records. In a quiet voice, Toby said, "Henny, did you call me?" and then she heard the voice answer, "Calm down, don't take it so hard, it will be all right." It was a girl's voice, and yet there was no one to be seen. The time was about five o'clock in the afternoon, and since it was in June, the room was still fairly light.

Toby had hardly recovered from this experience when still another event took place. Sharon had moved out and another girl by the name of Madeline had moved in. One day her brother came to visit them from Chicago, and he brought a friend along who had had some experience of a spiritual nature. His name was Joey, and both boys were about 20 or 21 years old.

Madeline and her brother were much interested in the occult, and they brought a Ouija board to the house. On Saturday, December 19, while it was snowing outside and the atmosphere was just right for a seance, they decided to make contact with the unhappy ghost in the house. They went upstairs into the living room, and sat down with the board. At first it was going to be a game, and they were asking silly questions of it such as who was going to marry whom, and other romantic fluff. But halfway through the session, they decided to try to contact the ghost in earnest. The three girls and Madeline's brother sat down on the floor with their knees touching, and put the board on top. Then they invited Henny to appear and talk to them if she was so inclined. They were prepared to pick up the indicator and place their hands on it so it could move to various letters on the board.

But before their hands ever touched it, the indicator took off by itself! It shot over to the word yes on the board, as if to reassure them that communication was indeed desired. The four of them looked at each other dumbfounded, for they had seen only too clearly what had just transpired. By now they were all somewhat scared. However, Toby decided that since she was going to be interested in psychic research, she might as well ask the questions. She began asking why the ghostly girl was still attached to the house. Haltingly, word for word, Henny replied and told her sad story.

It was a slow process, since every word had to be spelled out letter by letter, but the young people didn't mind the passage of time—they wanted to know why Henny was with them. It appears that the house once belonged to her father, a medical doctor. Her name was Cesa Rist and she had lived in the house with her family. Unfortunately she had fallen in love with a boy and had become pregnant by him. She wanted to marry him and have the baby, but her father would not allow it and forced her to have an abortion. He did it in the house himself, and she died during the abortion.

Her body was taken to Denver, Colorado and buried in the family plot. She realized that her boyfriend was dead also, because this all happened a long time ago. Her reasons for staying on in the house were to find help; she wanted her remains to be buried near her lover's in New York.

"Do you like the people who live in this house?" "Yes," the ghost replied. "Is anyone who lives here ever in any danger?" "Yes, people who kill babies." This struck the young people as particularly appropriate: a close friend, not present at the time, had just had an abortion. "Will you appear to us?" "Cesa has," the ghost replied, and as if to emphasize this statement, there suddenly appeared the shadow of a cross on the kitchen wall, for which there was no possible source, except, of course, from the parapsychological point of view.

The girls realized they did not have the means to go to Denver and exhume Cesa's remains and bring it to New York, and they told the ghost as much. "Is there anything else we can do to help you?" "Contact Holzer," she said. By that time, of course, Toby had become familiar with my works, and decided to sit down and write me a letter, telling me of their problem. They could not continue with the Ouija board or anything else that night, they were all much too shaken up.

On Monday, Toby typed up the letter they had composed, and sent it to me. Since they were not sure the letter would reach me, they decided to do some independent checking concerning the background of the house, and if possible, try to locate some record of Cesa Rist. But they were unsuccessful, even at the Hall of Records, the events having apparently transpired at a time when records were not yet kept, or at least not properly kept.

When I received the letter, I was just about to leave for Europe and would be gone two and a half months. I asked the girls to stay in touch with me and after my return I would look into the matter. After Toby had spoken to me on the telephone, she went back into the living room and sat down quietly. She then addressed Henny and told her she had contacted me, and that it would be a couple of months before I could come to the house because I had to go to Europe.

Barbara decided not to wait, however; one night she want upstairs to talk to Henny. She explained the situation to her, and why she was still hanging around the house; she explained that her agony was keeping her in the house, and that she must let go of it in order to go on and join her boyfriend in the Great Beyond. Above all, she should not be angry with them because it was their home now. Somehow Barbara felt that the ghost understood, and nothing happened, nothing frightening at all. Relieved, Barbara sat down in a chair facing the couch. She was just sitting there smoking a cigarette, wondering whether Henny really existed, or whether perhaps she was talking to thin air.

At the moment, an ethereal form entered the room and stood near the couch. It looked as if she were leaning on the arm of the couch or holding onto the side of it. She saw the outline of the head, and what looked like braids around the front of her chest. For half a minute she was there, and then she suddenly disappeared.

It looked to Barbara as if the girl had been 5'4", weighing perhaps 120 pounds. Stunned, Barbara sat there for another ten or fifteen minutes, trying to believe what she had seen. She smoked another five cigarettes, and then walked downstairs to try to go to sleep. But sleep would not come; she kept thinking about her experience.

At the time Sharon left, they were interviewing potential roommates to replace her. One particularly unpleasant girl had come over and fallen in love with the house. Both Barbara and Toby didn't want her to move in, but she seemed all set to join them, so Toby decided to tell her about the ghost. She hoped it would stop the girl from moving in. As Toby delineated their experiences with Henny, the would-be roommate became more and more nervous.

All of a sudden there was a loud crash in the kitchen, and they went to check on it. The garbage can had turned itself over and all the garbage was spilled all over the kitchen, even though no one had been near it. The new girl took one look at this and ran out as fast as she could. She never came back.

But shortly afterward, Toby went on vacation to California. There she made arrangements to move and found employment in the market research department of a large department store. Under the circumstances, the girls decided not to renew the lease, which was up in July, but to move to another apartment for a short period. That September, they moved to California. Under the circumstances, they did not contact me any further, and I assumed that matters had somehow been straightened out, or that there had been a change in their plans. It was not until a year later that we somehow met in California, and I could fill in the missing details of Henny's story.

On the last day of the girls' stay at the house on Clinton Street, with the movers going in and out of the house, Toby went back into the house for one more look and to say goodby to Henny. She went up to the living room and said a simple goodbye, and hoped that Henny would be all right. But there was no answer, no feeling of a presence.

For awhile the house stood empty, then it was purchased by the father of an acquaintance of the girls. Through Alan, they heard of the new people who had moved in after the house was sold. One day when they had just been in the house for a few days, they returned to what they assumed to be an empty house.

They found their kitchen flooded with water: there were two inches of water throughout the kitchen, yet they knew they had not left the water taps on. Why had Henny turned the water on and let it run? Perhaps Henny didn't like the new tenants after all. But she had little choice, really. Being a ghost, she was tied to the house.

Following her friends to San Francisco was simply impossible, the way ghosts operate. And unless or until the new tenants on Clinton Street call for my services, there is really nothing I can do to help Henny.